LIBRARY

P9-CRW-601

4604 9100 000

Mystery Gor
Gordon, Alan
Jester leaps in

stained 4-01

JESTER
LEAPS IN

Also by Alan Gordon

Thirteenth Night

JESTER LEAPS IN

A MEDIEVAL MYSTERY

ALAN GORDON

ST. MARTIN'S MINOTAUR M NEW YORK

SALINE DISTRICT LIBRARY
555 N. Maple Road
Saline, MI 48176

NOV 2008

Excerpt from *The History of the Siege of Lisbon,* copyright © 1989 by Jose Saramago and Editorial Caminho, SA Lisbon, English translation copyright © 1996 by Giovanni Pontiero, reprinted by permission of Harcourt, Inc.

JESTER LEAPS IN. Copyright © 2000 by Alan Gordon. All rights reserved. Printed in the United States of America. No part of this book may be used or reproduced in any manner whatsoever without written permission except in the case of brief quotations embodied in critical articles or reviews. For information, address St. Martin's Press, 175 Fifth Avenue, New York, N.Y. 10010.

www.stmartins.com

Library of Congress Cataloging-in-Publication Data

Gordon, Alan (Alan R.)
  Jester leaps in : a medieval mystery / Alan Gordon.— 1st ed.
      p.   cm.
  ISBN 0-312-24117-8
    1. Fools and jesters—Fiction.   2. Middle Ages—Fiction.
  3. Crusades—Fiction.   I. Title.

PS3557.O649 J47 2000
813'.54—dc21   00-031761

First Edition: November 2000

10 9 8 7 6 5 4 3 2 1

SALINE DISTRICT LIBRARY
555 N. Maple Road
Saline, MI 48176

To my parents, Anita and Louis Gordon,
thanks for the heredity, the environment, and the music

ACKNOWLEDGMENTS

I would like to thank Jessica Jones, my agent, for taking me on when nobody else would; Keith Kahla, my editor, for his refined vision and fine revisions; www.abebooks.com, for helping me locate some rare and useful tomes; Peter Tremayne, for taking me more seriously than I deserve; Niketas Choniates, for living to tell the tale; Harry J. Magoulias, for telling it in English; the Legal Aid Society, for letting me have a leave of absence; my colleagues there, for covering for me while I was gone; my son, Robert, for keeping me young; and my wife, Judy Downer, for everything.

Stultus. A man that lacketh naturall knowledge, an ideote.

—*Bibliotheca Eliotae,* Thomas Cooper (1559)

Fol. Arse, goose, calfe, dotterell, woodcocke, noddie, cokes, goose cap, coxcombe, ninnie, naturall.

—*Dictionary of French and English Tongues,* R. Cotgrave (1611)

Fool, n. A person who pervades the domain of intellectual speculation and diffuses himself through the channels of moral activity. He is omnific, omniform, omnipercipient, omniscient, omnipotent. . . . He is from everlasting to everlasting—such as creation's dawn beheld he fooleth now. In the morning of time he sang upon primitive hills, and in the noonday of existence headed the procession of being. His grandmotherly hand has warmly tucked-in the set sun of civilization, and in the twilight he prepares Man's evening meal of milk-and-morality and turns down the covers of the universal grave. *And after the rest of us shall have retired for the night of eternal oblivion, he will sit up to write a history of human civilization.* [Italics added.]

—*The Devil's Dictionary,* Ambrose Bierce (1911)

JESTER
LEAPS IN

ONE

What think you of this fool...? Doth he not mend?
—*TWELFTH NIGHT*, ACT 1, SCENE 5

The sun rose through the gap in the eastern ridge where the river cuts through. I watched it come up, lying on my back on the riverbank. A few months ago, I had prayed that God would grant me the gift of seeing one more sunrise. He had granted that prayer, along with a few others, in a manner more generous than my situation merited, but that's the sort of thing He does. I make no pretense of understanding His ways, but ever since I survived that dreadful night, I've made a point of trying to see every sunrise that I could. And I've continued to pray. Not for myself, mind you. I've been rewarded enough so that I can pass along some prayers for the rest of the world. It seems only fair.

As the warmth of the rays began removing the night's chill from my limbs, I took my right knee, brought it to my chest, and held it there for a slow count of ten. Then I did the same with the left knee, though the leg protested vehemently. Pain coursed through it, rounding the turns at my ankles and surging back toward my hip until I released it, gasping. Then I repeated the exercise, right knee without pain, left with.

I sat up, kept my right leg straight, and brought it up by degrees until it was pointing to the sky. I let it drop, then looked at my left leg as if it belonged to some stranger, one who had yet to earn my trust. Reluctantly, I grabbed it and started pulling it up.

I couldn't get it to the vertical, and had to settle for the diagonal. I thought I could hear the scar tissue cracking, but that may have been my imagination. I let it go and stood up.

Roosters crowed on the farms surrounding the town. I stripped to my linens and dove into the river, kicking hard. The water came directly from the snow still visible on the distant mountain peaks, pausing on its way to the nearby Adriatic to chill me to the marrow. I made it across to the opposite bank, then swam back. I did five circuits before the left leg gave up; then I dragged myself back up the bank like a shipwrecked sailor. Not bad, I thought. Only four months since a bolt from a crossbow had fixed my thigh to a wall, one month since I could walk without crutches. Lucky I still had a leg to stand on.

I dried myself off, donned my motley, and rubbed the flour-chalk mixture onto my face until it took on its normal macabre aspect. Kohl for the brows and lines, rouge for the lips and cheeks, then malachite for the green diamonds under the eyes. Finally, the cap and bells on my head, and I was ready to face the world again.

"Good morning, Fool," said a woman behind me.

I spun, startled; then I relaxed and bowed.

"Good morning, milady," I said. "I trust you slept well."

"Quite well, thank you, Feste," replied Viola. "I am ready for my lesson."

She glanced around and made sure that no one was near. Then she walked up to me, placed her arms around my neck, and kissed me.

"There, you've gone and smeared my makeup," I protested, admittedly some minutes later.

Viola stepped back and surveyed the damage. "I suppose some of it got on me," she said. I nodded. She pulled out a handkerchief and wiped her face while I made repairs to mine. "The perils of kissing a fool," she remarked. "I had no idea that loving someone so simple would be so complicated. How is your leg today?"

"Improving. Still weak and stiff, but less than before. Now, my lovely apprentice, let's see how you've progressed."

She took three balls out of a bag and started juggling.

"Good. Switch hands."

She shifted the pattern from a left-handed start to a right-handed one.

"Good. Two and one. Other way. Over the top. Excellent. Overhand grabs, now. Have you tried going under the leg?"

"In my room," she said, concentrating on the pattern. "But I can't do it here in this gown. Oh, dear." A ball dropped out of her reach and rolled toward the bank. I retrieved it before it plunged into the river and handed it back to her. "Why did you go over there?" she asked it sternly.

"Because that's where you threw it," I replied. "Start over."

She sighed and sent them aloft. "When do I start on four balls?"

I tossed another one at her. She wasn't expecting it. She made a late grab, and three of the four balls ended up at her feet.

"When you've mastered three," I answered.

"Yes, Teacher."

She went back to work while I resumed my stretching.

"That trick won't work on me again, you know," she said, tossing one behind her back and catching it over the opposite shoulder.

"That's today's lesson," I replied. "A good fool is ready for anything at any time. We'll start on four balls tomorrow. In the meantime, switch to clubs. When you're ready, we'll work on some four-handed moves."

I stopped and listened. "Do you hear that?"

She nodded, pulling three gaily painted clubs out of her bag. "Someone singing. Coming from the town toward us."

"Not just someone."

In the Fools' Guild, we are trained how to make contact with each other. The exchange of passwords is one method, of course, but only when you know where to find a particular colleague. In the vast expanses of the world, however, we have many ways of signaling when we need to find each other. A certain type of birdcall; a peculiar clapping rhythm; a song.

Our troubadours call it a *tenso*: a debate in verse and melody, a call and response between two singers on any topic, though usually on love. The best can improvise on a theme for hours at the contests held at the Guildhall and the great tournaments in southern France where a sparrow hawk is perched on a tall pole throughout and awarded to the winner.

But this particular song was a call to any Guild member to respond in kind. The verse was sung, and then the singer paused, waiting. Then he moved on and repeated it.

Thus it was that I heard in the distance a sweet tenor soaring over the faint strummings of a lute:

> *How sweet to meet the soft-lit Dawn*
> *When the world lies still aborning.*
> *Farewell, Philomel, I must move on.*
> *I have miles to go this morning.*

I cleared my throat and sang out in the direction of my unknown friend:

Yet stay, I pray, my pretty Faun,
Or my love you will be scorning.
The Sun will run, and then be gone.
Let tomorrow's Dawn be our warning.

"Shouldn't the second part be sung by a woman?" asked Viola, keeping her eyes on the clubs dancing in the air over her head.

"When one's available," I replied. "Now, hush, Apprentice."

Tantalo once told me that the art of being a troubadour is to sing, play the lute, and look magnificent in a cape, all while simultaneously riding a horse. And there he was, the embodiment of his own definition, perched on a beautiful, black, Spanish stallion prancing daintily down the hill, both horse and rider bedecked in black-and-red checkered silks. His Insouciance guided his steed without reins, leaving his hands free to continue plucking away at a lute that was far nicer than mine. His horse, I swear, kept time with its hooves. They descended the slope toward us. When they stopped, Tantalo swung his leg over the saddle and leaped lightly to the ground, continuing the melodic line in the lute without break.

"You must teach me how to do that trick," I said. "You're in fine voice this morning."

"This morning, this afternoon, yesterday and tomorrow," he replied. "You, on the other hand, sound a touch hoarse."

"I've been swimming," I said, a bit defensively.

He turned, doffed his plumed hat, and nodded to Viola, then turned back to me.

"Introduce me to your charming companion, if you would be so kind."

"Viola, this is Tantalo, an old friend. Tantalo, this is my apprentice, Viola."

"Apprentice?" he said in surprise. He leaned toward me and muttered, "Looks a bit long in the tooth for an apprentice, don't you think?"

I reached forward and caught a club an inch away from his skull.

"Oops," said Viola sweetly, keeping the other two clubs going with her right hand. I tossed back the wandering third. She caught it adroitly and continued practicing.

"Rather ungallant for a troubadour, commenting on a lady's age," I admonished him.

"Oh, a lady, is she? Forgive me. I mistook her for a fool's apprentice. As a Guild member, it is my right and obligation to insult apprentices, and their responsibility to come up with some witty retort."

"You're funny-looking, and your horse smells," Viola called out.

"All right, so that part needs work," I said hastily. "But she's no ordinary apprentice. She's fluent in nine languages, sings and plays beautifully, and is a superb actress and mimic. I can vouch for that."

"Well, if you say so," he said, somewhat dubiously. "Anyhow, that is not my business here."

"What *is* your business?"

He straightened up and puffed out his chest. "Theophilos, I have traveled from the Guildhall to Venice, and by boat from Venice to Capodistria, and then ridden down the Adriatic coastline to this lovely town of Orsino, to ask you but a single question: how is your leg?"

"Is that personal or official?"

"Both."

"Personally, it hurts like hell. Officially, I can no longer do a standing back flip, and I still limp fairly badly, but I am otherwise back to my old self."

"Good," he said, nodding. "Your report of your success here was duly noted. Father Gerald was so delighted, he was observed to kick up one heel. More cannot be expected of such an ancient. But you are back in his good graces."

"Hooray for me. What does the Guild want?"

"Now, now, gossip before business. You know the rules."

I debated with myself over whether or not I would intercept the next club flung in his direction. He pulled out a large handkerchief, opened it with a flourish, and placed it on the ground. He then sat upon it and leaned forward.

"You'll never guess, my friend, who showed up at the court in Hagenau recently."

"I haven't been in Germany in years. Tell me."

"Alexios."

"Which Alexios?"

"Alexios of Constantinople. Son of the usurped and blinded Isaakios, former emperor. Nephew of the usurping and blinding Alexios the Third, current emperor. Alexios, who seeks to become Alexios the Fourth, the next emperor."

"Which would be a neat trick, considering his father and uncle both live. When did he escape?"

"Sometime in the fall, we think."

"And this was not the Guild's doing?"

"By David's lyre, no. The Guild has no interest in disrupting the Byzantine throne. The results are too unpredictable, and besides, they do a fine job of that all by themselves. The immediate agents who arranged his escape were Pisan, but we suspect his sister Irene was behind it. She's married to Philip of Swabia, you know."

"He escapes, goes north to big sister, and has a ready-made entry to the German court. What does that have to do with the Guild?"

"Well, there's this little matter of the Crusade gathering in Venice."

"Which is going to Constantinople, according to Domino."

He shrugged. "Maybe. Domino's been the chief fool in Venice forever, and usually knows which way the wind's blowing. But not everyone in the Guild thinks Constantinople is the intended target. There's a whole lot of French and Flemish soldiers sworn to liberate the Holy Land, and nothing but the Holy Land. Then there are some who want to invade Egypt first, one infidel territory being just as good as the next. So, most of us thought Constantinople was a long shot. But Alexios's arrival complicates matters. You know who else was at Hagenau? Boniface of Montferrat. Here the Guild is, making every effort to keep the Crusaders from slaughtering Christians, at the very least, and now the commander is meeting with the chief claimant to the Byzantine throne."

"What's the Guild doing about it?"

"The usual. The troubadours are in a tricky position. Unlike you, we can't just go around making fun of our patrons. We're supposed to be out there singing their praises. And if the particular lord is taking the Cross and swearing to bring an army with him, then we're supposed to be out rousing the rabble. So, we roused them. Now that we've roused them, we're trying to douse them. Lyrics that once glorified the noble quest now speak of the girl we leave behind. Some of our gallants are becoming homesick before they even depart."

"Very good."

"We're also taking the opposite tack of inflaming their fervor to such a pitch that they must to Beyond-the-Sea immediately.

[8]

Several hundred have skipped Venice altogether and dashed off to Apulia, which is doing a nice business in transporting them. They'll arrive in inadequate numbers to fight the Mohammedans, while depriving their Venetian-bound comrades of their promised numbers. We're hoping that not enough of them show up in Venice to justify the journey. In Venice itself, we're spreading rumors that the Crusade is being subverted to Venetian ends. Some of those who came there because they took the Cross are now crying betrayal and going home."

"Well done. But it won't work. Venice has committed too much of its monies to this expedition. If they don't get repaid with profit, they won't be happy."

"Agreed. And just when we were hoping everything might fall apart nicely, along comes little Alexios with his big requests. Oh, you should see how grown men and women weep to hear of his travels and travails. Fortunately, Rome won't support him. Innocent may be one of the most conniving popes in recent memory, but even he won't absolve an attack like this. Unfortunately, events have their own momentum, which is why the Guild wants you to go to Constantinople."

I was waiting for it, I was expecting it, and he still managed to sneak it in and wallop me.

"Constantinople? Me? Now?" I almost shouted.

He looked at me and shook his head sadly. "Theo, you have to do better than one-word questions if you're to uphold your reputation as a wit. But to respond in the same manner: Yes. You. Now."

"But doesn't the Guild have half a dozen people there already?"

"We did," he replied.

Suddenly, I was afraid. "What happened to them?"

"We don't know," he said slowly. "That's what we'd like you to find out. They've disappeared. All of them."

"Dead?"

"We don't know. We received word from Fat Basil in Thessaloniki. The troubadour riding the circuit from Constantinople reported that all of the fools had vanished without explanation. He left, saying he would try to find out what happened. That's the last we heard."

"When was this?"

"Maybe six or seven months ago."

"Who did the Guild have working there?"

He counted on his fingers. "The dwarf brothers were with the Emperor. Thalia was with the Empress. Tiberius and Demetrios worked the streets, the Hippodrome, and the Great Palace. The troubadour was called Ignatius."

"You're using the past tense. About people that I know."

"Then I hope that you may know them again. Thalia was a particular friend of yours, was she not?"

Some troubadours should stick to singing. When they talk, they just get people in trouble. I glanced over at Viola, but she was absorbed in her juggling, some distance away.

"When can you leave?" Tantalo asked.

"There's a complication," I said.

"What is it?"

"I'm married," I replied, indicating Viola. "Meet the Duchess."

"Married?" he guffawed. "Well, my goodness. Congratulations, I suppose." He turned to Viola. "And to you, Apprentice." She nodded, and he turned back. "I guess...." Then his jaw slowly dropped in the first uncalculated expression I had ever seen on him. "When you said, 'Duchess,' you meant... Good God, Theo, you've rejoined the gentry!"

"Dragged me down to his level, more the like," said Viola.

He got up and swept his hat off in a superb bow.

"Forgive me, milady. Little did I know that such magnificence was consorting with such a lowly man as this."

"You're still funny-looking, and your horse still smells," she replied, curtsying.

"Ha, ha, excellently put, milady," he said, rolling his eyes at me. "Well, this is a priceless piece of news to take with me. I could dine out for a month on it at the Guildhall."

"Fine, so long as you don't noise it about locally. As you might suspect, it was done in secret."

"I'm certain of it. Last I heard, she was a recent widow and you were a bedridden cripple. Did she nurse you back to health?"

"She did."

"Then you fell in love and married in secret. What a scandal!"

"There might have been a greater scandal had we not married," I said. "And we had been in love for a long time. We just didn't realize it."

"Now she's your apprentice. How much have you told her about the Guild?"

"Who we are. What we do."

He sighed. "Is that all? After all these years, you'll give up our secrets for love?"

"Because I trust her, and because she'll become a member in due time."

"But that takes years of training, Theo."

"As I said, she has a head start. All she really needs is repertoire, juggling, and tumbling, and she'll be ready for initiation."

"I imagine she could give you a pretty good tumble if she wanted to," Tantalo whispered, leering. Then he turned and caught another club directed at his noggin.

"Oops, again," called Viola.

Tantalo flipped the club experimentally, then lofted it high over her head. She walked backward, gazing upward while keeping the other two clubs going in one hand. At the last moment, she tossed them high, cartwheeled backward, and caught all three. Tantalo and I applauded.

"All right, she does show some promise," he said begrudgingly.

"In the meantime, she has taken the Oath of Apprenticeship and will honor it," I said.

"How much does she really know about you?" he asked quietly.

"More than you do," I said. "She knows my real name. I had to give it to the hermit who married us."

"My word," he said, impressed. "But there is quite a bit more to you than that."

"True. I've promised one revelation for each wedding anniversary."

"Then, milady, I wish you a long and happy life together," he said, bowing again. "You'll need it if you want to learn all of this fellow's secrets."

"Oh, I have a few of my own," she replied.

"No doubt, no doubt. Well, Theo, you're right. This is a complication."

"Not necessarily," said Viola.

I looked at her for a long moment.

"Will you excuse us?" I asked Tantalo.

He bowed and withdrew. I turned to my beloved. "What are you up to?"

"A good fool is ready for anything at any time," she replied. "The answer is simple. I go with you."

"Impossible."

"Why?"

"Because it's dangerous. You have no idea what you're getting into."

Her face darkened. Always a warning signal, although one I

[12]

usually catch too late. "I married you. I became an apprentice of the Fools' Guild. I made both commitments knowing what they involved. I knew that at some point the Guild would be sending you on another mission. So, I'm going with you."

"What about your children?"

"My opportunity to be their mother disappeared when my sister-in-law was appointed as their regent. Mark is a few years away from his independence. Once he has full power as Duke, maybe I'll be allowed to be his mother again. But for now, I choose to be your wife rather than a useless appendage to my own family."

"You may get killed in the process."

"As may you. Don't forget, I've already had the experience of sitting home while my first husband went sailing off to the Holy Land to fight Saladin. Years of wondering if he was coming back. I won't do that again. I refuse to grow old waiting to see if you've survived. If you're going to die, I want to be there." She stopped. "That didn't come out the way I meant it to."

"Viola, this is no pampered life. A traveling jester lives on his wits and a handful of bronze. You'd be sleeping in haylofts if you're lucky, and on the cold, hard ground if you're not."

She walked up to me and looked up into my eyes. "But I'll be sleeping with you," she said simply.

I thought about that for all of a second. "All right, you can come. But your training continues. When we are working, you are my apprentice, not my wife."

"Agreed," she said, and she went back to her juggling.

I walked back to where Tantalo had withdrawn, a distance far enough to appear discreet while allowing him to hear every word we said.

"Problem solved?" he asked innocently.

"We'll leave tomorrow morning. Can you stay until then?"

"Alas, no," he said, mounting his horse. "I have a few more errands to run before I rejoin the Crusade."

"You're going with them?"

"Someone has to keep an eye on them. There'll be a few of us. Raimbaut's with Boniface, of course, and some of the other high and mighty are bringing along troubadours to record their prowess in verse. Things should get going this summer. The fleet will probably work its way down the coast demanding support. Most of the towns have quietly gotten in touch with Venice to arrange peaceful passage. Including yours, milady."

"We know," she said.

"Yes, that Jewish steward of yours is very efficient. You should get by with a relatively minor tribute and a few dozen men. But I have to visit Zara next. The Doge has it in for them, and they may want to consider some serious negotiating before the fleet shows up at their doorstep."

"I hear the place is a haven for heretics, brigands, and exiles."

"My kind of people. Well, I'll see what I can do about persuading them to settle peacefully; then I'm back to Venice. I'm worried Domino may take it upon himself to dive into the Grand Canal with a spike in his teeth and scuttle the fleet single-handedly. Oh, by the way, Brother Dennis was inquiring after that horse he gave you."

"Zeus is well," I said. "His manners have not improved over-much. Does Brother Dennis want him back?"

"No. He said, and I quote, 'If he can stand that vicious, willful, cantankerous bastard, he might as well stay with him.'"

"That's a fine way to speak about a horse."

"He was talking about you. Good-bye, Theophilos."

"Good luck," I said, reaching up and clasping his hand.

"And to you," he replied. "Perhaps I'll see you in Constantinople."

He started strumming his lute as his horse turned north back toward the town.

"One more thing," I called. "Let's say I'm sitting there, and war breaks out. What does the Guild want me to do?"

"Try and stop it," he called back.

"How?"

He shot us a wicked grin over his shoulder. "Do what you always do. Improvise!"

Viola watched him leave, flipping a club in her right hand, gauging the distance.

"I don't think you can hit him from here," I commented.

"I'll wager a kiss that I can," she said, still eyeing him.

I took the club from her hand and kissed her.

"I prize them too highly to cheapen them by wagering," I said. "Let's go pack."

Two

Never approach a goat from the front, a horse from the back,
or a fool from any side.

JEWISH PROVERB

I greeted the following dawn on horseback, riding Zeus through the northwest gate of the city.

"Good morning, Feste," called the guard. "No swim today?"

"The problem with having a horse is that he expects to be ridden once in a while," I called back. "And this one has to be ridden at the gallop. I'll see you later."

He waved, and I loosened my grip on Zeus's reins. He charged up the road that would eventually take a traveler to Capodistria. The forest soon enclosed us. I reined him to a walk, glancing back to see if we were followed. When I was certain that we were not, I cut through the woods on a little-used path that emerged on the northern road near the cemetery.

A man stood in a small clearing, holding a sorrel mare by its reins. I slowed Zeus to a halt and dismounted.

"Good morning, Malachi," I said.

"Good morning, sir," he said, bobbing his head. "The Duchess instructed me to bring her horse to this place, and to turn it over to you. She'll be joining you for a ride sometime later."

"Very good, Malachi. I'll look after the creature. I'll see you at dinner."

"Yes, sir." He looked away for a moment. "When you see milady . . . ," he said, hesitating slightly. Then he cleared his throat. "Tell her that I wish her a pleasant ride."

"I will," I promised.

He began walking back to the town, then turned toward the cemetery. "Might as well visit my family while I'm here," he called, and I waved good-bye.

A small, round, bearded man emerged from the woods and watched him go. Then he turned to me, tears running down his cheeks.

"Explain to me, Fool," said Viola, for it was she in men's garb, "why it is that I am sadder to part from my chief servant than I am from my own children?"

I didn't know the answer, so I kept silent.

She pulled out several saddlebags from her hiding place, and we loaded up the two horses and mounted. She looked down the hill toward her home. "Oh, God, Feste. Am I making the right choice?"

"There's no way of knowing," I said. "You can still turn back."

She shook her head quickly, and spurred her horse north. I caught up with her and we galloped on, side by side.

We had decided that it was safer to travel as two men, rather than as a man and a woman. I knew how capable Viola was with the sword she wore, but your average ruffian lacked that knowledge. Two men, like it or not, would seem slightly more intimidating to those who would seek to waylay us.

"Besides," she had said when we reached this conclusion, "if things get to that point, I'd rather die quickly as a man than slowly as a woman."

As the northern ridge rose in front of us, we came to a path that went east. We rode along the base of the ridge until we came to the upper bridge over the river.

"Why did you want to take this route?" she asked as we crossed.

"I didn't think your loving sister-in-law would approve of us running off like this," I replied. "She'll send Captain Perun after us as soon as she finds out. I figure that he'll follow my lead to the northwest, while we, in the meantime, will be cutting down to the south road."

"I see," she said, slowing her horse to a walk. "There's just one problem with that plan."

"What's that?"

"That's Perun waiting for us up ahead."

The captain was seated on a piebald steed. Both were in full armor. When I first returned to Orsino, Zeus and I had beaten him in a race. I heard that afterward he spent half a year's wages seeking a superior horse. I suspected that this one could match mine, stride for stride.

Perun was alone. This frightened me more than if he had the entire guard with him. At least there would have been witnesses. There was no love lost between us, despite a hard-earned respect for each other's abilities. Indeed, his appearance in our chosen path moved him up another notch in my estimation.

As we approached him, he saluted us. We came to a stop, our horses almost nose to nose with his.

"Good morning, Fool," he said. "And milady, I believe?"

"Captain," acknowledged Viola.

"I thought you might wish to partake of a little something before you left," he said. "I took the liberty of preparing a light repast. Forgive the meager choice, but I had such short notice." He pointed to his left. There was a table set up, a cloth draping it, with settings for three. He dismounted and stood by the head of the table.

"I am a bit hungry," I said. I stood at the opposite side of the table. Viola joined me. There was a pitcher of wine, three goblets, a basket with a cooked chicken, and a loaf of bread.

"I am forced to be both carver and butler," he said, pouring the wine. He lifted his goblet. "To your good health, and success on your upcoming venture." He drained it, then looked quizzically at us and our untouched wine.

"Surely you don't think me that crude," he sighed. "Shall I be taster as well?" He picked up our goblets and took a sip from each. "Satisfied?"

"Yes," said Viola. "I drink to the Duke." She drank. I joined her.

"What venture, Captain?" I asked as he sliced the bread.

"I'm not sure, and I truly don't care," he replied. "My spies weren't close enough to hear your little chat with that overdressed warbler. But my responsibility is for the security of Orsino. When the Duke's mother reverts to her old habit of dressing as a man and then runs off with the village idiot. . . ."

"Fool, please."

"Then the scandal could suggest to our enemies that we are weak, perhaps worthy of chastisement. Or even conquest."

"A bit far-fetched, don't you think?" said Viola, digging into the chicken. "I'm of no consequence here."

"You're the Duchess of Orsino and the Duke's mother. Still of marriageable age, and therefore still of strategic value to the city."

"Not anymore," she said. "We're married."

He was unfazed by the news. "Odd. I don't remember receiving an invitation."

"It was a private ceremony," I said.

"Conducted by that crazy hermit in the woods, I suppose. Such unions are of dubious validity, milady. Did you really expect to sneak off like this without any repercussions?"

"I left letters with my maid for each of my children. Mark and Celia will know everything within the hour."

He reached inside a pouch and pulled out two scrolls. "You mean these?"

"You had no right!" she shouted. Odd to hear such feminine fury emanating from a bearded face.

"Nevertheless, I have them. Quite beautifully written. I was almost moved. I may even give them to your children."

"When?" I asked. "What are you looking for? You obviously want something. Otherwise, you wouldn't be here alone."

He nodded. "I was wondering when you would ask. It's very simple. Right now, you are both under the Duke's protection. How long that will last depends on how he reacts to the news of your happy nuptials. These letters certainly would help your case. Promise me one small thing, and I'll see that they're delivered."

"What is it?"

"Wherever it is that you're headed, Fool, stay there. Don't come back to Orsino."

"And my wife?"

He grimaced at the word. "She is the Duke's mother. I'll use my influence to guarantee her safety anytime that she wishes to return. Perhaps they'll even let her wander in the courtyard on pleasant days rather than penning her up for this fit of madness. Go and have your little adventure, Duchess. You won't last, I promise you. And then come back to us where you'll be safe."

Viola reached for the pitcher, poured wine for herself and me, then lifted her goblet.

"To our journey, my loving husband," she said, and drank. I did as well. She turned to Perun.

"We thank you for your hospitality, Captain," she said. "But

I think that you have underestimated my resolve. I take my leave of you."

She mounted her horse. I swung myself onto Zeus, and we galloped off.

"Wait, I've packed you a lunch!" called Perun, and his laughter followed us out of the environs of Orsino.

"Well played, milady," I commented as we picked up the south road.

"Thank you. Imagine his chagrin when he finds out those weren't the real letters. I never did trust that girl."

"Where did you leave them?"

"Celia's is under her pillow. Mark's is on his chessboard. He'll have it before Perun gets back."

"How do you think he'll react?"

"He loved his father, but he loves you, too. I think he'll like the idea, even though he won't be able to admit it officially. And by the time we get back, he'll no longer have a regent telling him what he can and cannot do."

We forded the stream that marked the southern boundary of Orsino's domains.

"Which way now?" she asked.

"We'll follow the coast to Durazzo, then cross along the Via Egnatia to Thessaloniki."

"Why not just cut west over the mountains? Wouldn't that be quicker?"

"Not necessarily, and certainly more dangerous. There's all manner of bandits and rogue soldiers up in the mountains. If we stick to the main road, we'll be able to go from town to town in daylight, and spend the night under a roof. With luck, we may fall in with a group making a pilgrimage."

She looked up through the canopy of leaves at the blue sky

and breathed deeply. "I don't need a roof, you know. I'm a fool's apprentice. I practiced last night."

"How?"

"I slept on the cold, hard floor."

"Completely incorrect, Apprentice. A fool never turns down the chance at a bed when one's available. There will be all too many opportunities to sleep on the ground."

The first arose that night, as it turned out. The road down the coast was relatively deserted, so we found a comfortable spot in a stand of pine, hobbled the horses, and ate. We didn't bother making a fire. The food we had was fresh from the town, but we had laid in enough dried meat and biscuit to tide us over should we find ourselves far from taverns and hostels.

We spread out our bedrolls and settled down as the moon came up. Viola nestled into me. The nestling gave way to snuggling, which in turn led to an actual worrying. Finally, gasping, I gave in.

"But please, I beg of you," I panted. "Take off the damn beard."

Reality set in the next morning in the form of a rainstorm, but it failed to dampen our spirits in the least. I can't say that the horses shared our happiness. Maybe we should have hobbled them closer together, but I took no responsibility for Zeus's love life.

It was a new sensation, this feeling of contentment. A jester's life tends toward melancholy abetted by drunkenness, and I had been a prime example in my time. Yet here I traveled with a loving companion in the middle of spring, singing as we rode, and I could think of nothing in the world that I'd rather be doing, including the events of the previous night.

The singing was by way of instruction, of course. While you can't practice juggling on a horse—well, actually, I can, but nevertheless—it was ideal for teaching her songs and dialogues, switching languages at a moment's notice. Viola dropped her singing voice down to the low end of its range. I thought in a pinch that we could pass her off as a castrato, although the beard might present problems.

When we came to any decent-sized town, we set up in the market, and I entertained while she watched the horses and passed the hat. A short routine without tumbling, as I was still working my leg back into shape. After a few such performances, she picked up my lute and started accompanying me. I added improvisational composition to my growing list of her skills.

"You don't seem to be in a particular rush to reach our destination," she observed after lunch one day as we practiced some four-handed juggling.

"There's no great urgency," I replied. "Whatever happened to my colleagues happened six months before the Guild decided to send me. It will be eight months by the time we get there. I'm going there to find out what happened, not to save anybody in the nick of time."

She looked at me through the flurry of clubs between us. "You think they're all dead."

"Most likely."

"What exactly are we supposed to do when we get there?"

"Find out what happened. Make Constantinople a safe place for fools again."

"If someone's out to kill fools, then he'll try to kill you."

"Most likely. That's one of the reasons the Guild is sending me."

"Because they don't like you?"

"No, Apprentice. Because I have a talent for survival. Besides, I'll have you watching my back."

"Won't they try to kill me as well?"

"Perhaps. But you'll have me watching your back."

"What if they go after both of us at the same time?"

"Then we use Routine Eleven. Which we should practice some more."

It was mid-May, the year of our Lord 1202, when we left Orsino. A week's ride brought us to Durazzo and the Via Egnatia, which was still a good road these many centuries after the Romans built it to carry their armies east to conquest. Many armies have used it since, not all of them heading east and not all of them Roman. The people who build roads sometimes forget that they run both ways.

The ride east was almost without incident, but the incident that did take place was significant. We were riding through the most mountainous part of the journey to Ochrid when I motioned to Viola to rein her horse to a slow walk.

Two men blocked the road ahead of us. They wore scraps of armor, leather and iron, pieced together by thongs and cords, gleaned from whatever battlefields they had fled. Each had a short sword and a long knife at his waist.

"We're in trouble," I muttered.

"There's only two of them," said Viola softly.

"It's not the two in front that I'm worried about," I replied. "It's the five coming up behind us."

"Oh," she said, glancing behind her. "We're in trouble. How do we get out of it? Fight our way through?"

"A fool only fights when he can't talk his way out of something. We'll try that first."

"And if it doesn't work?"

"Routine Eleven. Follow my lead."

We trotted up to the two men in front, as the others, attired similarly, closed around us. I held up my hand in greeting.

"Hail, noble sirs!" I called in Greek. "You look in need of entertainment. How fortunate for you that we came by!"

Most of them looked at me blankly. One of the two in front muttered to the other in Bulgarian, then addressed me in heavily accented Greek.

"What are you that dresses so strangely?"

"A jester, good sir. A Christian who travels Christian lands to bring joy to Christian souls such as yourselves. Allow me to introduce myself: I am Feste, Lord of Misrule. Juggler, mimic, storyteller, and magician."

He gestured at Viola. "And this other one. He is no fool."

"My faithful servant, Claudius. A mute, alas, but a stout fellow. Are you gentlemen perhaps pilgrims?"

He laughed, then translated my comment to the others who laughed in turn. Well, laughter *is* what we seek in my profession, but I wasn't sure that this was the right kind. The leader said something, and our interpreter turned back to me.

"It must be life of great wealth, being fool."

I shrugged. "I have lived in castles and slept in caves. At the moment, I am looking for work."

He translated, and the leader laughed and barked something.

"He say, so are we," explained the interpreter. "Until then, we collect toll for road."

"How much is the toll?"

He smirked. "How much do you have?"

"Alas, no money. We can share what little provision we have, if that would suit your needs."

Viola gave me an anxious glance.

"Or," I continued as the two in front grumbled to each other, "may I suggest some entertainment to brighten your dreary day?"

The leader pointed at me and said something.

"He say, if you are jester, why do you carry sword?"

"This rusty old thing?" I exclaimed in surprise. "Merely a prop, my dear fellow. Allow me to demonstrate." I slid to the ground and drew my sword. They all began to grab at their own, but I held my other hand out to quiet them and quickly placed the weapon, hilt down, on the bridge of my nose. I let go and balanced it there.

They started laughing. I walked around them, faster and faster, skipping occasionally to and fro, the sword staying on my nose as if it had been soldered there. They started clapping. I removed it and commenced twirling it in one hand, spinning it around my neck and waist, over my head and through my legs. Viola slipped carefully off her horse and stood by it, her hand resting on the hilt of her own weapon.

Finally, I caught the sword, threw it high into the air, and stood under it confidently, one hand waiting to catch it. Then, at the last second, I ran screaming in terror as it plunged into the spot that I had just vacated. My audience laughed and clapped some more, chattering excitedly.

"That was a small sample of what I have to offer," I said cheerfully. "Would a full show be ample payment for our passage?"

The interpreter said something to the leader. He thought for a moment, then nodded and said something back. The interpreter turned back to me.

"He say, all right. You give show, we let you pass."

I bowed low, which amused them further, then beckoned to Viola.

"Routine Eleven, Claudius," I called, and she blinked, then bowed and pulled out three clubs from her bag. I took out three of my own, and we both started a simple pattern, walking casually toward each other. The men gathered around us. I caught her eye, nodded, and we started passing the clubs back and forth. One sequence, two . . .

"Gentlemen, for your pleasure, we will attempt to break our record for passes without a single drop."

Three, four, five . . .

"Gather around. The closer you get, the more fascinating it is."

Six, seven . . .

"As you see, we are but traveling players, simpletons who quail before your mighty arms."

Eight, nine . . .

"No need, with your numbers, to fear two small men such as ourselves."

Ten . . .

"Besides, I rarely kill with a sword."

Eleven.

The interpreter was momentarily too surprised by my last remark to translate it. Or maybe it was my dagger flying into his throat that prevented him.

Routine Eleven requires two jesters and six clubs. At the eleventh sequence, the clubs go flying out at anyone nearby. With a little bit of luck, you distract them long enough so that you can start evening the odds. With more luck, you might even send one or two sprawling.

Only one of the six went down, but in the second it took for the rest to duck, I plunged my knife into the side of the man to my right. I glimpsed Viola's sword out and active, but I was too worried about the two men coming at me to watch her.

There are plenty of ways to fight. There's the way they teach you to fight in castles, and the better way in the army. These fellows had clearly been good enough soldiers to survive some battles, and sneaky enough to take on all comers in this mountain pass.

But the Fools' Guild teaches us ways to fight that even a rogue can't anticipate. As the man nearest me came close, I ran at him, knife point-forward, then dove and tumbled by him as his sword passed over me. As I somersaulted past his leg, I opened up his thigh with a quick slash, then regained my feet as he fell to his knees. I slit his throat from behind.

Which left the leader, advancing cautiously, a weapon in each hand. I charged at him. He started to crouch, anticipating that I was going to repeat my successful maneuver against his late friend. My plan, however, was to fake a low move and then go high, flipping over him with my knife slicing through his neck.

That was my plan. It was a good plan, as plans go, and might even have worked, had not my knee chosen that moment to give way.

I hit the ground hard, my knife flying out of my hand. The leader watched for a second, suspecting some trick, but I was fresh out. He started laughing as he walked toward me. Again, not at all the right kind of laugh. My leg throbbing, I scuttled backward toward where my sword still stuck in the ground. He took another step, reversing the knife in his hand to throw it.

Then there was a faint *twung* from off to the right. He sat down heavily, an arrow piercing his neck. We looked at each other for a long time, sitting there a few feet apart. I shrugged. He shrugged back, then fell over, blood streaming from his mouth.

Viola stood some twenty paces away, a bow in her hand, another arrow notched and ready. Three men lay dead around her.

"Do you know," she said conversationally, "I somehow made it through the first thirty-two years of my life without killing anyone. Then you reenter the picture, and that's five dead men to my account since the New Year."

I forced myself upright, my leg on fire. "All justifiable, my love."

"As for that, why was Routine Eleven necessary? The nice man who spoke bad Greek said they would let us go."

"But what the leader actually said was, 'Let them put on their little show, and then we'll slit their throats and take their horses.'"

She looked around for her sword. It was embedded in the chest of one of them. She pulled it out and wiped it off on the nearby grass.

"What language were they speaking?" she asked.

"Bulgarian."

"You speak Bulgarian?"

"Fluently."

She sheathed her sword. "You must teach me. It sounds like a useful language to know."

I limped over to Zeus and pulled a rope from my pack. I looped one end around the feet of the nearest casualty and tied the other to the saddle.

"We're not going to bury them," she said, taking a rope out of her bag and following my lead.

"No. They may be missed soon. But I don't want to leave them lying in the middle of the road." I threw myself up onto the horse, then sat and waited for the pain to subside. "Remind me not to use that move next time."

"Sorry. I was a bit busy at that particular moment."

There was a whinny from off to the left of the road. I leaned over, snatched my sword from the ground, and rode in that direction, dragging the body behind me.

Seven horses were tied there, shying away from their late master. Viola rode up behind me as I dismounted. I pulled the body into the bushes where it would be out of sight. There was a slight rustling, and Viola called, "Feste! Behind you!"

I whirled, sword in hand, to see a boy of eight standing before me, a knife in his hand.

"Put it down, boy," I said in Bulgarian. "My quarrel is not with you."

"Mine is with you," he replied. He charged, brave stupid soul that he was. I sidestepped, caught his knife-hand in my left, and thumped him solidly with the hilt of my sword on the side of his head. He dropped like a stone.

We looked at him, lying on the forest floor, looking like any nonmurderous child lost in dreams.

"I suppose we have to take him with us," I said finally. She nodded, relieved. I tied his hands behind his back, then tied him to a tree. We hauled the remaining bodies off the road. Viola kept the bow she had picked up. I added another to my gear, and as many arrows as we could find. I then went through the pockets and saddlebags, collecting whatever coins and provisions I could find.

Viola looked at me distastefully. "Doesn't that make us as bad as them?"

"Not yet, my love. Give me some time."

I slapped the boy a few times until he came to. He gave me a look of pure hatred.

"These were your family?" I asked him.

He nodded.

"Father?"

He nodded again. "And brother. And uncles and cousins."

"Are there any women you can go to?"

He shook his head. "All gone."

"How far is home for you?"

"I don't know. I don't know where I am now."

I untied him from the tree, leaving his hands bound, then hoisted him onto one of the horses.

"Your family would have killed us, you know," I said, getting onto Zeus.

He nodded.

"You've seen them kill others, haven't you?"

"Yes."

"It would have been a simple thing to add your corpse to the rest of them. It might even have been a smart thing. But our quarrel ends now."

He sat, impassive. I leaned over and snatched his reins up.

"Let's go," I said.

"What about the other horses?" asked Viola.

I shrugged. "There's grass hereabouts. Someone else can claim them. I don't deal in livestock."

The reaction hit her that night. She sat hugging her knees to her chest, shaking, saying, "Seven men dead," over and over. I held her until she was too exhausted to continue. When she fell asleep, I covered her with a blanket, then looked up to see the boy, sitting against the tree to which he had been tied, wide awake. He had been watching the entire time.

We rode on in the morning. Outside of Ochrid, overlooking the great lake, was a monastery. I banged on the gate. A disheveled monk eventually came out.

"This boy is an orphan," I said. "He speaks only Bulgarian. Take him, teach him Greek, give him a decent trade. You can have his horse."

He nodded. In this part of the world, there were no questions. I lifted the boy down and untied his hands. He turned to face me.

"That one called you Feste," he said.

I shrugged. "That name will change."

"I will remember that name. I will remember your face. I will remember what you did. And someday, I will find you again and kill you."

"Maybe. Others have tried and failed. I suggest you devote your life to something a little more useful."

He turned and went inside. The monk made as if to follow. I tapped him on the shoulder. He turned, and I gave him the money I had found on the boy's family.

Viola was looking at me as I remounted Zeus. "So, that was his inheritance," she commented.

"No," I replied. "It was for the toll."

THREE

[T]he instruction of fools is folly.
PROVERBS 16:22

When were you last in Constantinople?" asked Fat Basil.

We were sitting in his cottage, a small stone building near the river. He was a slender man, tending a small kettle of stew on a small stove by the window. He had been in Thessaloniki for over twenty years, which meant that he had seen more than his share of horrors. When he smiled, even in full makeup, there was something dead in his eyes. Perhaps it was just a reflection.

He had received us without surprise, as though he had been cooking just for our arrival. We put our horses in back, then gratefully sank onto a pile of cushions that served as his only furniture. Viola remained in male garb. I was waiting to see how long she could sustain the illusion before another professional. She had fooled me on more than one occasion.

"About eight or nine years ago," I said. "Coming back from Beyond-the-Sea. Spent maybe six months there."

"All right, so you knew everyone except for Ignatius. He started working the troubadour route about four years ago. From here to there, entertaining along the way, then back again. I used to see him every two months or so. The last time was only six weeks after he had left, which meant that he had ridden straight back without stopping. His horse was practically dead from exhaustion, and Ignatius wasn't far behind."

"When was this?"

"Early December. 'They're all gone,' he said. He couldn't find a trace of any one of them. Their rooms were untouched, except there were signs of a struggle in Niko and Piko's house."

"Any blood?"

"If there was, it would have been two months dried when he was there. But he didn't notice anything like that. That's not to say it wasn't there, but the dwarves weren't the neatest of folk."

"Where was the message drop?"

"At the Rooster. Ignatius found nothing. Then he did the smart thing. He panicked and fled."

Despite the stove and the near-summer weather, I felt cold. "But he went back," I said.

"Of course," said Fat Basil, stirring his pot. "He had to. And I've heard nothing since. Not news, not gossip, not the vaguest hint of a rumor. Six of us vanished in a city of four hundred thousand. Nobody cares why."

"Except for the Guild."

"Yes," he said. He ladled out an unidentifiable but delicious brown mess into three bowls and handed them around.

"Why didn't they send you?" asked Viola in Claudius's voice. It was her first question.

"Because, Apprentice, I'm needed here. Someone has to tell the Guild when the two of you don't come back alive."

"If I don't come back alive, I'll come back to haunt you, just for the fun of it," she retorted.

He grimaced. "Join the crowd. There's always room for another shade in Thessaloniki." He gestured at her, looking at me. "Is this guy going to be of any use to you? He's awfully green."

"He already has been of use," I replied. "Is there anyone there that you know of who I can turn to in an emergency?"

"Maybe the innkeeper at the Rooster. I don't know of anyone else. No, wait. I don't know for certain, but they say Zintziphitzes may still be around."

"No!" I exclaimed in astonishment, and we both started laughing. Claudius looked back and forth at the two of us.

"Who was Zintzi . . . Zintzi what?" she asked.

"Zintziphitzes was, or is, a fool," I said.

"But not like us," said Fat Basil.

"He's a short man, with unusually long arms. . . ."

"An ugly man, with hair all over . . ."

"He's been compared to an ape. . . ."

"Unfavorably!" we finished together.

"So, he was in the Guild," she said.

"For a while," Fat Basil explained. "But he didn't particularly like following orders, or doing anything for anyone else's benefit."

"He was a mocker, pure and simple," I continued. "He prowled the seats at the Hippodrome. No makeup, no costumes, no tricks or artifice of any kind. He would seize upon a target and spew venom in the form of rhymed couplets, improvised on the spot yet never less than hilarious and brilliant. As hideous and misshapen as he was, he could mimic anyone and make you forget who you were actually looking at."

"Which was a blessing when you consider who you were looking at," added Fat Basil. "Once, someone insulted the Emperor's son by saying he resembled Zintziphitzes. The Emperor considered it so grievous a slander that he had the man put to death."

"My goodness," exclaimed Viola, impressed.

"Ignatius mentioned a few visits back that he had heard he was still around, but we didn't discuss it any further. Zintziphitzes may not have liked the Fools' Guild, but he was friendly enough with the fools. He might know something."

"Where does he live?" I asked.

"Last I heard, somewhere near the Hippodrome. He doesn't perform there anymore, but he couldn't tear himself away from it."

"All right, I'll track him down." I yawned. It had been a long ride, and we still had another two weeks' journey ahead of us. Our host scattered some cushions about.

"You can each have a corner," he said. "I have my usual rounds to make tonight."

"We can share," said Viola, pulling her wig off and shaking out her hair.

Fat Basil stepped back and collapsed onto the cushions, laughing uproariously.

"Well done, Apprentice," he gasped. "You took me in completely. Who is she, Theo?"

"Meet the Duchess Viola."

He sat up and nodded. "You're the one who killed that Malvolio fellow while yonder hero was pinned to a wall."

"That was me," she admitted.

"Took his head clean off, I heard."

"Not entirely," she said briefly. "And it was far from clean."

"You got the job done, in any case."

"It wasn't a job back then. I killed him strictly as an amateur."

"Well, I'll leave you two fools together. I suppose that I should be chaperoning, but I have prior commitments." He gathered his gear, then leered at me. "I do hope you're married."

"Of course," I said.

He sighed. "I should have been a traveling fool," he said, and he left.

We lay side by side on the cushions as the sun set. I traced the curves of her eyebrows with my finger, and she smiled at me. It was worth everything good that I had ever done in my life to be on the receiving end of such a smile.

"Tell me why he's called Fat Basil," she said. "Some inside joke of the Guild?"

"No joke," I said. "He was once the fattest fool in the Guild, yet a nimble man for all that. He came to Thessaloniki when he was still a young man. He was an immediate success, particularly with the children. He had a childlike nature himself, or so they said."

"I don't see it," she commented.

"This was a long time ago. In 1185, the city was taken by Norman invaders, led by William the Good, who was only called that because he was a little less bad than William the Bad. It was a massacre. They violated the women, looted the houses, slew anyone who objected, and set fire to churches filled with people who had sought sanctuary inside. They seized all of the food and glutted themselves on it, while the Thessalonians watched and starved."

"And Fat Basil starved with them."

"They found him singing to a dying child and dragged him into a great house they had occupied. They forced him to perform, and threw him what scraps of food they deemed unworthy of finishing. He ate only what he could survive upon, and smuggled the rest out. By the time the invaders were driven out, he was a wraith of a man, wandering the city, looking for survivors to help. And he's been here ever since, and we still call him Fat Basil. To honor him."

She sat up, the moonlight glinting off the tears on her cheeks. "I never knew," she whispered. "These Normans—they were from Sicily, were they not?"

"They were."

"You know that I am Sicilian."

"Yes, fair Messaline. I know."

"My people did this."

I shook my head. "Your people no longer. You've joined another tribe. The invisible nation of fools."

We embraced our host in the morning and rode off. The Via Egnatia stayed under our horses' hooves for the next two weeks as Thessaly gave way to Thrace and the Aegean called to us over and over from the south.

I used the journey to tell Viola everything I knew about the great city that awaited us. Who was in it, who was allied to whom, and why that was a bad idea. Where the best meals were, when to draw the line in haggling, when to cross it.

We spoke of the fools that prowled Constantinople, where they lived, where they worked, what predilections might have led them into traps.

"And Thalia was a particular friend of yours, was she not?" she teased me at one point.

"First anniversary for the next revelation, my dove," I said.

"That's not a secret I need to know," she replied. "From the way you're reacting, I'd say it's not even a secret. There's no need to be coy with me, Feste. We are not blushing young virgins entering marriage."

"Fair enough."

"But tell me more of the dwarf brothers. Were they dwarves who were also fools, or does the Guild go around recruiting dwarves just because they are dwarves?"

It stung when she hit the mark so accurately.

"It is an area of some controversy," I admitted. "Even some shame. It is an old story, how the little people are seized from their villages, carried away from their homes and families, solely for the amusement of kings and their children. If the Guild hears of such persons, we try and enlist them before it happens, give them the training they need."

"The training they need to serve the Guild?"

"That, and the training they need just to survive. They are treated cruelly, these small folk. They're dressed up as monkeys, put on leashes, led around by toddlers, and thrust into iron collars that are never removed."

She rode in silence for a while. "It seems to me that you're no better than anyone else, if all you seek to do is use dwarves to suit the Guild's purposes."

"Perhaps. Yet we are different in one aspect. We treat them as human, as full-fledged members of the Guild. We are all used to suit the Guild's purposes, milady, and the dwarves are used equally. And many of them flourish as a result. There once was a dwarf named Scarlett . . . well, that's a long tale, and best left to another day. Niko and Piko were twins, recruited by us when they were still children. We were able to place them in Constantinople. They were a brilliant team, verbally, physically, and musically. They managed to survive the many sudden changes of emperor and still advance the Guild's goals with each successor."

"I suppose they would have been less than adequate at defending themselves."

"You suppose wrong. Niko was a superb knife-thrower, and Piko an adept poisoner. If they were taken, it must have been at their house."

"They must have been quite successful to have a house of their own."

"You'll understand when you see it."

We came over a rise, and she gasped, reining her horse to a walk.

"Is that it?" she cried in wonder. "The walls of Constantinople."

"Not even close," I said.

"But those walls . . . they're enormous."

"A mere trifle, a pile of children's blocks compared to the city walls. These are the Anastasian walls. Impressive, but they've been breached many a time. We're still two days' ride from Constantinople."

The walls were guarded, of course, so our audience that evening was mainly soldiers. Claudius was part of the act by this time, playing the traditional apprentice role of dupe and stooge. She had affected an air of dignity to the point of caricature, and combined it with a taciturn style that led to a wonderful slow burn as I took increasing liberties, though I had to forgo my beard-pulling ways to help her maintain the disguise.

And we played with her persona: this short, grumpy, hairy fellow would pick up a lute and suddenly sing in an exaggerated soprano, astonishing the rough fellows with its beauty. That such a high voice could emanate from such a masculine face—well, they had never seen anything like it, and we did quite well financially.

We ate with a few of them afterward, a group of Cumans who all spoke Greek fluently.

"It was lucky you came by today," said one. "We just got paid yesterday. Back pay for half a year. If it hadn't arrived and you came here next week, you might have found a deserted wall and no audience."

"It wouldn't have been the worst crowd I've ever had," I replied. "At least no one would have thrown anything at me. Has the pay been that irregular?"

Some grumbled, some laughed. "We are out of the Emperor's purview," said a second.

"And not being grapevines or whores, we rarely come to his attention," added a third.

"May I conclude that he only cares for things that cling?" I quipped, and they laughed. I stored that one away for further use in the city.

Two days later, we rounded a low hill, and Viola gasped, reining her horse to a stop. She stared for a long time.

"Now, that is truly a wall," she pronounced finally. "Two walls, in fact."

"Welcome to Constantinople, Duchess," I said. "Behold the walls of Theodosios, which were actually planned and built by his regent, Anthemios, but what good is being the emperor if you can't take the credit? The walls that no enemy has ever breached. If you were to take the bones of every soldier who was ever killed at the base of these walls, and legions of them were, you still could not pile them so high as to surmount them. Arab armies were decimated here. The great river of Huns was dammed and diverted by them. The Visigoths broke camp just upon seeing them, and Krum the Bulgarian, who laid waste to the entire countryside, who had as his personal drinking cup the skull of the Emperor Nikephoros, took one look at them and wept, knowing that he had at last reached the limit of his conquests."

"When so many great kings and armies have been stopped by this mountain of stones, how are the likes of us supposed to get in?" complained Viola.

I pointed to the left. "How about through one of those gates over there?"

She looked, then pointed to the right. "What's wrong with that one?"

There was a stone arch set into the wall atop two giant pillars of polished marble. Where the rest of the wall was made up of layers of brick and limestone, this section was comprised entirely of marble blocks, including the towers, and was covered with friezes and statuary. The doorway could have admitted the Colossus of Rhodes had it been brought to life, with enough room left over for it to wear a plumed hat.

"Once a duchess, always a duchess," I sighed. "Your ambition rears its ugly head yet again. That's the Golden Gate, my dear, and even you are not worthy of its passage."

"Really?" she sniffed. "Who would I have to kill or sleep with to change that?"

"The Emperor, in both cases," I replied. "And he can only use it for military triumphs or coronations. Theodosios himself entered on the back of an elephant without even ducking his head."

She leaned forward and patted the neck of her mare. "That's all right, dear," she said to it soothingly. "I like you just fine even if you're not an elephant. Shall we take one of those gates to the left?"

The land walls separated the peninsula from the mainland, running from the Sea of Marmara by the Imperial Landing to the Blachernae Palace on the southern bank of the Golden Horn. Someone once told me that a map of the city boundaries resembled a horse's head facing the east. The land walls met up with the seawalls at both ends, built by some emperor named Theophilos, of all names. One of the smarter ones, as I recall, and that rare Byzantine emperor who came to the throne after his predecessor died of old age. He had a fool, according to Guild lore, a fellow named Dandery who kept him from killing too many people.

The overall effect of the encircling stone to one viewing it from a distance was that some ancient god of pottery had manufactured a massive bowl, into which he had poured a city.

We rode along the outside of the moat, while Viola glanced nervously at the fortifications to our right. The outer wall was some thirty feet high, the inner wall twice that, and towers—

some square, some round—interrupted both of them, alternating between the inner and outer walls. The towers on the inner wall looked a hundred feet high or more.

We couldn't see much of the city from this angle, although the Xerolophon, the Seventh Hill, loomed beyond the inner wall, with the Pillar of Arkadios at its peak. If you had never seen a mountain, you might very well assume that the top of that pillar was the highest point in the world. It certainly tended to remove the element of surprise from any attacker, whether they approached by land or sea.

We passed by military gates, by the Gate of Xylokerkou, by the Gate of Pege, by the road to Selivrias, and by the Holy Springs. By this time, Viola's glances were directed toward me.

"You know, it really is a pity that we've come all this way, and then decided not to visit," she commented. "They'll think us rude. Or were you planning to make the assault by sea after all?"

"I want to go in by the Rhegium Gate."

"Oh. I see. Because that is a much nicer gate than all of these closer ones."

"Not particularly."

"Why the Rhegium Gate?"

"Because if someone is killing all the fools, then he may be expecting the Guild to send someone. Since the Guildhall is to the west, he'll most likely be having the gates watched from that direction. So, we'll go a few gates north."

We rode on while she thought about that. "You're thinking that there's more than one person involved."

"I'll assume that for safety's sake."

"But they'll get word from the guard post at that Anastasian wall, won't they?"

"Possibly. But no messengers passed us on the way."

The ground rose a bit toward where the wooden bridge crossed the moat. I pulled up Zeus and looked at the gate, the twinned towers flanking it on both the outer and inner walls. Viola followed my gaze, then looked back at me.

"Shall we?" she said.

I kept looking.

"You're afraid," she said softly.

"Yes," I said. "I've never encountered a task quite like this one. I have to find someone I don't know in a city of four hundred thousand. And he, or they, will be looking for me. And they'll have the advantage, because I do stand out in a crowd."

"There are two of us," she pointed out.

"There were six of them," I replied. I took a deep breath, then exhaled. "All right, let's go."

The horses' hooves clopped loudly on the wooden bridge as we crossed the moat. It was dry, revealing the ancient stonework of the scarps as well as piles of refuse at the base.

"Maybe I'm just ignorant of such manly things, but shouldn't there be water in there?" asked Viola.

"Should be," I agreed. "Last time I was here, there was. I wonder what happened?"

From the bridge, it was some fifty or sixty feet across the peribolos to the opening in the outer wall. No grass grew there, either because of the constant foot patrols or because the blood-soaked earth would permit none. The wall itself was maybe seven feet thick. I knew that the towers on both sides could rain rocks, arrows, boiling oil, or Greek fire down on anyone they didn't like. I hope they liked us.

But that was a silly fear. There was a stream of commerce flowing in and out of the city through this gate: ox-drawn wains, peasant-drawn carts, children with baskets of dates and figs balanced on their heads, women with pails of milk hung from yokes on their shoulders, all the daily turmoil from the countryside needed to keep the city supplied. Even in full makeup, I barely received a second glance.

I noticed some deep cracks in the masonry as we passed, perhaps remnants of some minor earthquake. Man could not breach these walls; God still could.

It was late in the day, and the sun was fleeing back down the Via Egnatia, abandoning us to the shadows of the walls. Another sixty feet across the parateichion, wide enough for an army to race from one entrance to another, and we were at the inner gate, the real monster, a tunnel through thirty feet of stone, brick, and concrete with the only light coming from the end. The various animal and human noises, squeaking wheels and clanking chains, all mingled in the gloom into a fair representation of what Hell would sound like in my dreams. Our horses were pressed together in the crowd, and I felt Viola's leg brush against mine. Well, that belonged to a different dream altogether.

We emerged, blinking in the daylight, into a profusion of garrisons, stables, carpenters, armorers, blacksmiths. Huge ramps, broad enough to carry the larger engines of war, led to the ramparts high above us.

Yet for all the show of force, sections of wall had crumbled, and there were no workers in sight repairing them. It was late afternoon, yet some of the towers had no watch posted upon them, and the noise from the blacksmiths' anvils was sporadic at best.

"Woe to the emperor who neglects his walls," I muttered to Viola.

But she was looking everywhere else. The garrisons gave way to farmland, which seemed almost incongruous with the fierce stonework protecting it. Off past it lay the other six hills of this walled city, the great aqueduct of Valens spanning two of them, and then building after building, spire after spire, clusters of palaces to the left and right, and beyond them all, the immense dome of the Hagia Sophia, the church that dwarfed all churches.

But, glorious as it was, I had seen it before. I chose instead to observe my beloved as she beheld it. She turned her head slowly, her eyes darting everywhere, trying to take it all in at once. She almost seemed a child again, despite the wig, despite the beard, her face suffused with wonder.

"I've been to Paris, Rome, Vienna, Ravenna, and Venice," she said finally. "None of them compare to this. It's enormous."

"All of those cities and thirty more would fit inside these walls with room to grow, my dear Claudius."

She winced slightly at the male appellation, but we were here, and it was time to stay in character. There was a rumbling noise behind us, and we turned to see the several gates of Rhegium being pushed closed and the great beams used to bar them swung into place.

"We are trapped, my dear Feste," replied Claudius. "The world is shut out, and we are joining the rest of the inmates in this magnificent prison."

I slid off Zeus and started leading him to a nearby stable. Claudius did the same.

"On the contrary, the entire world is a prison, but we have escaped to another world. Walls can keep things out as well as keep them in. At least there is safety here."

"Unless you happen to be a fool."

I clapped her on the shoulder as men are wont to do to each other. She staggered under the blow and glared at me.

"There is freedom behind locked barriers, Claudius," I continued. "Did not Aristotle say that a city defended by walls has a choice of alternatives, but a people without any walls are a people without any choice?"

She looked at the Vigla, the night watch, assembling, fully armed, for their evening patrol.

"Aristotle got it wrong," she said.

ƒOUR

Make not thyself an underling to a foolish man.

SIRACH 4:29

It would take me several books to describe the grandeur of Constantinople but let me at least give you an idea of the city.

I mentioned that it was shaped like a horse's head. Take the line made by the horse's mouth—that's the Mese, the main road, starting at the Milion, the marker for all distances. I suppose the horse would have to be smiling slightly for this to be accurate, much as my friend Zeus does when I do something stupid as opposed to merely foolish.

Now, put a bit in the horse's mouth. That marks the Forum Amastrianum, where the horse dealers do business. This is where I threaten to bring my friend Zeus when he smiles at me for doing something stupid.

Attach a bridle to the bit. This would show how the Mese divides after the Forum Amastrianum, with one branch going off to the southwest, much as the rein would at rest. This road ultimately connects with the Via Egnatia.

The other branch goes northwest, parallel to the Golden Horn, and passes through the Charisios Gate to the road to Adrianople.

The vast majority of the buildings and people fill the space from the seawalls to the Mese and its branches, from the Golden

Gate all the way around to the Golden Horn. The quarters maintained by foreign cities—Venice, Pisa, Genoa, and Amalfi—are all by the seawall fronting the Golden Horn, each with its own piers and warehouses.

The Muslims, though possessing a seaside mosque outside the city walls, have their quarter up the Golden Horn near the stone bridge that crosses to the Galata district. The Jews, once in the city proper, have been relocated across the Golden Horn near the Galata Tower. I think the Venetians may have bumped them out, but that was a long time ago.

The Great Palace complex, where the emperors used to live before it became too full of ostentatious architecture, is just below the horse's nose. The Blachernae Palace, where they live now, is up by its ear. The ear is pricked up and alert for signs of danger, both from without the walls and within. The Blachernae complex is the only neighborhood in the city that is walled on every side. Empires also face threats from their own people. The large triangle made by the forks of the Mese and the land wall is mostly farmland, hills, and the odd ravine.

Those of you who have been to Constantinople and who feel protective toward it may be somewhat offended by my choice of animal for comparison. Let me say in my defense that there are cities that I would compare to an entirely different portion of a horse's anatomy. Consider yourselves fortunate.

By now, fellow fools, the clever ones amongst you will have deduced that I survived this particular story to write about it. Naturally. Historians are always survivors. But rest assured, not everyone you will meet in this tale will have the same luck.

We stabled our horses, paying a week in advance, and hoisted the saddlebags onto our shoulders. We hurried along as best we could, for the sun was setting, and to be caught out after dark by the Vigla would have meant our immediate arrest. As newly arrived foreigners, one in disguise, we would have faced some unpleasant forms of interrogation.

Viola was puffing slightly under the weight of her bags. "Several leisurely weeks on horseback," she grumbled. "Now, all of a sudden, we have to run? I don't even remember how to walk after all that riding. My legs will never forgive me. I may never forgive you."

"Look up for a moment, Apprentice," I suggested.

She glanced over as the setting sun bounced its beams off the variegated domes and spires of the city proper, gold leaf and porphyry and a dozen different colors of marble transmuting the rays into something altogether glorious.

"All right, I forgive you," she whispered.

There was a small neighborhood that had sprung up where the Rhegium and Romanos roads met, a grouping of taverns and hostels seeking to beguile weary travelers before the bulk of the city had its way with them. In the center of this larcenous cluster was the Rooster, an inn of uneasy repute that nevertheless set a fine table and, more to the point, possessed a worthy wine cellar. It was a two-story, brick construction, and the second floor projected out over the street, sagging slightly. The red, rounded roof tiles gave the inn the appearance of having a cockscomb.

Dinner, mostly of a liquid nature, was taking place, as the several men who stayed there had just returned from a day's honest labor before sneaking out again for a night's dishonest labor. The room, which was at the level of a general roar, became somewhat quieter as we made our entrance. Claudius, I observed approvingly, had adopted not so much a fierce expression as a studied bland one. The most dangerous men are those who choose not to reveal it, and the cautious appraisals of the toughs in the room acknowledged this truth.

I drew my usual stares, of course, mingled with some anticipation of entertainment. At least, I assumed that anticipation was
there, though it may have been my vanity whispering in my ear.

The tapster was a tall fellow, heavily scarred about the face
and neck, his knuckles thick and calloused. I caught his eye, and
he limped in my direction.

"Drink or what?" he rasped. His Greek was fluent, but with
an accent I couldn't quite place.

"Drink, victuals, and lodging, my good fellow, assuming you
are the proprietor."

"I am. The name's Simon. You're together?"

"Indeed. My name is Feste, and this is my manservant, Claudius. How much for your best room?"

"My best room is taken. So is the second best. The two of
you can have the last room on the right upstairs. You'll have to
share the pallet. How long will you be staying?"

I smiled. "It depends on how well we do."

"Then I want two weeks in advance. Now."

I sighed and paid the fellow.

"Claudius," I said. "Take the bags upstairs. I'm going to introduce myself to our new neighbors."

Oh, the resentful glare from my newly appointed manservant!
Muttering invectives in my direction, she hoisted my bags on top
of hers and staggered up the steep stairway.

"So hard to get good help these days," I commented to the
room in general, and a mild chuckle went around the crowd.

I secured enough space for Claudius and myself at the end of
one bench, and helped myself to a portion of the jellied calves'
feet and a chunk of brown bread to sop it up. I think it was
jellied calves' feet. Jelly there was, and some species of foot in it.
The wine was sweet and thick, almost a syrup. It was delicious.

"Syrian, is this?" I called to the tapster across the hubbub.

"Well done!" he shouted. "From the hills of the Krak des Chevaliers, where the brave knights of the Hospitalers protect us from the infidel. Good Christians with fine vineyards. Have you been there?"

"No, but this wine is ample argument for making the pilgrimage."

Claudius rejoined us and went at the dinner with an appetite.

"You know your wine, Fool," said a deep voice from across the table. I looked up to see a cowl with shadows inside. Only a sharp chin was visible.

"I've traveled a bit," I replied. "A fool lives from meal to meal, and from drink to drink. One learns to savor the experiences, because occasionally all one has to dine upon are the memories of previous meals."

"And that is what you are? An entertainer?" asked the priest, if that was what he was.

"I have many talents," I said. "But being a fool has kept me in my cups for many a year."

"Then let me counsel you," he said. "They call me Father Esaias. I run this neighborhood. I watch my flocks very carefully, especially by night."

"When the fleecing is done."

"Exactly. I have no interest in entertainment. In fact, I have very little sense of humor, and what amuses me, many find terrifying. The last time I laughed was when an overly ambitious young cutpurse went beyond his assigned territory. He was found hanging by—well, the details aren't important."

"Not at all."

"So, as long as I see you doing your little tumbling routines in the markets, I will have no need to bring God's wrath down upon you. But interfere with any of our activities, or try your luck without our permission or our participation in the proceeds, then I will laugh at your antics myself."

"I understand entirely. And if I need further religious instruction, where may I find you in my hour of need?"

"At the church, my son. Saint Stephen's, down toward the river."

I reached into my purse and handed him a coin.

"For the orphans, Father."

He stood, took it, and glided out of the inn.

"That was well done," commented a man to my right. He held out his hand, and I took it. "Peter Kamantares."

"Feste, the Fool, at your service. My manservant, Claudius."

Claudius nodded politely, her mouth full.

"Does everyone here end up working for him?" I asked.

"When times are good, there's no need. Some of the fellows here prefer the night."

"You are not one of them, I take it."

He shrugged. "Times have not always been good. But I work in the slaughterhouse. There's always a demand for fresh meat in this city."

He introduced us to some of the other residents of the inn. There was Michael, a huntsman; Asan, a small, lithe fellow who had the look of a pickpocket if ever I saw one; Stephanos, a burly, heavily bearded man who I certainly would want on my side in a fight; and a table full of Russians who kept to themselves. Peter told me they had rowed across the Black Sea in a boat filled with furs, sold them at a huge profit, and then drank, whored, and gambled their way to the Rooster, where they now had too little coin to resupply their way back.

The fire was down to embers. I stood, stretched, and bade our new companions a good evening. Simon was wiping the cups with a rag that looked far from clean. I leaned on the counter and beckoned to him.

"If by chance you see another fool by the name of Tiberius, tell him I'm in town."

He scowled. "What would you with that rascal?"

"He owes me money," I said. "A considerable sum. He is truly what drew me back to this city."

"Join the club," replied Simon. "He owes half of Constantinople. There's been plenty looking for him, but he's vanished."

"When?"

"I couldn't say exactly. Sometime before Christmas. He used to come in here a lot. I made the mistake of letting him drink on credit. I won't make that mistake with you."

"I won't give you cause, my dear sir. Tapsters are my closest friends in the world."

"No need for friendship, Fool. Just pay up front, and we'll get along fine."

I lit a candle and led Claudius upstairs.

The room was not even the third best room, if I was any judge of quality. The pallet was a pile of moldy straw with a ragged sheet thrown over it, and I had the distinct feeling that we would not be the only creatures sharing it this evening. Viola laid out our bags as far from it as she could, which in the space allotted us was maybe three feet away.

"Could we go back to the woods?" she asked.

I held a finger to my lips and listened at the doorway. There was no actual door, just another sheet tacked onto the lintel for privacy. I took a length of twine and fastened it across the entrance about a foot from the ground.

"Keep your disguise on," I whispered. "Do you want first watch or second?"

"I'll take first," she said.

I stretched out on the pallet. She came over and hauled my boots off, then sat down for me to return the favor. She pulled a blanket from her bedroll and huddled on the other side of the doorway.

"You told Simon that story to give you an excuse to go looking for Tiberius," she whispered as I blew out the candle. "I like that. I never thought I could fall in love with someone who could lie as proficiently as you do."

"Thank you, milady."

"How long will we have to keep watch in this lovely hostel?"

"At least for the first few nights."

A little bit of moonlight came through the window, enough for me to discern her eyes gleaming from the corner, like some nocturnal rodent watching me for an opportunity.

"You realize, of course, that if I am to remain in male garb, that we will have to forgo conjugal relations," she remarked.

"I thought you were tired of riding."

She gave a quick, quiet bark of laughter, fortunately still in Claudius's voice. I closed my eyes.

I am a light sleeper, partly by nature, partly by training. Something stirred my dreams enough for me to lurch to my feet, knife in hand, before I was entirely awake. My eyes, when they had finally adjusted to the dark, saw Claudius, sword drawn, sitting on top of a dark form.

"What have we here, my good man?" I asked.

"A rat, sir," she replied. "A veritable vermin."

"Isn't this my room?" protested the man. I pulled the sheet over the doorway and lit the candle. It was Asan, one of the fellows from the evening table. He was dressed in dark clothing, and had smeared his face with charcoal.

"Didn't your mother teach you to wash your face before bed?" I asked him.

He muttered something that reflected upon my mother. I chose to ignore it, and knelt down by his head, my knife resting on his neck. He became still.

"You're a poor excuse for a burglar," I said.

"Can't blame a fellow for trying," he replied.

"Oh, yes, I can. Now, my first inclination is to slit your throat and be done with it, but I'd hate to be thrown out of a place when I've already paid for two weeks in advance. I suppose I could turn you over to the authorities."

"But I have the feeling that you'd rather have no contact with the guard if you can help it," said Asan hurriedly.

"I wasn't talking about them," I said sharply. "Father Esaias might be interested in this little incident. The Rooster is off-limits, isn't it?"

"How did you know that?" he whispered.

I cuffed him. "You're a puppy," I said. "I was picking pockets when your mother's milk was still wet on your lips. You think I don't know this city? Maybe I'll just give you to Esaias and be done with you."

"Please, sir, I'm sorry. I didn't know," he babbled.

I cuffed him again, and he shut up.

"What say you, Claudius?" I asked. "Shall we let him live?"

"I don't see what use he could be to us," said Claudius slowly. "He bungled this job."

"No, no, I'm no good at nightwork, but I can pick pockets, and I'm a good lookout, and I can find you anything you want here."

I raised my hand, and he quieted. I lowered it.

"As it happens, I am looking for someone," I said. "A fool like myself. His name is Tiberius."

"I know him!" he said excitedly. "You see? I'm useful!"

"I'd like to know where he is," I continued. "Find him, and

there may even be a little something in it for you. Although continued existence seems ample profit under the circumstances, don't you think?"

"Yes, yes. I'll have word for you by sundown tomorrow."

"Search him, then let him go," I commanded.

She rummaged through his clothing, found no weapons, and then let him stand, her sword constantly at his chest.

"Until tomorrow, my friend," I said. "Go get some sleep. And wash that face. Our landlord may not appreciate the mess on his fine linens."

He slunk into the hallway. I leaned outside the doorway and watched him until he entered his room.

"Well done," I said to Viola. "Only use your knife next time. Swords are a liability when there's no room to swing them."

"All right. Shall we assume that's it for the evening?"

"Not at all. Get some sleep. It's my turn to keep watch."

We left the Rooster at midmorning, a jester's normal working time. I took only my working bag with me, leaving most of my gear behind. I left my sword as well. We could afford to appear less belligerent now that we had made it inside the city walls. Viola kept her sword. It was the day's plan that I would do the performing, and she would keep an eye on the crowd.

"Is that our entire plan?" she asked.

"No," I replied. "But I have to establish myself immediately. A fool who does not care about entertaining is clearly a spy. At some point, we'll go search out where my colleagues dwelled."

The road from our immediate neighborhood carried us south, following the gentle rise of the Xerolophon toward the southwest branch of the Mese. Bakeries on both sides of the road scented the air until we could stand it no longer and bought enough bread for two meals. Although the road was more or less straight, the side streets twisted and turned in a labyrinth of passages, houses of stone and brick crammed together, the upper floors projecting over the streets, greedily seizing every possible square foot while blocking the sun from reaching the pedestrians.

People swarmed everywhere. Constantinople is the crossroads of the world, and every nation sent its representatives to seek their fortunes, or to seek someone else's fortune. Franks, Vlachs, Pechenegs, Turks, Russians, Alans, and Latins all scurried about, speaking Greek with varying proficiencies and in a profusion of accents.

Our road met the Mese in the Forum of Arkadios. The pillar erected to the memory of that emperor overlooked us, a pile of immense, squared stones stacked to over a hundred feet. They say there had once been a statue of Arkadios himself on top, but an earthquake had sent it plummeting long ago.

There were pillars all over the city, as various emperors and their wives competed for posterity. Many in this superstitious time would observe which personage's representation was struck down by one calamity or another and try to interpret what it portended. Some of the more cynical would merely place elaborate wagers on which statue would be the next to topple.

A small squad of soldiers marched by, their body armor almost cylindrical in shape, enormous single-edged axes carried casually over their shoulders. Their standard was a dragon, spewing flames on a blue field. A few of them were chattering as we passed.

"They were speaking English," exclaimed Viola in astonishment.

"The Varangian Guard," I explained. "A lot of them are English. They first came after the Norman Conquest. More have come since then, especially after the Crusades stranded a few. Very devoted to the emperor, at least until he's been overthrown. Then they're very devoted to the next emperor."

Another squad passed us, consisting of extremely tall, fair-haired men, similarly attired.

"Those are also Varangians?" she asked.

"Yes."

"But they weren't speaking English. I don't recognize that language."

"Danish," I said. "Those who aren't English are usually from the north. They send them down here for experience."

"You speak Danish?" she asked.

"Fluently."

"Strange," she said. "Why would you need that language? I thought you spent most of your career around the Mediterranean."

"I don't need it. It was thrust upon me by accident of birth."

"You're Danish?"

"Originally."

"But how did you end up . . . ?"

"Second anniversary, Duchess. Here's a likely spot. Let's get to work."

The market was in full haggle as farmers in from the outlying regions vended their produce, huntsmen sold freshly killed venison from their bloodied carts, and woodsmen stood before stacks of, well, wood. The smaller children ran screaming around the forum, dashing fearlessly around and occasionally under the hooves of the passing horses, while the older ones watched their parents' goods. A clump of them saw me and scampered over expectantly. I arranged them in a largish circle with as much pomp as I could muster, then shook my head in mock dissatisfaction and rearranged them several more times. Then, I pulled out five balls and sent them flying, occasionally sending a ball at one of the children and catching the return toss.

Out of the corner of my eye I saw Claudius drift over to a

nut seller and engage in some spirited negotiation, which conveniently provided her with a good view of my performance and the crowd that gathered.

I continued for an hour, working knives and torches into the juggling, pulling out my tabor and flute and playing both simultaneously, singing a number of silly songs, and finishing with a lengthy encomium to their glorious city, thanking the crowd for their most gracious and heartfelt welcome. Then I picked up the scattered coins thrown in my direction. All bronze—this was not the wealthiest of forums, but when one is new in town, one should start at the bottom.

"Thank you, good people," I shouted. "Should you desire further entertainment, leave word at the Rooster for Feste, the Fool."

I picked up my gear and walked out of the market. I ventured a few hundred feet down the Mese, then turned onto a side street where I saw a likely tavern. A few minutes later, Claudius sat by me and silently held out a cloth bag filled with nuts. I took some.

"You weren't followed," she said. "I didn't see anyone in the crowd who looked unduly interested."

"I wouldn't have expected it the first day," I said.

"What shall we do after lunch?"

"Let's go look at Demetrios's room. It's time to revert to our other function."

"So, in this case function follows forum."

I winced. "I don't think you're quite ready to go solo, Apprentice, but keep trying."

We walked together down the Mese. Claudius glanced wistfully back at the Pillar of Arkadios.

"Will we have a chance to go to the top?" she asked.

"Sometime," I said. "There's much to do first."

"And the holy relics. They say they have most of the True Cross here."

"That's what they think. There's a big chunk of wood at the Church of the Theotakos at Blachernae, supposedly excavated by Helen, Constantine's mother. She was sainted basically for being conned by some Palestinian tricksters. They also sold her the crosses of the two thieves, the crown of thorns, Mary Magdalene's jar, the baskets that held the miraculous loaves, the slab on which the dead Christ lay, and that's just the Jesus stuff. They have all sorts of relics of the saints as well."

"I hear they have the head of John the Baptist."

"They do. In fact, they have two. We'll see them both."

She looked at me quizzically.

"I thought you were a believer," she said.

"I am. I just don't believe in worshiping pieces of dead people."

We walked on toward the Forum Bovis. Demetrios had lived in an inn near it. As the Mese opened into the great rectangle, we came up against the great Brazen Bull, in which the tyrant Emperor Phocas had, according to legend, been roasted to death. The area was now, appropriately, the main meat market for the city. The beast glowered at us, but did not charge. Claudius looked happily around at the throngs of people streaming through the forum, swirling around one bronze masterpiece after another.

"I do want to see this city," she said.

"We will," I promised. "If we live long enough."

FIVE

Behold: I have played the fool, and have erred exceedingly.

I SAMUEL 26:21

Demetrios lived in a small hostel south of the Forum Bovis. Lived, past tense. His landlady, a large, slovenly woman with wine-stained clothing, snored on a bench in front. When we roused her from her nap, she took one look at my makeup and shouted, "Go away! We'll have no more of you people."

"My apologies for disturbing you, Madame," I said, sweeping my cap and bells off my head and bowing low. "I was merely seeking an old friend who lived here. I had hopes that he might find me some employment. His name is Demetrios."

"I know who your friend is," she snapped.

"Then perhaps you could tell me where he is."

"Perhaps I can't," she said, and sat in her chair. I waited for her to speak again. "Vanished," she said finally.

I waited for her to elaborate. After some minutes of looking at each other, I decided to prompt her.

"Vanished, you said?"

"Yes."

"When was this?"

"What's it to you?"

"As I said, I was hoping he could find me some employment. We used to work together."

"Then you can pay me what he owes me," she said hopefully.

"We weren't that close. When did he vanish?"

"Beginning of November. One day he's here, the next he isn't, without so much as a by-your-leave. Ten years he'd been living here, and didn't even say good-bye. Leaving me to sort out his things."

I had a brief moment of hope. "Do you still have them here?"

She laughed. "Sold them after a month. That's what we do around here. Got pitifully little for the lot, mostly some hideous costumes of his."

"You have nothing left?" I said. "What about in his room?"

"Let it in December. Can't have it going to waste. Now, get on with you."

I turned to leave.

"Wait," she called after me. She got up from her chair for the first time and scurried into the building. She returned with a long, thin parcel, wrapped in rags, bulging at one end.

"He left this," she said. "I couldn't sell it. It has a cursed look to it. Do you want it?"

"Yes," I said, my heart sinking as I recognized the shape. I took it from her, and we left as the sun started setting.

We reached the Rooster before dark and went straight to our room. I unwrapped the cloth and held up a scepter with a small figure of a skull at the end of it, decked out in cap and bells.

"Demetrios's *marotte*," I said. "Look at the makeup. That was his style, with the red triangles ringing the eyes. He never would have left this behind."

"Does it shoot poisoned needles like yours?" Viola asked, edging away from it.

I turned it upside down. Nothing fell out. I located the hidden trigger and pressed it. There was a faint click.

"There's nothing in it, and it hasn't been used," I said. "Whoever killed him took him unawares."

"What did they do with the body?"

"Who knows? The landlady looks like she could sleep through Judgment Day given a decent wineskin, so it wouldn't have been hard to carry him out. Let's go see if our new employee found out anything."

Asan was at a table, digging into some gray slop like it was his last meal. He started as he looked up to see us seated on either side of him.

"Greetings and well met, my little burglar," I said.

"Hush," he said, looking around nervously, but the general din of the room drowned us out.

"Any news of Tiberius?" I asked.

He shook his head.

"He's gone," he said. "Been gone for months. Must have owed someone badly, because he left in a hurry. His things were still there."

"Who was he running from?"

He snorted. "Could have been half a dozen men tired of waiting for him to pay up."

"Any of them likely to kill him rather than take his money?"

"Most of them would want to do both. If he had anything belonging to you, it's long gone."

"Any friends? Did he keep a mistress?"

"A mistress?" he laughed. "He was a fool. He was a debtor with aspirations to poverty. What woman would want such a creature?"

"One never knows," commented Claudius.

"Any friends, then?" I asked.

"That other fool, Demetrios. They used to work together, entertaining the troops at the Great Palace garrisons, sometimes working the Hippodrome. But no one's seen him in ages, either. Maybe they left together."

"Maybe. That's most likely the case. Well, young thief, you are quit of your debt to me. Go and sin no more. Or as little as you can without going hungry."

We shifted to another table, taking some of the glop with us, washing it down with some brown ale. I craved more colors in my food.

There was a table of soldiers in the inn, and one of them threw me a coin and bade me sing. All in a day's work. I unslung my lute and launched into something appropriately martial, then segued into something more bawdy. The latter was apparently what they were looking for, so I continued in that vein, Claudius joining in, beating on my tabor. The wine and ale flowed freely, and when I came to the end, several of them clapped me heartily on the shoulders, some taking the time to pummel poor Claudius as well.

Simon was quite happy to have the free entertainment in his place, and even happier that it led to such free-spending inebriation. He came out from behind the bar with a pitcher of ale and plunked down in front of me.

"I should introduce you to these fine fellows," he said. "This one's Henry of Essex. He's a captain with the Varangians."

I saluted him. He was a flaxen-haired fellow of medium build, with a livid scar crossing from the bridge of his nose down to the bottom of his left cheek. He noticed me marking it, and bellowed, "You should see the other fellow!" I saw his axe leaning against the table, the lamplight bouncing off it.

"Just give me a shovel and show me where to dig," I replied, and he guffawed.

"This one's Cnut," continued Simon, throwing a massive arm around the shoulders of a tall lad of eighteen. A pale down clung to the boy's cheeks. "He's also a Varangian, from that Danish city I can't pronounce."

"Kjoebenhavn?" I guessed.

Cnut's jaw dropped. "How did you know?"

"It's the only city in Denmark I've been to. Let me guess. You're the third son of a merchant. The diet in Denmark is too bland, so they sent you to Constantinople for seasoning."

The other Danes at the table laughed and nudged the youth.

"And this is Stanislaus," said Simon, pointing to the only man at the table not wearing the Varangian armor. "He's a captain with the Hetairia. He gets to open the Great Gates of Blachernae Palace every morning."

"And then you're done for the day?" I exclaimed. "That's it. I've been working too hard. I'm going to join the Hetairia. You're up at the Anemas garrison?"

"Correct, Fool," replied Stanislaus, a dark-haired man with a weathered face. Also a foreigner, with an accent similar to Simon's. "Unfortunately, our commander permits no entertainment at the garrison, otherwise I'd invite you to perform there."

"We could use some jesting," said Henry. "It's been bloody dull around here. Come down to our garrison one of these days."

"It would be my pleasure. Which one are you at?"

"Hodegon, near the Arsenal, Do you know it?"

"I can find it. What would be a good time?"

He thought, then snapped his fingers. "Saturday afternoon, when my brigade takes its bath. We usually have music there, but if you don't mind performing for several hundred naked men, we could make it a profitable day for you."

"Done. I've never seen a Varangian unshelled before."

"It's an ugly sight, but seeing it en masse should dampen the blow. I'll show you the rest of my scars. Well, Simon, time for the real soldiers to depart. We're up at dawn guarding the Emperor's ravines. But we'll be back now that we know you have some real entertainment."

"My conversation was not good enough for you before?" protested the tapster in mock indignation. "My apologies, my lords and masters, for the ignorant level of discourse to which you have been subjected. I only thought to instruct you with the tales of my life."

"Yes, tell us again how you fought Saladin blade to blade," laughed Henry.

"He did?" exclaimed Cnut, and the older soldiers cuffed him affectionately until he managed to get his helmet back on. They exited, all save Stanislaus who sat staring morosely at the pitcher.

"I cannot believe they left some undrunk," he said. "I'll need your help finishing it."

I live for invitations like that. Claudius and I joined him at the table and commenced pouring.

"Long live the Emperor," I said, raising my cup.

"Long live both of them," he replied, raising his a little unsteadily. "To the most unholy pair of brothers since . . . since. . . ." He drank. "I can't think of a good example. No family like the Angeli for treachery, even in this part of the world. God, I wish I was home again."

"Where's home?"

He sighed. "A small town near Mainz. Took the Cross and followed Frederick Barbarossa on the last Crusade. You were on that one, weren't you, Simon?"

"Sure. I have many memories. I remember. . . ."

"We're not discussing your memories," interrupted Stanislaus. "We're discussing mine. We've heard your memories more times than I can remember. What a long walk that was! Men dropping right and left. Even Frederick didn't make it all the way."

"But you did," I said. "And then you ended up here?"

"Like I said, it was a long walk, and I didn't feel like walking all the way back."

"And there was this girl...." prompted Simon.

"Shut up. Yes, there was a girl, thank Christ. But then she left me. So, now I'm here, marching around, opening gates, propping up the Emperor when he's too drunk to stand, clearing crowds, quelling the occasional riot when it gets too close to Blachernae Palace, and watching the throne change hands suddenly. It's all very entertaining. It's not a bad life, being a mercenary. The pay is good, and I have a nice farm picked out for when I retire. And none of that silly fighting-for-honor stuff anymore. That's a farce. Look at my Varangian friends."

"What about them?"

"Do you realize that the last three emperors have come to the throne by violence against their predecessors, and the Varangians have not lifted a finger to prevent it? God knows that Isaakios was no paragon, but he was all right. Now he's a blind man resting in comfort at the Double Column, until our current ruler panics at some omen and has him strangled."

"Have there been any such omens lately?"

He laughed. "Everything's an omen here, and for every occurrence there are a dozen explanations from a dozen competing soothsayers. This from the heart of Christendom. Give me the Latin church any day. At least it's consistent. And give me a mercenary over a man of honor. Honor may be bent in any direction, but with a mercenary, you get what you pay for."

He upended his cup, then poured some more.

"How about you? Where are you from?" he asked.

"Originally? Or lately?"

"Lately."

"I was working up north, traveling from town to town, until they got bored with me. So, I came here."

"Someone will probably make an omen out of you," he remarked. "There used to be some other fools around. Used to see a couple at the games every now and then. Haven't seen them lately. And the Emperor used to keep a pair of dwarves. Twins. Funniest damn creatures you ever saw."

"I've heard about them," I said. "They're not still around?"

"No," he said. "They took off. Had enough, I suppose, and they were well off. Alexios is very generous when he wants to be. I tell you, my friend, if you could get in there, you could do quite well for yourself, if you're any good."

"That would suit me royally," I said. "How do I go about doing that?"

"Good question," he said. "There's no actual Master of Revelry like there used to be, at least not at the moment. There's this eunuch, Constantine Philoxenites. He's the Imperial Treasurer, which means he's the warden of the Emperor's greed and profligacy. He's probably the man to know, but he's a hard one to reach, there are so many layers of bureaucracy surrounding him. I see him every now and then. If you like, I'll put in a good word."

"I would be most grateful," I said.

We finished the wine. He lurched to his feet and looked out the window.

"Dark already," he said. "Your wine is too good, Simon. Point me home."

"I'll walk you," said Simon, grabbing a cloak. "Good night, Fool. Good night, Claudius."

He put his arm around the mercenary's shoulder and guided him through the door.

"I enjoyed that," said Viola, when we settled down in our room. "They were very pleasant for soldiers. And to think, on Saturday I get to see several hundred of them naked. I do so enjoy this life."

"Yes, they were pleasant," I said yawning. "I wonder if any of them was checking up on us."

She stretched the twine across the doorway and settled into her corner.

Nothing happened this night. I let her sleep late, the sunbeams crossing her bearded face. I had known an actual bearded woman once, during a short stint with a traveling circus. She had her own little tent, and her boy would stand in front and charge a penny a peek. She'd let the observer tug on her beard to ascertain its veracity, then would sit and chat with her visitor. It was the chat that kept bringing them back, for she had a jolly disposition and a wealth of stories. I think she could have lived off the stories alone, but she welcomed her oddity as it brought her an audience.

Viola woke and looked at me reproachfully as she realized the time of day.

"Why didn't you wake me?" she asked.

I motioned to a low stool by the bed where I had placed a washbasin.

"All of the honest folk have gone to work," I said. "The dishonest folk as well. I thought you might enjoy washing your face before we began our day."

She removed the wig and beard, sighing happily, then plunged her face full into the basin. I had procured a bit of soap and a cloth. She scrubbed herself thoroughly, then looked up at me.

"I must look a horror," she said.

"Absolutely beautiful," I said.

She snorted. "You're an expert husband for one who's been out of practice for so long." She attached the beard, replaited her hair, and stuffed it under the wig. Then she looked at me. "When do I get to be a woman again? I survived the journey."

"I've been thinking it would be useful to keep that identity a secret. It's like having another person in reserve. Carry women's clothes and makeup in your kit for a quick change."

"And when do I perform again?"

"Soon, Apprentice. I need you watching the crowd again. And then we'll check out Thalia's quarters."

I set up at the Forum Amastrianum, Claudius wandering among the horses. She kept her purse tucked safely away. This was an area known for attracting the worst elements, and that wasn't even counting the horse traders. There was a statue of an honest scale and measure in the center of the square, a stern advisory to the local merchants. A sterner one was the use of the square for public executions. One of the less scrupulous local merchants was dangling from a gibbet nearby, swaying gently with the breeze.

It was a decidedly more masculine crowd than I had previously seen. Horse-trading was traditionally a man's profession in these parts. So was horse-thieving. The beasts varied in quality and breed, some showing Arabian heritage, others the short but study mixes of the north. Some had battle scars equal to any I'd seen on a soldier, and it was these who drew the attention of a number of military types.

I performed for a few hours, and did moderately well. Several in my ever-changing audience inquired about my lodgings, I hoped for the purpose of retaining my services rather than slitting my throat while I slept.

As I was packing my gear, an emaciated, ratlike man of some fifty years sidled up to me, clutching his threadbare cloak about his body.

"You look like a man who could use a little luck," he said out of the side of his mouth.

"What man couldn't?" I replied.

He nodded rapidly several times. "Sure, sure, what man couldn't? But luck doesn't just happen, you know. It needs encouragement."

"Does it?"

"Yeah. Sure it does. How do you think people get rich?"

"Inheritance? Light fingers amongst the gentry?"

He shook his head. "You don't know anything. There's luck. And it doesn't..."

"...just happen. You mentioned that before."

He smiled, showing blackened gums and nothing else.

"I know how to get luck," he said. "I can help you."

I looked at him. He was bald, scrofulous, and missing part of his right ear.

"Do you practice what you preach, friend?" I asked.

"No, no, you can't get luck for yourself. But if you give the right talismans to someone, they can get lucky."

"You are proposing a gift, then."

He shook his head.

"It's an exchange of luck," he said. "You give something to me, I give something to you."

"You look like someone already gave you something, and feel free to warn me away from her."

He opened his cloak slightly. Sewn into the lining was an astonishing array of odd trinkets: bits of bone, locks of hair, shriveled frogs, lizards, pieces of other animals, small vials, boxes, rings, and all manner of talismans.

[71]

He launched into a well-rehearsed patter. "Troubles in the marriage bed, place these under it and all is well." He pointed to what appeared to be a decaying pair of bull's testicles. "Wax from the tomb of Saint Stephen, rub it on your doorstep and no evil will dare enter. The thumb of Saint Simon, the Canaanite. Menstrual blood from a black witch, no need to tell you its powers. The actual ring that Saint Edward the Confessor gave to a beggar. The beggar, on his deathbed, passed it on to me. It cures all manner of fits. A toadstone, place it by your drink, it will detect any poison; place it in someone else's drink, and if they be sinners, they will not live out the night."

"And if they are not sinners?"

He showed me his gums again. "We are all stained with original sin. The stone does not discriminate."

"Well, my friend, I'll pass for now, but if you'll tell me your name, I may seek you out when the occasion demands."

He backed away from me hurriedly, wrapping his cloak around his spindly body.

"No name, no name," he muttered. "My enemies would pay highly to learn my whereabouts, and would gladly murder me for these treasures. When you need luck, I will find you."

He hobbled away, glancing over his shoulder several times. I signaled to Claudius. She ambled by, not looking at me.

"That relic seller who approached me?" I said under my breath. "Follow him."

She nodded slightly, and walked in the direction he had taken.

I quickly packed my gear and waited until she was just at the edge of the forum. Then I threw my cloak over my motley and began trailing her.

It's an old test in the Guild: direct the apprentice to follow a designated fool through a crowded city. The first part of the test is to successfully follow the target without being spotted. The second part is for the apprentice to figure out that he or she is also being followed.

I walked quickly to the south end of the forum in time to catch sight of Viola as she disappeared into a warren of covered stalls. I skirted the local Scyllae and Charybdises, stopped my ears to the Sirens of the oaken casks, and otherwise avoided or rejected every invitation to purchase, haggle, fondle, gamble, or imbibe, never losing track of that short, bearded, beloved wife of mine.

Then, on a particularly narrow, winding street, shielded completely from any memory of sunlight, she disappeared. I poked my head cautiously around the corner, slipping my dagger surreptitiously into my hand, waiting to see if an ambush had been laid. No one accosted me, so I made so bold as to enter the street itself.

The noise of the sellers from the stalls faded. The gloom increased the further I ventured. The passage finally opened between two buildings onto a view of the Kontoskalion Harbor, where the Imperial Navy had its dockyard.

I heard a throat clear behind me. I whirled, dagger ready to be thrown, to see Claudius, hands on her hips, glaring fiercely.

"There I was, thinking that you actually trusted me to accomplish something on my own," she said. "Then I noticed a cloaked fool following me. I suppose this was some kind of test."

"Indeed, Apprentice," I replied, wondering, not for the first time, whether a teacher/apprentice relationship was practical for a marriage. "And if you can tell me where that walking pustule went, you pass."

"He's in that shack by the dock," she said.

"Good. Let's go pay him a visit."

"You mean he actually matters to us? I thought you just wanted me to practice following someone."

"He matters. I recognized a ring that he had among his collection. It's a Guild ring. I think it belonged to Demetrios."

I took a step. She grabbed my arm and pulled me into a doorway.

"Since you're such an expert," she whispered, "then you know, of course, that someone has been following you."

Six

[T]ime, the transformer and perpetual engenderer of dissimilarities...
O CITY OF BYZANTIUM, ANNALS OF NIKETAS CHONIATES,

P. 291

I gaped at her stupidly, then looked back into the passage from which I had emerged.

"He's gone," she said. "Whoever he was, he elected not to follow you into a dark alley. He must have thought you were cleverer than you are. Or maybe someone was following him. I'm beginning to think that everyone in this city is following someone else. No wonder it's so crowded."

"Full marks and extra credit, Apprentice," I said. "What manner of man was he?"

"I don't know," she said. "I saw a cowl and no face."

"Interesting. Father Esaias, perhaps?"

"The cowl was different," she said. "That doesn't mean it wasn't him. Do you think someone from the Church was on your tail?"

"If it was a cowl, then it would be anybody except someone from the Church. They would most likely disguise themselves as something else. In any case, the cowled stranger's not a problem at the moment. Let's go visit our shack-dwelling friend."

I decided not to knock, choosing instead to barge in, knife drawn. I caught the fellow attempting to light a small metal bowl of incense. I grabbed him by the scruff of the neck and held my knife close to his eye.

"Well, here's luck," I said. "I changed my mind. I'm interested in your wares."

"Sure, sure," he gasped. "Anything you want, just don't hurt me."

Claudius closed the door behind us and kept watch. I let the relic seller go, keeping an eye on his hands. He fumbled at the cord holding his cloak closed, then opened it. I pointed my knife at the item I had marked before, a pewter ring with a Death's-head set in black enamel.

"A good choice," he babbled. "That will ward off enemies, bring..." He stopped as I brought my knife back to his throat.

"Look here," I said, holding up my other hand.

He drew in his breath sharply as he saw a similar ring on my finger.

"It wards off no one," I said. "It may even attract enemies. I took it from the finger of a dead fool, along with his clothes and gear. I've been a jester ever since. Sometimes I tickle people's humor. Sometimes I tickle them with this."

I touched him lightly with the blade, and he started crying.

"Now, that ring belonged to a fool named Demetrios," I continued. "I've been looking for him. He has something that belongs to me, and I want it. I don't care what I have to do or who I have to kill to get it." I flicked my knife at the thread holding the ring to the cloak, and it fell. Before it hit the ground, I caught it with the end of my knife and flipped it into the air. It fell onto my waiting pinkie, beside its mate. The relic seller watched the whole routine in terror. I pointed the knife back at him.

"Talk," I said.

"I took it from a dead fool as well," he said. "Demetrios."

"When? Where?"

"Early November, out in the forest."

"Who brought him there? Tell me everything you know."

"They were dressed like monks, but they weren't," he said. "I was out gathering herbs and trapping rabbits. I like a stewed rabbit every now and then. The Emperor's forests are untouchable. No one's allowed in, not even the woodsmen or the shipbuilders or anyone. So, when I heard the noise, I hid."

"How many were there?"

"Three, lugging the body. I recognized him right away. I've seen him work for years; I knew the pattern of his motley. And that's the only way I would have known him. His face was beaten to a pulp.

"They had shovels. They dug a grave, put him in, covered him up."

"Did they say anything?"

He thought. "One of them said, 'No fool like a dead fool,' and they laughed."

"Would you recognize the voice if you heard it again?"

"No, no," he whimpered, shaking his head emphatically.

"But he spoke in Greek?"

"Sure, sure."

"With an accent, or without?"

"I heard none."

"Go on."

"I remembered about the ring, and the earring. I figured he wasn't using them anymore."

"Did you find anything else on him?"

He fumbled through a pile of odds and ends by his pallet and produced a worn, leather pouch.

"There was no money in it," he said in a most unconvincing tone. "But there was a piece of paper with writing on it. I don't know what it means."

I snatched it from him and opened it. There was a scrap with faint lettering. It was in German. I looked at it, passed it to Claudius, and opened the door.

"You never saw me," I said. "If you forget that, you will see me again."

"Go away," he whispered.

We stepped outside.

We walked toward the harbor and sat on the edge of a pier. Claudius held the paper up to the sun.

"'Can't make it tonight. T.,'" she read. "Tiberius?"

"Or Thalia," I replied. "We may never know."

We looked out upon the shipyard. There was no activity there. There was a time when the Byzantine navy could send over two hundred ships into the Bosporos to take on whatever fleet the Arabs had sent. Now, there were maybe twenty aging hulks, half in dry dock, all in need of repair. Yet there were no sailors standing guard, no caulkers boiling pitch in vast cauldrons, no rope-makers splicing and gabbing, no carpenters repairing the hulls and decks.

"This city is ripe for the plucking," I commented.

"There are still the armies," she replied. "And the walls."

"The walls were badly in need of repair," I said. "And they weren't being patrolled overmuch. The troops at the Anastasian walls were being paid so irregularly that they were thinking of deserting. Something is going horribly wrong in this city."

"Does it have something to do with the disappearance of the fools?" she asked.

I shrugged. "Part of what we do is maintain the peace. Without the fools, there's one less source of good advice or well-intentioned manipulation. But I can't think that whatever is happening here came about because someone decided to eliminate five jesters and a troubadour."

I stood, stretched, then bent over backward until I could touch my heels. She watched me with amusement.

"Does that help you think?" she asked.

I thought for a moment. "No," I concluded, and straightened up.

"Where to?" she asked. "Do you want to check out Thalia and the dwarves?"

"No," I said. "They all lived up by Blachernae. We'll do that tomorrow. Let's go by the Hippodrome and find out what one has to do to be admitted to perform there."

We walked along the seawalls, cutting north just before the Bukoleon Harbor. There was a marble grouping of a bull and a lion, looking out to sea. They were the most vigilant creatures we had seen since we had come to the city.

We came up on the southern end of the Hippodrome, the great curving facade with its huge marble arches, easily six hundred feet in width. The hill on which it was perched sloped sharply away from this end, forcing whatever ancient architect had been responsible to support it on massive columns. Under the shelter of the stadium was an immense stable set into the hillside, complete with its own set of smiths, carpenters, and chariot builders. It was here that I chose to make my approach, rather than through the public entrance at the north end.

While protecting the city was apparently not a current priority of the Emperor, entertaining it still was. Horses were being led everywhere, exercised, shod, curried, examined for any trace of injury or illness. It took some time to locate the man I had to see, but by dint of constant shouting and pointing, we were able to locate him. He was a massive fellow, with arms as thick as my body, and a trunk as thick as the Pillar of Arkadios, or so it seemed. He was heavily bearded, and what little face was uncovered was grimed by the smoke from the blacksmiths' fires. He wore a thick leather cap and leather breeches. At the moment, his torso was bare, and large rivulets of sweat left streaks in the soot covering him. He looked at us without expression.

"My name is Feste, the Fool," I shouted. "This is my assistant, Claudius. I am told that you are the man to see about our performing in the Hippodrome."

"You were told right. My name is Samuel. Who sent you?" he asked in a deep rumble.

"I sent myself," I said. "But I used to work with Demetrios and Tiberius. They can provide good report of my talents."

He frowned at the mention of the other fools. "They've not been around in months," he said. "How do I know you've worked with them?"

"Would you like me to give you a brief demonstration?"

He nodded. I pulled off my cloak, threw it to Claudius, and went through a quick juggling routine, there being too much noise for music or banter to have much effect. He watched without reacting until I was done.

"Fine," he said. "As long as you have the entry fee, you can come for the games in three days."

"What's the fee?"

"A gold histamenon to me, in advance, plus ten percent of what you make inside."

"That's a bit steep for one performance."

He smiled. "The rates vary. If you become established here, it's just the percentage."

"Fair enough. What's the occasion for the games?"

"Some relative of the Emperor has a birthday. The usual excuse. There'll be chariot races, some acrobats, musicians, a man who says he can fly, and now you."

"I'll see you in three days."

"How can he charge us so much?" sputtered Claudius in protest as we emerged into the street.

"Because he can," I said. "It's not unusual, or even that out-rageous. They only want the best performers, and any jester who can't raise the entrance fee from fooling in the markets is probably not worth seeing."

We came upon a small square that had a number of stalls selling fruits, nuts, and spices to the neighborhood. A crowd was gathered before a street preacher, who stood on a boulder and harangued them for their instruction, or at least their entertain-ment. He was an old man and clearly not of the main church, for he lacked the rich vestments one would expect even of a lesser deacon in this city. He wore a long, tattered wool robe, patched in many places. He was clean-shaven and bald to boot, and his dome was so perfectly round that his head could have been used for a football.

He was quoting extensively from the Gospel of Matthew, pick-ing out parts of the parables and sermons and applying them quite effectively to both the audience and the mere passersby. Some clerical folk crossed the square, minor functionaries from the vast Byzantine bureaucracy on some taxing mission, and he immediately pointed to them and cried, "Woe unto you, scribes and Pharisees, hypocrites! For ye devour widows' houses, and for pretense make long prayer: therefore ye shall receive the greater damnation!"

The bureaucrats frowned and scuttled on, while the crowd laughed. I wondered if there were any Pharisees in the crowd. This being Constantinople, it was quite possible.

He then singled out the spice sellers and screamed, "For ye pay tithe of mint and anise and cumin, and have omitted the weightier matters of the law: judgment, mercy, and faith. These ought ye to have done, and not to leave the other undone."

"He's quite good," commented Claudius as we walked by. "I wonder if he knows anything outside of Saint Matthew."

He must have heard us, for the moving finger pointed my way. I prepared a retort for whichever denunciation of jesters he might summon up, but when he caught my eye, he merely said, "And you, Fool, ere you twist in everlasting Hellfire, I bid you remember the instructions of Saint Luke, chapter one, verses three and four. Live by them, and you shall find salvation."

I stared at him, at the finger still pointing at me at the end of his long arm, and could think of nothing better to do but stick out my tongue in reply.

"I apologize, Fool," he cried. "Mark ye, my brethren, here is a Holy Fool indeed, for he speaks only in tongues!"

The crowd laughed. At my expense, they laughed. It galled me.

Claudius looked at me curiously.

"Are you going to let him get away with that?" she asked.

"Come on," I said roughly. I seized her by the arm and dragged her out of the square into a nearby tavern. We sat down at a table in the corner.

"Well, that was disappointing," she commented. "I was waiting for a comeback, something good. And what did he say that was so devastating that it quieted you? What was the verse?"

"Luke, chapter one, verses three and four," I said.

She thought. "I can't even remember how it goes. It's just some introduction, isn't it?"

"Yes," I said. " 'It seemed good to me also, having had perfect understanding of all things from the very first, to write unto thee in order, most excellent Theophilos, that thou mightest know the certainty of those things, wherein thou hast been instructed.' "

Her eyes grew large.

"He knows your Guild name?" she said. "Who is he?"

"I think that was Zintziphitzes."

Her eyes narrowed again.

"You told me that Zintziphitzes was an ugly, hairy man," she said. "That man, while certainly no beauty, was completely devoid of hair."

I leaned forward and tugged gently on her false beard.

"Hair doth not make the man," I said. "I want you to do something for me. Go back into the square, and when he is done preaching, go ask him to join us for a meal. Tell him Genesis, chapter twenty-seven, verse eleven."

"That one I know," she said happily, and she left.

Two cups of wine later, she returned, preacher in tow. He had a staff that he leaned on, and was a shriveled man compared to the robust simian of my memory. But his eyes were keen and mocking still, and fixed me with that same quick appraising leer that I saw every time I thought about him.

"A good choice of verse," he said. " 'Behold. Esau, my brother, is a hairy man, and I am a smooth one.' "

"Here's another one for you. *Stultorum numerus*," I said quietly.

"None of that Guild nonsense," he said, laughing. "I left them long ago, and I left foolishness when I came to preach the Word."

"Well, then," I said, motioning for him to sit with us. "If it would not compromise your hallowed state to be in this tavern, allow me to buy you a meal and some wine."

"If publicans and harlots were good enough for Our Savior, then this place is good enough for me," he said, sitting. "Verily, this is my flock."

I bought enough for the three of us, and he dug in with a will.

"Preaching must stir the appetite as well as the soul," I observed.

"The body must have its sustenance," he said. "And collections are uncertain in the open air."

"Why don't you preach in an actual church?"

He gave a quick, derisive burst of laughter. "A Guild member asking that. For the reasons you would expect. The Church here is just as corrupt and worthless as the one in Rome."

"And when did you see the light?"

He leaned back. "About three years ago. In the middle of working the nobility at the Hippodrome. I was brilliant. I had just finished reciting a long, satirical poem that incorporated the names of a hundred people sitting there. Funniest thing since Aristophanes, or at least since the *Timarion*, and completely improvised on the spot. There was gold raining down upon me, enough to keep me going for years. I was at the top of my game, and as I scooped it up, I heard a voice in my head say, 'Render unto Caesar....' And that was it. Made my whole existence to that point meaningless. I went to church, prayed, dumped the gold into the poor box, and began preaching. I recommend it. You should try it."

"I'll pass, thank you."

He leaned forward. "You can't be a fool forever, Theo."

I leaned across the table until my face was an inch from his. "First, the name at the moment is Feste. Second, the difference between your fooling and mine is that the Fools' Guild has a higher purpose, one you abandoned a long time ago. So, don't preach to me, Saul of Tarsus. I've been doing God's work a lot longer than you."

He smiled. "Competing for God's favor, are we? The Guild is trying to save the world, and I'm trying to save a few souls. Who has been more successful? Which is more realistic? Where does it get you?"

"In this city, dead."

He stopped smiling.

"I was wondering who the Guild would send," he said slowly. "I thought it might be you, if you still lived."

"Instruct me, preacher, with your perfect understanding. Who is responsible for the deaths of the fools in Constantinople?"

"I suppose, in a way, that I am," he said, and resumed eating. Claudius drew in her breath, then let it out slowly.

"Could you explain that in a way that won't make it necessary for me to kill you?" I requested, my right hand resting on the handle of the knife in my boot.

"You would, wouldn't you?" he said. "Bastard. I didn't kill them, of course. But I think I inadvertently set events in motion that led to their deaths."

"Explain."

"I will, but not here."

"Why didn't you contact the Guild after you heard?"

"I tried to, but that troubadour was in too much of a hurry. He didn't know me, and wouldn't stop to listen to the ravings of an old man. And by the time I heard he'd returned, I guess they got to him as well. I saw his horse up for sale in the Amastrianum. After that, I decided to lie low for a while."

He wiped his bowl clean with the last piece of bread and then stood.

"Put your cloak on and your hood up," he said. "No one followed us in here, but I don't want to chance being seen with a fool outside. Give me a moment's lead, then follow me."

He walked out. I threw my cloak over my motley, and we followed him.

His route took him back toward the Hippodrome. Claudius and I walked separately. I made damn certain that no one was following us this time. Just as the stadium loomed over us, Zintziphitzes ducked into an alleyway that neither of us would have noticed otherwise. We stopped at the entrance and looked down it. It cut between two stonecutting shops and had no apparent outlet other than the one in which we stood. Zintziphitzes stood at the end of it, waving merrily.

"I don't like the smell of this," said Claudius.

"Now, now," I admonished her. "He's an old man. He's bound to smell a little bit."

"He had Guild training once. That means he knows how to kill."

"Among other things. But why would he want to kill us?"

"I'm just bringing up a possibility."

"Fine, Apprentice. No reason not to be careful." I walked into the alley.

"This is your idea of careful?" she muttered, but she followed me, glancing behind her.

"Well done," commented the preacher. "Time for me to let you in on a few secrets."

"I'm listening," I said.

"The other fools always envied my ability to get information," he said modestly. "I had the most intimate details at my beck and call, and all of the freshest variety. The Hippodrome was my personal theater. And there was a reason for that."

He reached down and pulled up a pair of large flagstones, revealing a hole that a slender man could enter. He then lowered himself into it.

"Come on," he said.

We looked down inside. There was a tunnel, going toward the Hippodrome. Zintziphitzes fumbled in the darkness, and a small flame came up. He was holding a candle.

I lowered Claudius, then jumped down. The hole was about five feet deep. I pulled the flagstones into place, which forced me into a crouch.

"I normally do this in the dark," said the old fool. "However, one must be more accommodating when one has guests, don't you think?"

The tunnel was carved into the earth, shored up in places with some inexpert timbering. We followed our guide for about sixty feet, crouching all the way. Then the tunnel joined a larger one, with ancient stonework and some actual Roman-style arches. A trickle of water ran past us down the center of the tunnel. Several dozen pairs of small, red eyes picked up the candlelight.

"It's all right, my friends," called Zintziphitzes. "They're with me."

It was an act, I was sure. I doubted that he truly knew the rats well enough to speak to them. But they avoided us as we traversed the length of the tunnel, which was fine with me.

"We're in a drainage tunnel," he explained. "I don't know when it was built. It may go back to Severus for all I know. Good old-fashioned Roman engineering. It will outlast the empire. Here we are."

What I took for a jumble of stones was actually a stairway, leading to a hole in the side of the tunnel some six feet up. The old man scampered up the stones and disappeared. We followed before we lost sight of the candle.

What we found was a good-sized room with stone walls on three sides and a newer wall of concrete opposite the entrance. There was a proper bed in a corner, a bookcase with six shelves, completely filled with ancient tomes, scrolls, piles of scrap paper, and some empty bottles used for paperweights. There was a bureau at the foot of the bed, and a pile of carpenter's tools, which explained how the furniture had gotten there in the first place. There was a small table and a single chair by the entrance. The wall to our right had only a plain, wooden cross to adorn it.

Zintziphitzes bustled about, setting food on the table, lighting some sputtering torches set in sconces on the concrete wall.

"I apologize for not having enough chairs," he said. "Give me some time and a few scraps of lumber, and I'll build a few. I've become quite the carpenter, you know. I'll have to ask you to keep your voices low, however. The stables are just on the other side of the wall here, and we don't want to frighten the horses."

"Where exactly are we?" I asked.

"Under the Hippodrome, of course. This room was sealed off during renovation some thirty years ago. I figured out where it was, and broke through from the drainage tunnel. Thought it would be a useful little hidey-hole in emergencies. Then I made a very useful discovery. So useful that this became my home for most of the last three decades. Cheese?"

"No, thank you," I said. "The dead fools? Did they know about this place?"

"Tiberius knew I had a place, but didn't know exactly where or how to get here. It wasn't important to him. He respected my privacy, and I liked him for that. Probably my only real friend in this city. He's the one I went to."

"With what?" I prompted, trying not to be impatient.

He led us to the exit and pointed into the darkness.

"This stadium is very ingeniously constructed," he said. "There are drains in all the tiers. Makes it easier to get the place ready after a rainstorm. There are tunnels under every tier to carry the water off, large enough for a man to crawl through if he had a mind to. And then, all he has to do is sit and listen, and re-markable things will come down through the drains."

"You've been overhearing conversations," I marveled. "You've been crawling through drains and spying on people!"

"Oh, the things that people say when they think they're alone in a stadium box. I've exposed a hundred scandals to the delight of rich and less rich, embarrassed not a few high dignitaries and bureaucrats, and have aimed barbed couplets at more than one emperor. It's a sin, of course, and a terrible addiction. Even when I began preaching, I still would come here seeking the choicest tidbits, for the preacher may use them as well as the fool. But then I learned something that was too big for me, so I brought it to Tiberius. I assume that he told the others, and that whatever actions they took led to their deaths."

He looked at me, the rapture of the storyteller gradually subsumed by the horror of what he had to say. Suddenly, he was an old man, sagging in body and spirit.

"Go on," I said.

He shook his head abruptly.

"I told them, and now they're dead," he said. "That's on me. If I tell you, it's because you wanted to know, and that will be on you. I'm warning you, this may get you and your little friend killed."

"I came here to find out," I said. "I'll accept the responsibility for my death if that's what you want me to do. I'll be better armed knowing."

He nodded, then sat on his bed, cross-legged, and resumed speaking.

"The voices came through one day. Two of them, both men. 'He's gone. It's safe to speak,' said the first. I perked up immediately and moved toward the voice. 'The timing is crucial,' he said. 'You have to be ready on a moment's notice.' 'Fine,' said the second man. 'You just make sure that once I get in, I can get out again.' 'That's my lookout,' said the first. 'That's why I am where I am. You'll have the passwords to get past the guards. Once it is done, you'll be safely out of the city before the cock crows.'"

He paused, mopping his brow.

"Then the second man laughed," he continued. "A soft, evil sound. 'This will be interesting,' he said. 'I've never killed an emperor before.'"

SEVEN

The wise man's eyes are in his head; but the fool walketh in darkness.

ECCLESIASTES 1:14

There was no sound other than the sputtering of the torches and, somewhere in the distance on the other side of the concrete wall, a hammer hitting an anvil. Zintziphitzes sat on his bed, his knees pulled up to his chest, his eyes closed.

"But the Emperor still lives," said Claudius finally.

"I suppose the appropriate time has not yet arrived," replied Zintziphitzes.

"Did they say what they were waiting for?" I asked.

"The conversation ended there," he said. "I didn't recognize the voices. The first spoke unaccented Greek. The second I would guess was from somewhere north, but he didn't speak enough for me to pin it down. Nor have I heard him since then.

"I brought this to Tiberius, figuring it was more his business than mine. I'm not particularly concerned with who runs the ever-dwindling empire.

"Tiberius was interested, of course. He thanked me and said he'd let the others know. I told him to keep me out of it, and he promised he would. About two weeks later, it occurred to me that I hadn't seen him or Demetrios in the area. I dropped by the stables and chatted with Samuel, and I learned during the course of casual conversation that they hadn't been at the Hip-podrome in a week. I went by their places, but they had vanished. Demetrios's landlady was busy selling his belongings.

"Now, I was well and truly worried. I decided to change my appearance by shaving off everything that could be shaved. I'm much colder now, by the way. Then I hobbled up to Blachernae, but no trace of Thalia, Niko, or Piko. And that was that. Your troubadour showed up, apparently got wind of something, and took off like a bat out of hell, which was smart. But then he returned, and no more troubadour."

"Why didn't you warn the Emperor?" asked Claudius.

He looked at her with scorn.

"An apprentice, right, Theo?" he spat, and I saw her head snap back with the sting of the remark. "Because the Emperor is shielded from rabble-rousers like me. He's surrounded by an outer layer of guards and walls, a middle layer of courtiers and cour-tesans, and an inner layer of boneheadedness that no helm rivals for protection."

"Is there no one close to the Emperor who you could trust?" I asked.

"Theo ... I mean Feste," he said hurriedly as I raised a finger in warning. "I don't think you understand what's happening. Where do you think I was when I heard this?"

"You said already. Under the tiers."

"But under which tier, Feste? I was just outside the Kathisma, the imperial box. Only those of great privilege—either by wealth, position, or power—sit that close to the Emperor. They lie back on silk cushions, surrounded by the Imperial Guard and wined and fed by servants, and watch the games while they play their own. The plot against the Emperor is coming from someone very close to him, which is usually the case. And if I go traipsing in, bellowing about an assassination, they'll look at me and laugh, saying, 'Isn't it that old fool, Zintziphitzes? I thought he was dead. What a funny fellow!' And then one of them will arrange to have me quietly snuffed out after the show is over."

"You're the boy who cried wolf," I said.

"Isn't it the truth?" he replied, chuckling. "Just when I need them to take me seriously."

"Was there any talk about the fools all disappearing like that?" asked Claudius.

"Less than you might suspect," he replied. "The Emperor apparently whined for a day or two about missing his pet dwarves, but found solace in old wine and a very fetching young flutist from Alexandria. The Empress and he rarely consort, so no one was particularly aware of Thalia vanishing at the same time. The other two worked this part of the city. It may be that the only person who noticed it was me."

"What has to happen before they go ahead and kill the Emperor?" I wondered.

"That's what has me puzzled," he said. "There's been ample opportunity, especially if he has the passwords to get past the Imperial Guard. The Emperor has not been reticent about being seen in public. He hunts, he feasts, he makes the requisite appearances in the Hagia Sophia, does his ceremonial distributions for charity. Hell, I could probably kill him if I had a mind to."

"I'd like to get into Blachernae. How would a fool get admitted there?"

"I'd start by performing here," he said. "Are you in the Hippodrome yet?"

"Playing the games in three days," I replied. "After the entrance fee is paid."

"What's Samuel charging nowadays?" he asked curiously.

"A piece of gold and a tithe."

"Really? I must have gotten the old-timer's rate. Just as well I got out when I did."

"For many reasons," I said.

He pulled a blanket over his frail body.

"I'm tired," he announced. "Can you find your way back?"

"I think so," I said. "Lend us a candle."

He waved to one on the table. I lit it, and we cautiously picked our way down the pile of rocks to the tunnel.

"He must. . . ." began Claudius, but I hushed her.

We continued on for some distance before I spoke softly.

"Sound travels here," I said. "I don't know how well Zintziphitzes can hear, but I don't want to take any chances. What were you going to say?"

"He must get trapped in that room when there's a heavy rain," she said, looking back into the darkness. "I think that I would go mad under those circumstances."

" 'The prophet is a fool, the spiritual man is mad,' " I said. "He may have been mad from the start. That's why it's difficult to know if this is how it all started. But it certainly has the ring of truth."

"Do you think the event that will lead to the assassination is the coming of the Venetian fleet?"

"Good girl. That's my best guess. And thanks for not bringing that up in front of him. We don't know who he gossips with."

"But why wait so long?"

"Because the way things are going, Alexios is an invader's best friend. He's completely mismanaged the defenses of the city. The Crusaders lay siege, the population realizes there's no navy to drive them away, and before you know it, they're rioting against the throne. And then our unknown killer sneaks in and eliminates him just when his usefulness has come to an end. The Crusaders march in to the cheers of the liberated populace, take the traditional three days of rape, sack, and pillage, and then install their puppet on the throne."

"It sounds plausible," she conceded. "But what did the fools have to do with it? I thought the Guild didn't care who was on the throne here."

"That's true up to a point. But we'd favor whichever outcome produced the least amount of slaughter. The fools here had to operate on their own most of the time because it took so long for instructions to go back and forth from the Guildhall. Niko and Piko generally were in charge of the others. Tiberius sounded the alarm, and they must have decided that this was something that had to be stopped. But the something stopped them first."

We came to Zintziphitzes' tunnel. She stopped me before I went in.

"Before we go back up, there's something I want to do," she said, and she hauled me down into a fierce kiss. "It's been a while," she said when we finally came up for air. "I'm getting a bit tired of being a man."

"Agreed," I said. "But this is not exactly the place for anything further."

"True enough," she said, looking around. "I prefer to make love without rats watching. It's a peculiarity of mine."

I lifted the flagstone a crack and peered out. The alley was deserted. I clambered out.

"Come, Eurydice," I said, holding out my hand. "Your Orpheus has brought you safely from the underworld."

"Don't say that," she said hurriedly. "That was an ill-fated match. And you're looking back before I'm out. It's bad luck."

She climbed out quickly and covered the entrance. We merged easily into the stream of commerce in the street.

———

We came back to the Rooster with no apparent tail, had a quiet dinner for a change, and retired for the evening.

"I'll take first watch," I said, settling into position.

"I'll let you," she said sleepily. "So, now we know what we're up against. I should be terrified. But I think I'm more nervous about our performance at the Hippodrome. How many people will be watching us?"

"If it's full, about a hundred thousand."

"Oh, is that all? Silly me to be nervous. Why, I've played to literally dozens of people at a time."

"Just make your gestures grand, Duchess. Otherwise, it's exactly the same."

"Who says I married beneath myself?" she sighed. "A few months with you, and I'm a Grand Duchess."

"Keep that one," I said, and she smiled as she fell asleep.

I often found myself up at this hour. Normal for a jester returning from an evening of entertaining. Too tightly strung to fall asleep, yet too exhausted to move. My mind loosened by wine. I did my stretches silently in the moonlight, while my beloved breathed deep nearby. I watched her, wanting her to be a woman again, to be Viola, my wife, and wondering when we would have time for each other.

So we had the why of it at last. Someone had killed six of my colleagues. Friends. Lover, briefly, in one case. Bad idea, getting involved like that, but I had returned from the last Crusade Beyond-the-Sea only slightly scathed, and in the full flush of my survival had wanted her embrace. I never knew why she wanted mine. But then the lesser king who was my assignment ended his own dalliance in the city, and off I went. I couldn't say good-bye—she was a street performer back then, and we'd only find each other at sunset. I left a hurried note for her, and that was the last contact I had with her. I trusted that she would understand. Now, I would never know if she had.

Those were fine times for fools back then. Isaakios was Emperor, always one for entertaining. He had deposed Andronikos, who was a true horror, so Constantinople was beholden to him no matter how badly he ran the place. He had married a Hungarian princess for the political alliance, which was not unusual. She was nine at the time, which unfortunately also was not unusual. By the time she grew to womanhood, he had long given way to licentious parties with all manner and combinations of women, which was the least unusual for a Byzantine emperor. It could have been worse. Andronikos would have had no compunction about taking a child-bride into his bed.

Niko and Piko came to the city then, and there was a witty fool named Chalivoures to whom we reported. He indulged himself in the Emperor's leavings, which probably led to his own early demise a year or two later. It was one long party, was old Constantinople, and now the century's passed, the city's falling apart, Isaakios is a comfortable but blind prisoner, and all the fools are dead.

Except for me, my bearded duchess, and an old man who lives in a drain.

Now, I had to find my way into the Emperor's chambers, sort out the powers surrounding him, figure out which one was organizing the assassination, and then...

Well, then what? Did the failed efforts of my colleagues mean that I had to follow the same course and succeed? Maybe the assassination of the Emperor would be in the Guild's interest, depending on who would ascend to the throne.

Which would mean that the deaths of my colleagues would go unavenged.

But vengeance was not part of my mission. I was hoping that it would be a gratifying corollary, but the Guild's goals came before any personal ones.

And if that meant that six of us had died in vain, then so be it. That's the way of the world sometimes.

I was getting ready to wake Claudius when I heard a faint noise in the hallway. I held my knife up, waiting. In the streak of moonlight coming through the window, I saw a hand reach through the lower part of the doorway and feel around until it encountered the twine stretched across. Then a foot came in, stepping carefully over it.

I held the knife in the moonlight so that the blade reflected it into the face of Asan. He blinked once when it hit his eyes, then several more times when he saw the source of the reflection.

"Good evening," I said.

"Um, just checking to see everything's all right," he said quickly.

"Very considerate of you," I said. "Everything's fine here. I trust that it will remain so."

"Certainly," he said. "Well, I'll be off to bed, then."

"Good night," I said politely.

"Can't blame a fellow for trying," he muttered as he left.

"Keep the day job," I called after him.

Claudius stirred. "Is everything all right?" she asked, rubbing her eyes.

"Another nocturnal visit from Asan. Your turn to watch. Good night."

I wanted to finish checking out the residences of my late colleagues, so in the late morning we crossed the Lycos and walked north. We crossed the northwestern branch of the Mese, picking our way through the fast-moving carts and wains with some difficulty. As we reached the other side, there was a sudden commotion nearby.

Dozens of Imperial Guards fanned onto the street, using their bronze shields to force the pedestrians to the sides of the road. I pulled Claudius into the shelter of a doorway, and we watched as the guards then halted the equestrian traffic, driving back the riders with whips and clubs. In a remarkably short time, they had cleared a wide space leading to a bronze statue of some ancient emperor whose name had long been forgotten, standing in full armor, his left hand beckoning beyond the walls to the north.

"Take my advice and start cheering," called a captain. "You don't want her angry."

A reluctant huzzah poured from the crowd, which became more enthusiastic as the guards began poking the quieter ones with clubs. Soon we heard the clopping of several horses, and murmurs of, "There she is! The Empress approaches!"

A team of four matched white mares trotted around the corner, pulling a white chariot covered with intricate gold decorations. The charioteer was garbed in a garish getup that combined red leather with all manner of dyed feathers, yet the sword he carried was huge, and his arms looked perfectly capable of swinging it through anyone who chose to ridicule it. I chose not to. You have to pick your moments.

The Empress Euphrosyne lay back on a seat covered with red silk cushions. She had introduced the scandalous custom of appearing unveiled in public, and she now flaunted her still potent charms to the world. She wore a gold tunic with fitted sleeves covered with raised embroidery and uncut gems. Her collar was wide, made of several rows of beads of faience. Over it she wore a necklace that looked to be a string of pierced gold coins. Her hair was braided in a complicated pattern and covered with a golden crown shaped as a two-tiered skullcap with a small golden cross on top, a lattice of hanging drop pearls dangling from either side. Still more gems swung from her ears, encircled her waist, and gleamed from her golden shoes. Even the falcon resting on her left wrist was adorned, its leather hood encrusted with the precious stones.

The procession halted in front of the statue. The Empress whispered something to an adviser who rode on horseback by the side of the chariot. He nodded, and she stood.

"So, you think to betray us, do you?" she cried, addressing the statue. "No longer satisfied with your own glory, you must drag your descendants down so that you may appear even greater. Well, we can't have that, can we? I will give you one chance. Lower that hand that invites our enemies from the north, and I will let you alone."

She waited, her arms folded. There was no word from the crowd. Even the horses were still. This went on for an impressively long time.

"Very well," she said finally. "You brought this upon yourself."

She nodded to her driver, who stepped down from the chariot and drew his sword. He swung it once over his head, then brought it down in a streak of light. The statue's offending arm clattered to the ground.

She turned to face the uncomprehending crowd.

"So shall all of our enemies be punished," she cried. "Doom to those who oppose our city!"

"Long live the Empress, our gracious protectress," prompted the guards, and the crowd took up the cheer somewhat uncertainly.

She basked in her assumed glory. The driver boarded the chariot, took up the reins, and was about to turn it around when a harsh dissenting voice began screaming from a rooftop.

"Strumpet!" it cried. "Strumpet! Strumpet! Strumpet!"

It was a small, dark bird that someone had apparently trained for the occasion. Many in the crowd burst into laughter, quickly stilled by the raised clubs of the guards. The threat didn't appear too serious, as many of the guards were stifling smiles as well.

The Empress turned a shade of red darker than the considerable amount of rouge already covering her face. Slowly, she removed the hood from her falcon. She whispered something to it, then loosened the jesses.

The falcon shot straight through the air. There was a squawk and a spray of blood and feathers from the rooftop, then silence. The falcon returned, dripping gore, and settled on its mistress's waiting wrist. She held it up to her face and kissed it gently. Some of the blood got onto her mouth. I don't think she noticed. Or perhaps she didn't care.

The chariot turned and retraced its route. The guards disappeared. Normal traffic resumed.

"I wonder where I could get one of those talking birds," I remarked. "Might be fun to work it into the act."

"I want a falcon," declared Claudius. "She may be insane, but she's insane with style. Has she always been like this?"

"I didn't see her when I was here last," I said. "But this behavior is completely consistent with the stories I've heard."

"But I've heard she also practically runs the place," said Claudius.

"That's been true on and off," I said. "She's been in and out of favor. One of her more blatant adulteries was once brought to the Emperor. Alexios was too frightened of her to confront her directly, so he had her servants tortured to get the details. He had her lover dismembered, and his head brought to her in a sack. Then he threw her into a convent for a while. But now she's back."

"And the city statues have been trembling ever since," said

Claudius. "Do you think it would be worth trying to warn the Emperor through her?"

"Possibly," I said. "Zintziphitzes said they don't see each other much nowadays, but she certainly would have an interest in keeping him alive. He's the source of her power. There's a problem with that, however."

"What is that?"

"She won't have a male fool. That was why Thalia was so important."

We walked on, Claudius thinking.

"May I suggest something obvious?" she said.

"Yes?"

"Present appearances to the contrary, I have been known to be a woman. Why not let me become fool to the Empress?"

"Not a chance, Apprentice. You're not ready."

She stopped.

"When *will* I be ready?" she asked. "I've been training for months. You haven't let me perform since we've come to town."

"I need you watching my back right now. And as for the length of time, Guild training takes years."

"For the children they recruit," she snapped. "I am no child, Feste. I deserve a little credit for everything I've done with my life."

"You're not ready," I said. "And I'm not going to send a novice into the lion's jaws. Especially when she's married to me."

"You're protecting me."

"We protect each other."

We walked on in silence. Not a companionable silence at that particular moment.

Thalia had a couple of rooms in a house near the seawall fronting the Golden Horn. Her former landlord was out front mending a fishnet when I inquired about her.

"And who are you?" he asked suspiciously.

"An old friend of hers," I said.

"She had a lot of old friends, didn't she?" he said, winking. "Very friendly girl was our Thalia. They'd be dropping by at all hours, you know. If I wasn't so sure she did it for free, I would have run her out for keeping a bawdy house."

"Do you know where she's gone?" I asked.

"Not a clue. Ran off with some sailor is my guess. I didn't even notice. She was paid up through the end of the month, and it wasn't unusual for her not to come home for several days at a time, if you know what I mean. Not to mention keeping Her Battiness amused."

"What about her belongings?"

"Oh, some relative came by and picked them up," he said.

"Who?"

"Some cousin. Don't remember his name."

"Well, there's a trip wasted," I said. "If you see her, tell her I said hello."

We walked off.

"That will be difficult," commented Claudius. "As you never told him your name."

"Didn't I? How careless of me. So, this one is different."

"Yes," she agreed. "They came back for her things. I wonder why."

"She must have found something. Maybe they tortured her and learned what it was, then had to come back for it."

My voice sounded strangled, even to myself. Claudius looked at me with compassion.

"It may have been a quick death," she said. "We can't know. I'm sorry, Feste. I know what it's like to lose someone you love."

"It was a long time ago," I said. "I don't know that it was love. But I cared for her. What could she have found?"

"Is there any point in going to the dwarves' house?" she asked. "We're probably too late to find anything."

"That may be the one place where something could still be turned up," I said. "You'll see why."

The Emperor Isaakios Angelos had so adored Niko and Piko that he built them a palace. It was an exact replica of the palace at Blachernae, except that it was about twelve feet high. All of the columns, arches, friezes, and so forth were recreated in miniature, with marble blocks the size of a child's hand.

"How wonderful!" exclaimed Claudius as we walked by it.

"You see why it hasn't been occupied by anyone since then," I said. "Now, I need you to go in and search the place. I'll set up across the square and create a distraction."

"Glad to be useful," she said. Then her face fell. "You're letting me do it because I'm shorter than you, aren't you?"

"And for your training, sweetness. In particular, I want you to check one place that an outsider may have missed. The dwarves maintained an escape tunnel in the lower level. There's probably a trapdoor somewhere. I expect that's where they kept anything they didn't want found. Wait until I draw a crowd, then go to work."

"Yes, milord," she muttered, and drifted off.

I worked the square for a good hour or so, thinking that would be enough time for her to accomplish the task. I paid particular attention to the guards passing through, calling to them and abusing them mildly to bring them over and get them involved—anything to keep their attention away from that tiny palace opposite.

I was in good form, and even attempted a few tumbles with success. The leg had definitely come a long way since we left Orsino. But as the hours passed, there was no sign of Viola. I was running out of my street material, and was improvising off the crowd and worried that I was going to have to bring in some lengthy ballads when I saw her staggering back across the square. She was white as a ghost. I finished quickly, plucking from the air the silver thrown to me. Then I collected my gear.

Viola looked ready to faint. I took her by the arm and steered her into a nearby tavern. It took a large cup of wine to pull her back. I had one myself as a precaution, just in case what she had was contagious.

"I found something," she said finally.

I waited. She reached into her pouch, pulled out three things, and placed them on the table in front of me: a knife, dried blood still visible on it, and a pair of studded leather collars that might have fit a brace of large dogs or small men.

"They never left the house," she said. "They were in the tunnel."

EIGHT

I insert these events into my history to show my readers how unreasonable a thing wickedness is and how difficult it is to guard against it.

O CITY OF BYZANTIUM, ANNALS OF NIKETAS CHONIATES, P. 63

The place had been ransacked," Viola said. "Everything had been turned over. The cushions were slit and the stuffing pulled out. The pallets had been cut to pieces, and every item of clothing had been ripped to shreds.

"I went through it all, just in case they had missed something. I looked in places that a small hand might use and a large one miss. There was nothing. Finally, I found the trapdoor to the tunnel."

She took a long sip of wine and refilled her cup.

"I've seen dead people before. But they've always just died, and they're laid out properly and dressed nicely. And since I've met you, I've seen my share of those who died by violence. But to see these two—they had been hacked apart. It was savagery, what was done. Someone must have kept at them long after they were dead, and then thrown them down there where the vermin could get at them. I cannot get the sight out of my mind."

"You will," I assured her, placing my hand on hers for a moment. "It will fade in time."

She gripped my hand hard.

"I still looked," she insisted. "Do you understand? I went down there, and I searched them, and crawled over them to search the rest of the tunnel. I found nothing, Feste."

"Then there was nothing to be found. I'm sorry you had to experience this."

"Why did they leave them there?"

"Maybe they couldn't leave the building safely with the bodies. Or maybe they left them as a message."

"A message for us?"

"For whoever came looking for them."

"Does that mean they know about the Guild?"

"Maybe. You've probably noticed I've been trying to come across as a rogue fool rather than a Guildman. It might buy us a little confusion when the time comes."

"You didn't send me down there knowing they'd be there, did you? As another test?"

I shook my head adamantly. "Guild training is not that cruel. Nor am I."

"Let's get out of here," she said.

I paid the tapster, and we walked home. Viola was unsteady at first, but regained her footing slowly but surely.

We spent the remainder of the day rehearsing. Two important performances were coming up: before the Varangian Guards at their weekly bath on the morrow, and at the Hippodrome the day after. I had had an idea for a routine that would be relevant to the locals, and purchased a small pile of red bricks, a few scraps of wood, and a cart to transport them.

"Are you planning to build your own garrison?" asked Claudius. "Must I lay siege to you to regain your affections?"

"Milady, I would capitulate without battle. Let me show you some tricks with bricks."

That Saturday was the hottest day we had had so far. Dogs slunk into what little shadow they could find, too parched and dispirited to even bother licking themselves. I gave my face a good, long scrub and made sure it was absolutely dry before applying my whiteface. Flour has a nasty tendency to cake up on a sweaty face.

Simon hailed us from outside the Rooster's entrance. He was hitching up a donkey to a wagon.

"We travel to the same place," he called. "Help me load my wagon, and I'll give you a ride there."

Four oaken casks stood ready to be taken to their execution. We lifted them together, Claudius straining mightily. She hopped in back, and I sat up front with our host.

"What good is that little fellow as a servant?" he muttered to me as he flicked a whip at the beast.

"Not much, but he's learning the act," I said. "He's actually quite talented."

Simon glanced back at her.

"Look, what goes on between the two of you is your business," he said quietly. "Just try not to be too open about it in public. The weight of hypocrisy can crush you in this city."

"Point taken," I said. "Are you just transporting wine, or will you be dispensing it as well?"

"I am the official tapster to the Varangian Guard," he said proudly. "Old Crusaders stick together. That's why so many of them come my way."

"That, plus the whorehouse down the alley," I commented.

"Fortunately, they don't serve drink there," he said, grinning. "A man can build up a powerful thirst anticipating the act of love."

"And a need to celebrate it afterward. You have an ideal location. One of Father Esaias's innovations?"

The smile vanished. "I'd rather not discuss him," he said.

I changed the topic hurriedly, and we gossiped the rest of the way there. The donkey began panting as it took the slow rise to the Akropolis, so the three of us jumped down and walked alongside it. It was in this manner that we made our entrance into the Great Palace complex.

There was no single great palace in the Great Palace complex. It was, instead, a series of buildings, each more magnificent than the last, the product of several mad or overweening emperors competing with their ancestors or pleasing their mistresses. All of this perched on a vast terrace overlooking the Bosporos. The Hagia Sophia loomed to our left, its vast dome reaching so close to Heaven that a man would be tempted to try to jump directly there. Claudius gaped at it, as all do upon seeing it up close for the first time.

"What holds it up?" she wondered.

"The hand of God," I said. "We'll visit it some other time."

One used to enter the Great Palace through an ancient pair of bronze gates, but Isaakios, in the full flush of his newly acquired divinity, embarked upon a series of misguided building projects. "Renovations," he called them, but he ransacked the grand old buildings of this area and carted the materials all over the empire, mostly building churches honoring Saint Michael. Three laborers were crushed to death when they took down the entrance gates to transport them to the church in Anaplous. I suppose that they appreciated their martyrdom to holy construction, but they didn't even rate an inscription on the building.

The baths were near the Arsenal, which was situated close to where the Mangana Palace used to be. The palace was another victim of Isaakios, despite its dedication to Saint George. In truth, Saint George was never of much use around these parts. If he ever went toe to toe with Saint Michael, I'd put my money on the commander.

The baths were new, made of mismatched marble blocks pirated from the razed structures. They were a gift to the Varangians from Isaakios in gratitude for the inaction of the guard when he deposed Andronikos. One might even call the baths a bribe if one were the sort of person to say that sort of thing. Which of course, I am.

Henry, the English captain, was waiting outside with three of his men. He saluted us, adding a special bow to the wine. Then each of them picked up a single cask like he was swinging a toddler into the air and carried it inside, Simon following.

"Fine muscles," commented Claudius.

"Yes," I agreed. "Soon you'll be seeing them in all their glory. By the way, Simon suspects us."

"He does?"

"He thinks we're lovers."

"He knows I'm a woman?"

"Not in the least. He just thinks we're lovers, and cautioned us accordingly."

"Then I can stare all I want once we get inside, and still be in character," she said, chuckling softly.

"But you're still coming home with me."

"Probably."

The legendary baths of Zeuxippos supposedly had a slew of bronze and marble statues intended to inspire noble and artistic instincts. The Varangian baths were also surrounded by statues, but their intended purpose was to inspire soldiers. They were divided between the martial and the lascivious, with an emphasis on the latter. Aphrodite, Helen, Circe, Cleopatra, and many other unlikely idealizations of the female form beckoned across the waters to the scarred veterans who fought for their favors.

These waters poured from pipes in the walls, carried from the Aqueduct of Valens by lesser aqueducts, heated on the way by passing over braziers maintained throughout the day by teams of slaves. The main bath was big enough for several hundred men. There was a platform in the middle with a small bridge leading to it.

"That's where you'll be performing," said Henry, pointing to the platform, "after the musicians are done. The fellows all speak Greek, but if you could throw in something in English or Danish, it would be appreciated."

"I can do both."

The musicians were all women, a comely quartet that could have given some of the statues a run for their money. They were not wearing much, and the not much was made of transparent silk that left little to the imagination. But soldiers aren't known for possessing much imagination, so that was probably just as well. The ladies trotted across the bridge and set up on the platform. Then, when they had their instruments ready, they wrapped blindfolds around their eyes. Thus was modesty preserved.

"They're really quite good," observed Henry as they began to perform. "And they play well, too."

"They put the Muse back in music," I said.

A fanfare signaled the opening of the main doors, and a brigade of Varangians marched in, fully armored. They formed ranks at the side of the baths, axes gleaming in the torchlight. Then, on a command from Henry, they stripped in a matter of seconds, their gear placed beside them in identically formed heaps. They continued to stand at attention.

I glanced at Claudius, who had discovered something fascinating about a hangnail on her left hand and was busy examining it.

"Long live the Emperor, Alexios Comnenos!" shouted Henry.

"Long live Alexios, our lord and charge!" they shouted in unison.

"Company, bathe!" ordered Henry, and with a whoop and a splash they dove in.

Suddenly, a company of soldiers became a pack of little boys, racing and wrestling and splashing the musicians. The sopping wet silks clung to the women and virtually disappeared, prompting ribald hoots from the men. The women played on gamely, managing to keep time despite the occasional deluge. The water wasn't doing the harp strings much good, but the men didn't seem to mind the sogginess of the sound.

"Remember, lads, some actual washing should occur," called Henry as he joined them. Now that he was bare, we could see that he had more scars than any of them.

Simon was set up in a corner, serving cups of wine at such a pace that I was worried that four casks would be inadequate. I was especially worried that there would not be any left for me after my performance. The tapster was in his element, chatting with one soldier after another, greeting most by name.

After some time, Henry motioned to us to begin our performance. I walked to the center of the platform.

"Hail, noble Varangians!" I cried. "In honor of your esteemed traditions, I have come to recite a heroic saga that dates to the beginnings of the guard. It should last about another hour. I think it will take that long to get the likes of you clean again."

There was a happy roar from the men. I struck a declamatory pose.

" 'When Olaf was king,' " I began, and then they laughed as

a club struck me in the head. I turned angrily, but could not find the culprit.

"Really, gentlemen," I admonished them. "Have you no respect for culture? I shall begin again. 'When Olaf was king, and the very waves...'"

Another club struck me. I spun around. Claudius stood there, hands behind her back, an innocent expression on her face. I continued to look around futilely as the bathers roared.

"Very well. This is the last time," I warned them. "'When Olaf was...'" I spun and caught the club just before it connected. Claudius stood frozen in the follow-through.

"So, you wish to play games, do you?" I sneered. "Catch this." I hurled the club at her. She caught it and returned it even faster.

I picked up the two clubs that had fallen at my feet. I threw them, one at a time. She caught them and returned them, then added three more, and we had our basic pattern. The soldiers applauded.

"Claudius, my friend, there is something amiss here," I cried.

"What is that, Feste?" she replied.

"The Varangians have a policy of blindfolding their entertainers."

"So they do."

"No doubt because of what happened to poor Actaeon."

"Absolutely," she agreed, then paused for a beat. "Who's Actaeon?"

"A great hunter, according to the Greeks, who chanced to come across the goddess Artemis just as she had begun her bath. She's that one over there," I said, managing to point out a particularly voluptuous statue while still tossing the clubs.

She glanced over to where I had pointed.

"Nice," she said. "No wonder they made her a goddess."

"I don't think that's how it worked back then," I said, flipping the clubs behind my back just to vary the routine a little.

"So, she's naked; he's a hunter. I bet I know what happened next," she said, leering. Several of the Varangians cheered.

"I bet you don't. She was one of those virgin goddesses."

"That's what she told Actaeon, anyway," said Claudius.

"It was the truth. And so angry was she at being caught in her shame that she turned him into a stag for her to hunt."

We stopped the clubs, Claudius staring in shock. Then she went over to the statue and gave it a good hard slap. The soldiers applauded, then laughed as she did a delayed take from the pain in her hand.

"I'd say the same must have happened to these men," she called out. "It looks like a stag party's going on."

"In any case, I'm not going to take any chances," I said.

"What are you going to do?"

I produced a blindfold from my pouch and tied it around my eyes.

"Is being blind an improvement over being a fool?" she called.

I held up my clubs.

"You can't be serious," she said.

"I never am," I said, and started juggling. It's not a hard trick to do. Juggling is more a matter of timing and feel than seeing. Besides, there were tiny slits in the blindfold. Not that I needed them.

I caught the clubs to the applause of the crowd, and bowed.

"You see, gentlemen?" I said. "I could do the entire performance blindfolded if need be."

Then I turned, took a step, and fell into the water.

Simple humor, but it worked. I kept my head above water so the makeup would stay more or less intact and pulled myself back onto the platform.

Claudius brought my lute to the platform, and I slung it on and strummed a few chords. Then I launched into an old English ballad that was applauded by the English portion of the group when I was done.

"What about us?" called Cnut, who was floating just in front of me.

"Join me, my Danish cousin," I replied, switching to his language. "Let us ride the sea king's steed to Byzantium; let us not drive the plough through the field, let us plough with the watery bow...."

They all joined in. The song does sound better in the original, fellow fools, and it was one I had known from my own childhood. I had rarely sung it in the last thirty years, and it was a pleasure to revisit it. I looked at the Northmen, so far from home, and thought of paths not taken.

We finished in due course to much cheering. As we packed up on the side, the guards hauled themselves out, dried themselves off, and were in full armor in a matter of seconds.

"Company, dismissed!" shouted Henry. He turned to me. "Excellently done, my friend. Feel free to use the bath before you go. There may still be a patch of clean water in there somewhere. I'm glad we caught you before we left. We're rotating out of here."

"Where are you going?" I asked as he handed me a small purse.

"Off to the Double Column," he said, sighing. "Leaving the city and crossing the waters to guard a blind man. A full brigade being detailed to guard a blind man who reclines in a prison that's more like a palace. Imagine that."

"Isaakios? Since when does he rate that kind of security?"

"Ever since the child Alexios escaped," he replied. "Even though that was the Emperor's fault for being lax. He never should have taken the boy with him. Now he thinks his brother arranged the whole thing, blind or not. So we guard him to prevent any further plotting."

"Then God speed and protect you," I said. "It was a pleasure. Have me in for your return. I can do an entirely new set of songs. English and Danish."

He clasped my hand, and beckoned to the musicians who followed him out.

"Aren't they going to get paid?" asked Claudius.

"I don't think they are done performing," I replied.

"Oh," she said in a small voice. "Well, that was fun, anyway. How did I do?"

"Splendidly," I said. I started to peel off my motley.

"I don't think this is the time or place," she said, glancing around.

"I am taking a bath," I said. "Sorry you can't join me. I need you to go check on the horses and pay for another week of stabling."

"When do I get to bathe?" she protested.

"I will borrow a tub from Simon and carry the water myself," I said. "Be good, and I'll scrub your back."

She picked up her gear. "How long before I become a full-fledged fool?" she asked.

I shrugged. "You are progressing remarkably well."

She bowed briefly. "Thank you, Master. I'll see you back at the Rooster."

"Give my love to Zeus," I said.

I spread my motley out to dry and jumped in, scrubbing vigorously, still keeping my head above the water. Then there was an enormous splash nearby.

"Damn, this feels good," exclaimed Simon, floating on his back about twenty feet away. Unclad, he revealed a physique that matched any of the soldiers, with a fair number of scars to boot.

"You really have been to the wars," I observed.

"As have you, I see," he replied. "What happened to that leg? Looks like you caught an arrow."

"No war," I said. "I was accompanying a duke and his retinue on a hunt. Someone saw my motley through the brush and mistook me for a large, colorful bird. He was quite the marksman, unfortunately. I was laid up for months."

The truth was more interesting, of course, but I saw no need to tell that story.

"How about those?" he said, pointing to some old wounds on my side.

"This was from a jealous mistress when I stopped courting her," I said.

"And the other?"

"From her husband."

He guffawed. "Truly, I had no idea jesting was so dangerous," he said. "Are you one of those Guild fools?"

"Not I. They're not to my taste. Too many stupid little rules, and you have to pay them for the privilege. My income is uncertain enough without sending part of it to a pack of meddlers who don't do a damn thing for it."

He zipped by me with a few powerful kicks.

"I need to do this more often," he said.

"Does your leg hurt you much?" I asked sympathetically.

He ducked under, scrubbing his hair and beard, then surfaced.

"An Arab spear did that on the plains of Arsuf in '91," he said. He pointed to some other scars on his left arm and shoulder. "These I got at Acre, end of '89, but they didn't slow me down any. It was that spear that gave me this limp. But it was a blessing. Many of my mates never made it back, but I survived, and learned the local wines well enough during my recuperation there to set up shop here. Now I get bathing privileges as the official tapster to the Varangians, and good seats at the Hippodrome as long as I bring a few wineskins with me."

"Wine sellers are worthy of any honor man can bestow upon them," I said. We climbed out and dried ourselves off.

"Does your friend not bathe?" he asked as we dressed.

"He has a physical deformity that he's a little sensitive about," I explained.

"That would be no problem here," scoffed Simon, pouring wine from the single cask still containing any into a pair of cups. "You saw this group. A parade of the mutilated. A soldier without a scar is a soldier who has never seen battle."

"It's more than a scar. I don't want to pique your curiosity any further on the matter. Perhaps he might borrow a tub back at the Rooster?"

"No problem. There's one in my room you can use. Just make sure you pour the water out the window afterward."

"Very kind of you. Your noble health, milord," I said in salute, and we finished the cups, rinsed them in the bath, and loaded the barrels back onto the wagon.

I did not go back with him then, choosing instead to find a money changer in the Forum Amastrianum who could give me a gold histamenon for some of the silver, electrum, and bronze I had collected. I did not want to be barred from the Hippodrome for having the wrong coin.

Claudius had not yet returned from the stables when I got back to the Rooster. Peter, the butcher, had come back from his labors with a pair of suckling pigs, and Simon was setting up a fire in a small brazier in back to roast them. I was looking forward to dinner. I must say that I was enjoying my time in Constantinople despite the tasks that lay before me. I don't often work in the larger cities, and the variety of the meals alone more than compensated for the length of the journey here.

It was indulgent of me to dwell on my appetite. It was also careless. I should have noticed before I entered my room that someone was in there waiting for me. But I just blithely walked in and dumped my bag on the floor before looking up to see the cowled figure standing in the corner, out of view from the hall.

I whirled to face him, not going for a weapon just yet. He had his hands in view, the only part of his body that I could see.

"Greetings, Holy Father," I said softly. "Have you come to shrive me?"

"*Stultorum numerus,*" he whispered.

"Some Latin blessing?" I asked. "An incantation? A curse? I have little Latin, Father, not having been educated properly in my misspent youth."

"You speak it well enough," came the whisper again. "*Stultorum numerus.*"

I didn't reply. The Guild had been compromised enough in this city, and I was not about to exchange passwords with a face I could not see. I stood there, idly scratching my ear.

"No need to go for your dagger, Theo," said the voice. He stepped into the light and pulled the cowl down.

And I nearly dropped dead on the spot.

"What's wrong, Theo?" asked Thalia, smiling. "You look like you've just seen a ghost."

NINE

Thou speakest as one of the foolish women speaketh.

JOB 2:10

My feet were rooted to the ground as Thalia moved toward me. My mouth went dry, and my heart raced fast enough to compete in the Hippodrome.

She had a feline grace that she used to full advantage, mimicking cats of all kinds, tame and wild. When she walked, it was a series of undulations, yet the green eyes would remain fixed on her target. She could keep that stare steady no matter what contortions she put her body through, something I had witnessed in both public and private performances. Right now, those eyes were locked on mine.

"I promise you I'm not a ghost, Theo," she said. "I'm very much alive. Flesh and blood, still warm. And I'll prove it to you as soon as you give me the password."

She closed the distance between us, gliding across the floor so silently that it almost gave the lie to her denial of incorporeity. Then her arms slipped around my neck, and she gazed up at me.

"Give me the password, Theo," she whispered.

"*Infinitus est,*" I managed to choke out, and she hugged me tightly and pressed her lips against mine.

"All right, that's proof enough, my good monk," I protested, dislodging her as gently as I could. "If I had known the Church was that friendly, I would have rejoined years ago."

"I can't believe you're actually here," she said, her eyes brimming. "I was beginning to think they'd never send anyone."

"I think we're even in the disbelief category," I said. "We thought you were dead months ago. Along with the others."

"I almost was," she said, pulling me into the room. She sat on the pallet and patted the place next to her. I sat down, my body obeying her before my mind told it what to do.

"How much do you know?" she asked.

"I know that there's a plot against Alexios," I said. "That there is an assassin waiting for a particular event to take place before he makes his move. And that's about it."

"Where did you hear that?" she asked. "I didn't think any of us had managed to get the word out."

"Zintziphitzes," I said.

She nodded. "So that's where Tiberius got it from. I never knew. But I should have guessed. I didn't know the old fool still had his sources."

"Tell me what happened."

"Niko called a meeting. We usually just met in passing, because the Emperor and Euphy . . ."

"Euphy? You call the Empress Euphy?"

"Yes, I do. Don't interrupt, Theo. They don't get together much, so I wasn't working with the twins regularly. But we would pass messages to each other and to Demetrios and Tiberius. And when something like this came up, we all got together."

"Did it come up often?"

"In this city? There's always someone plotting something. That's what the meeting was about. Whenever there's a potential overthrow, we get together and try to figure out if the city is better off with the current Emperor or the claimant. Then we act accordingly."

"I thought the Guild stayed out of the Byzantine succession."

She sighed. "The Guild is two months' travel from here. We can't wait for them to make every decision. We started getting involved when Andronikos was Emperor and Chalivoures was running the fools. You weren't here then, so you have no idea how horrible it was, all the rape, murder, torture. We used to check out every possible rival to the throne to see if any of them was strong to take on Andronikos and then run the empire without destroying it. Unfortunately, Andronikos was very good at weeding out the opposition before we could build them up. Finally, we decided that Isaakios was better than nothing. When Chalivoures got wind that Andronikos was sending someone to kill Isaakios, he made sure Isaakios heard about it. Isaakios killed the executioner and suddenly found himself leading the rebellion."

"Proving he had what it took."

"To take over, yes. To govern, no."

"What about Alexios's coup? Was that helped along by you?"

Thalia shook her head. "That happened out of town. That was one we would have tried to prevent, but we can't be everywhere. Anyway, when Tiberius brought us the latest rumor, we agreed to start working our usual sources to see what we could find out, and then pool our knowledge. But there was nothing to find. Nothing out of Blachernae Palace, nothing from the Church, nothing from the Senate, nothing from the Blues and Greens in the Hippodrome, nothing from the Great Palace. Then I got a message that Demetrios had left at the Rooster calling for a meeting. Unfortunately, Euphy was in one of her moods and needed my shoulder to cry on for the rest of the night, so I couldn't make it."

"Then that was your message I found in his pouch. Do you know what he had discovered?"

"No. And then when I was coming home from Blachernae late that night, a man came out of the dark with a knife."

She was looking down, her hands shaking.

"He was fast, Theo. I barely had my own knife out before he was on me. And that was the last thing I remembered for a long time."

She stopped, and leaned into me, pulling my arm around her.

"Someone found me in a sea of my own blood," she continued. "Yet I survived. I lay on a bed for months before I could even speak. When I ventured out on my own at last, the others were long gone. So I hid, Theo."

"Why didn't you contact the Guild?"

"How?" she cried. "There was no one I could trust with a letter. I figured Fat Basil would come looking for us, or a new troubadour. Then I heard there was a new fool in town. I came to the Amastrianum, and there you were, come to rescue me at last. You were pretty good, by the way. You've lost a step or two since I last saw you, but you were still pretty good."

"Thank you. I almost lost a leg since I last saw you. Was that you following me in the cowl then?"

"Yes, but I decided not to interrupt you. You were intent on trailing that little bearded fellow, the one that's standing in the doorway with his mouth hanging open."

I glanced up. There was Claudius, looking daggers at us. Not just daggers, but swords, crossbows, poison, Greek fire, and stampeding elephants.

I stood up a bit too hastily and helped Thalia to her feet.

"Look who survived," I said. "Thalia, this is ... this is Claudius, my apprentice. Claudius, this is Thalia, still among the living."

"Hello," said Thalia. "I know I'm supposed to say something insulting here, but I'm tired. Forgive me for not following tradition."

"That's too bad," said Claudius. "I had a real good response ready. Nice tonsure, by the way."

Thalia turned back to me.

"What's the plan, Theo?" she asked. "I don't know how much good I can be to you. It took all I had to walk here. I'm not up to serious fooling yet. But I'll do what I can."

"There's no real plan," I said. "We're playing the Hippodrome tomorrow. Hopefully, we'll do well enough to worm our way into Blachernae. Who are the main players around the Emperor?"

"Apart from the Empress, there are several. The Eparch is Constantine Tornikes. He's a pathetic little man who'd flee his own shadow. The Grand Chamberlain is a eunuch named George Oinaiotes. He's a sneaky one. The Emperor once sent him as an envoy to a Vlach rebel. George ended up tipping off the fellow that there was a Byzantine army right behind him. The eunuch in charge of the Imperial Wardrobe is called John. No fashion sense whatsoever. You'll know him by his garments. He favors these horrible green buskins that make him look like a frog. The Keeper of the Imperial Inkstand is Leonitos, very lecherous and very bribable, a bad combination. And there's Constantine Philoxenites. He's another eunuch, but he has a head on his shoulders. He runs the Imperial Treasuries. Niko always said that for a eunuch, he had balls."

"What about other family members? Potential claimants?"

"There are three daughters: Irene, Anna, and Evdokia. The older two are each on a second husband. Irene's is Alexios Palailogos. He's very close to the Emperor, fights a lot of his battles. Anna's is Theodore Laskaris. I'm pretty sure he has ambitions, but he's close to Euphy, so he's probably not interested in overthrowing anyone, at least not yet. He'd be more likely to plot against his brother-in-law. Evdokia was kicked out of her marriage for adultery, which is a family tradition, so she came running back to daddy. She's still married officially, although that could be fixed in a hurry if anyone wanted to have her. I think they're waiting for the best connection they can make."

"And women?"

She snorted. "An ever-changing procession. The current favorite is this Egyptian courtesan."

"Egyptian?"

"Oh, don't worry, Theo. She's been checked out thoroughly."

"By the Guild?"

"No, by Euphy. The Empress has the best network of spies in the city, especially when it comes to the Emperor's women. The Egyptian is probably working for her."

"Isn't marriage wonderful?" I sighed.

"I used to think so," said Claudius.

"What a cynical little man you are," said Thalia. "I don't know if it's even worth my while flirting with you."

"It would be amusing to watch," said Claudius.

"Well, I'd better get back before the Vigla come out," said Thalia.

"Where can I find you if I need you?" I asked.

She shook her head. "I'll track you down tomorrow." She stood on tiptoe and kissed me again. "I'm so happy they sent you," she said, and glided out.

"Thalia was a particular friend of yours, was she not?" sneered Claudius. "Your makeup's smeared."

"Hush, Apprentice," I said. I slipped down the stairs and peered out the front doorway, but there was no sign of her. I went back to our room.

"You have this odd affinity for women who dress as men, don't you?" commented Claudius. "Why didn't you introduce me properly? Didn't want her to know you were married and had the wife along?"

"Something bothers me about her being alive," I said.

"Well, we're finally in agreement. I'm not happy about her being alive, either."

"A Thracian king once captured six wolves while hunting," I mused. "He put them into a dungeon in the lowest reaches of the palace and locked the door. He came back six months later and found one wolf."

She looked at me skeptically.

"Are you saying that you suspect her?" she asked.

"Do I detect some hope in your voice?" I responded.

"I found you in each other's arms."

"She needed comforting."

"She looked comforted."

"She caught me by surprise, all right?" I protested, nearly shouting. "It took me some time to finish picking my wits off the floor."

"A good fool is ready for anything at any time," she reminded me.

"Enough, Apprentice."

"Stop calling me that!"

"What do you want me to call you?"

She turned away.

"Wife," she said softly. "Beloved. Viola. Any endearment would be welcome right now."

I went up to her and put my arms around her.

"How about I give you that bath I promised?" I said.

"That's a start," she replied.

I went downstairs to the back where Simon had his rooms. The tub was beside his bed. The bed itself was a grand, four-posted affair that I eyed with envy. One's host should not sleep so much better than his guests.

I lugged the tub upstairs, then fetched a bucket and filled it with water. By the fifth trip, the tub was full and Viola was sitting in it, scrubbing vigorously.

"I remember you," I said, kissing her on the back of the neck.

She tossed a cloth at my face. I caught it and began doing her back.

"I used to have servants," she said. "A bevy of maidens caring for my clothes, my rooms, my children. To think that I gave up that life for a tub of cold water in a tiny flea-ridden room with you. And we don't even get to sleep together."

"We will again. Be patient."

She pointed to her right shoulder blade.

"Scratch right there, husband, and I'll forgive you much."

I did, and she sighed happily.

She got up and dried herself. I bailed out the tub with the bucket, heaving the bathwater out the window, first making sure no one was beneath it. Then I lugged the borrowed items back to Simon's room.

He was still out back, roasting the pigs. I noticed an immense wardrobe standing slightly open. I'm a nosy person by nature. I peeked in. There was the usual collection of linens, leather aprons, and cloaks. And a large white mantle with a red cross on it.

Oho, I thought, isn't that interesting?

Claudius had reassembled himself and come down to dine by the time I returned. The pigs were done to perfection and served to cheering from the gathering, with special thanks to Peter for providing them. I gathered that this was how he paid his rent.

I had first watch. As she pulled the thin covers over her, I told Claudius everything I had learned from Thalia.

"So far, we've drawn out a pair of fools," she said sleepily. "I wonder when the fool killers will come our way."

"Maybe they're long gone," I said. "Maybe they gave up."

"You don't really believe that," she said.

"No. Oh, and here's a bit of gossip. Our host wasn't just a Crusader. He was with the Knights of the Temple. I saw an old mantle in his bureau."

"Simon's a Templar?" she exclaimed. "He doesn't seem the type at all. He's too happy."

"Maybe because he survived," I said. "Now, he's gone back to the simple life of selling wine to drunks and telling war stories to soldiers."

"Preaching to the converted," she said, drifting off. "Funny, you wouldn't expect to run into a Templar in Constantinople."

"Sleep tight, beloved wife, Viola," I whispered, kissing her. "Tomorrow, we play the Hippodrome."

We were up at dawn for a change. We loaded our cart with the bricks and the rest of our gear and trundled it toward the Hippodrome. We passed through the square where we had encountered Zintziphitzes. He was there again, haranguing the merchants as they opened their stalls. I gave him a quick signal to meet us, then took Claudius to break our fasts at the same tavern we had been in previously.

He came in quickly, looking around until he saw us.

"You should be in church, sinners," he said.

"We are with a holy man," I replied. "What could be more religious than to worship at your feet?"

"Mockery, mockery," he sighed. "I sometimes wonder if Our Savior was ever heckled when He preached. And if He had the proper retorts ready. He certainly had His humorous side. Are you off to the Hippodrome for the games today?"

"We are," I said. "And I was wondering if you could give a more precise location as to where that conversation took place. If I can place the seats, I might be able to pin down who was using them."

"That's a bit tricky," he said, thinking. "The sounds trickle down from different directions, and if I can't recognize the voices, it's extremely difficult to say where they are coming from."

"It was just a thought," I said.

"I'll tell you what I can do," he said. "I'll take a bit of green wood and get it burning. The smoke will rise up through the same drain that the sounds came down. Watch the Kathisma at the first imperial fanfare, and look to the right."

"That would be very helpful," I said. "Thank you."

We rose to leave.

"Knock 'em dead," he said, giving the sign of the Cross in blessing.

"Peace be with you," I replied.

We entered through the stables, searching for Samuel. The activity was about triple the level of our last visit, with the horses being rubbed down and their manes being braided with gold ribbons. We passed stall after stall with their highly strung occupants whinnying after us. One stall brought forth a deep growl from its depths. Claudius glanced in, then leapt sideway a good eight feet.

"That is not a horse," she pronounced. "That is a bear. A really large bear with several hundred teeth."

"I'm sure he's friendly," I said. "Probably a trained one working with some acrobats."

"Actually, he's quite savage," shouted Samuel from the top of a ramp. "They're going to put him in a ring with a lion and see which one emerges. That's the lion to your left."

Claudius glanced that way and was greeted with a roar. This leap brought her to the exact middle of the path.

"I'll bet on the lion," she said.

"Greetings, noble patron," I said, handing the gold coin to Samuel.

"Pass, fools," he said after inspecting it closely. "The entertainment will stay in the pen by the euripos during the races. We're doing the usual four races in the morning, four in the afternoon. Barriers in the morning, chariots in the afternoon, with the usual footraces, gymnastics, animals, and the man who says he can fly. You can do your act between the races. Don't perform in front of the Kathisma until you are invited to do so. The Eparch will have his scouts watching the performances, and they'll let you know if the Emperor wants to see you."

We thanked him and pushed the cart up the ramps through the gates to the arena.

"What's the euripos?" Claudius asked.

"There," I said. "That structure in the center."

"Oh, my," she said.

The course was so long that you could launch an arrow from one end, walk for several minutes, pick the arrow up in the middle, and send it to the far end. At the center was a long, narrow, oblong platform on which was scattered a variety of columns and statues. This was the euripos.

The entertainers' pen was by the Egyptian Obelisk, brought in triumph by Theodosios himself nearly a thousand years ago. Near it was the Serpent Column, part of the tripod from the Oracle of Delphi, its carved serpents so lifelike you'd swear you could hear them hiss. At the other end was the Column of Constantine Pophyrogenitos, a giant pile of masonry sheathed in bronze that caught the sun and tossed it around the stadium like a plaything.

In between these rivals to Babel were the statues depicting

animals of nature and of nightmare, and humans of history and of myth. All bronze, they were all fighting for attention so that the observer would become dizzy as his eye was captured by one, then another. Of all these statues, my favorite was the giant Heracles by the legendary Lysippos. Rather than choosing a standard heroic pose, Lysippos sculpted the half-god without weapons, weary from the imposition of impossible labors, yet unbeaten. His refusal to bow before adversity had made him a favorite whipping boy of the Empress, yet even she had yet to conquer him.

"What happened to the nose of that poor boar?" asked Claudius as we set up our cart inside the pen.

There was a massive bronze boar facing down a lion. Its snout had been sheared away.

"Euphrosyne," said a young man limbering up with a group of acrobats, and that was all the explanation anyone needed.

"We have time for a walk," I said, and we ventured up the tiers of the Sphendone, the great curved end, to the colonnade that ran along the top of the stadium. More statues surrounded us, and we had a splendid view of the city, indeed, of the entire world beyond it. The Hagia Sophia loomed ahead of us, and we could see all the way across the straits to Chrysopolis.

"The Kathisma is that two-story building in the center of the south side," I explained. "The Emperor and his retinue sit in the second story. Most of the imperial staff sit to the right, and the senators sit to the right of them. That's where we have to watch when the fanfare is sounded. On the north side are the two great factions, the Blues and the Greens. That's where the trouble can come from. They each have their favorites in the races, and will use any small excuse to start a fight. That's why we're only doing physical comedy in here. No politics."

"But won't there be soldiers keeping the peace?" she asked.

"You'd better believe it. Several centuries ago, there was a riot that started right in that section. They say that the army ended up massacring thirty thousand people inside this pretty little stadium. Those drains must have run blood for weeks afterward."

"How horrible," she said.

We walked down to a sculpture of some long-forgotten charioteer.

"The races start down at the other end where the gates are," I said.

"Under that sculpture of the four horses?"

"Yes. Make sure you're well to the center of our pen before they start. If we're caught outside, just get to the euripos and climb up one of those statues."

"How will we know when they're going to race?"

"Listen to the fanfares. And do you see that bronze eagle there, the one with the snake in its claws? Look at the underside of its wings."

She looked at the sculpture, which was mounted so that it soared high over the rest. The wings had a series of lines scored on the bottom.

"Those will mark the hour according to the sun," I said.

"Wonderful!" she exclaimed.

We made our way back to our pen and began our preparations. I watched the gymnasts contort with no small amount of envy, but as we joined them in our stretches, I found that my leg was proving remarkably cooperative. On an impulse, I crouched, then did a standing backflip.

"Not bad, old man!" called one of the youths.

"Well?" I said, looking at Claudius.

She looked back impassively, then duplicated the trick.

"Well?" she said. I grinned.

The gates opened, and the Imperial Guard marched in, followed by members of the Emperor's administration and the Senate. Next came the two factions, waving flags of their respective colors and shouting clever things like "Green! Green!" or "Blue! Blue!" I was glad that purple was reserved for the crown, as the extra syllable might have been too much for these idiots to handle.

The crowd filled the stadium to the brink. The course inspectors bustled about the track, making sure no stray stones were present to trip up either human or equine competitors. The Guard took up positions all around the stadium, and soon several dozen heralds ran across, standing ready to take their signals. Claudius and I pushed our way to the side of the pen facing the Kathisma, keeping our eyes to the right of it, while our fellow performers craned their necks, looking for signs of the Emperor's arrival.

There was a flourish of drums, and the heralds began to scream at the spectators: "Rise, O senators, and render praise to the Emperor! Rise, O soldiers, and render praise to the Emperor! Rise, O citizens, and render praise to the Emperor!"

The great golden curtains that cloaked the Kathisma from the common view were pulled to the sides and secured. Then there was more drumming, and a score of trumpeters took their place on the roof of the building. They breathed as one, and the fanfare split the heavens.

Claudius stood with her gaze fixed on the spectacle, her hands clenching the top of the barrier. I leaned over and whispered into her ear, "It's showtime."

TEN

It is a vigorous blow to vices to expose them to public laughter.
MOLIÈRE, PREFACE TO *TARTUFFE*

Emperors don't have to walk if they don't want to. Six burly guards carried Alexios to the second level of the Kathisma on a litter with a throne affixed to it. They lowered it carefully, and he stood to the cheers of the crowd, stepping slowly to the front, though not so close that one of his men could succumb to the temptation of shoving him over the edge. He was clad sumptuously in purple robes and red buskins, a crown double the size of Euphrosyne's weighing down his head. His beard was suspiciously black for a man with three grown daughters.

I saw all of this out of the corner of my eye. I was focused on the section to the right, where the Imperial officeholders were standing, trying to peer around the edge of the royal box to glimpse their ruler.

A small wisp of dirty smoke rose by one of them. I nudged Claudius, and we followed it down to where a corpulent, bald man in blue robes was looking around irritatedly. He motioned to his guards, who were crawling about the tiers. One of them stood, pointing down. They all gathered around and looked at the source of the smoke. Then one of them left and returned with a bucket of water. He poured it on the offending embers, and the smoke stopped. They all nodded, satisfied, as if they had accomplished something important.

"Our preacher may have gotten himself baptized again," I murmured. "But we may have our man. Nice work, old fellow."

The horses, riders, and charioteers gathered for a grand promenade around the stadium, saluting the Emperor as they passed. He had some visiting ambassadors from somewhere seated behind him, and by his side a sullen, young boy, the relative whose birthday was the ostensible reason for the games today.

"Where's the Empress?" wondered Claudius.

"A woman at the Hippodrome?" I gasped, scandalized. "That would be completely improper. The only women you'll ever see here will be either entertainers or courtesans. Why, a proper woman appearing here would be giving her husband grounds for divorce."

"It's a good thing I'm an entertainer," she said softly. She glanced around, taking in a hundred thousand faces. "I hope they like me."

"You'll be fine," I assured her.

The horses for the first race lined up at the starting gate. A man I assumed to be the Eparch rode onto the course. He trotted in front of the Kathisma. He was a nervous rider, was this Constantine Tornikes, and he was sweating profusely under the morning sun. The horse sensed his unease and kept skittering sideways.

There was a fair amount of booing from the factions. Someone yelled, "It's Constantine Turn-and-flee!" and the crowd laughed derisively as the Eparch looked angrily over his shoulder.

He held up a large, white napkin that fluttered in the breeze. There was another fanfare. He looked up at the Emperor, who by this time was reclining on the throne, his legs up on cushions. He was being massaged by a dark-skinned beauty. The Egyptian, I guessed.

The Emperor motioned to the Eparch, who turned and faced the riders. There was a brief drumming, then silence. The crowd collectively craned their necks to see the napkin. He let it fall and galloped out of the way.

The gates opened simultaneously, thanks to the usual Byzantine mechanical genius in the service of leisure activities. The horses charged the turning post at the front of the euripos, then veered to the left and dashed past the Kathisma, the Imperial office-holders, and the Senate. They took the Great Turn, the riders leaning sideways to the right, and shot past the factions who were cheering wildly.

The first race was four laps of dodging around barriers, and as the riders passed our pen on the final turn, the various entertainers began gathering at the gate in preparation for their performances.

"We'll start by the end in front of the common folk," I instructed Claudius. "Then we'll work our way around the stadium during each lull between races. Have fun."

The winner, a favorite of the Greens, was led before the Emperor, while that faction celebrated across the stadium. A team of acrobats quickly sprang into action, jumping onto each other's shoulders and off again, spinning like madmen, and finishing in a human pyramid. The Emperor barely paid any attention.

Meanwhile, Claudius and I were doing well with the cheap seats. We timed our routine perfectly, scooped up our coins, and dashed back to the pen. And so continued the morning.

What I heard later on was that the Emperor noticed the laughter from the first performance, but we were too far away for him to see us clearly. After the second race, while a team of the city's young men took on a collection of foreigners in footraces, the laughter came from the Blues. The Emperor looked again, but was blocked by the euripos. Nevertheless, his curiosity was piqued to the point that he wondered out loud what was so amusing. Several of his servants scrambled to find out.

We returned to the pens and quenched our thirst at a water barrel someone had thoughtfully provided for the entertainers. The slaves were setting up the barriers for the next race, a steeplechase. This one produced the first casualties of the day, a pileup of five horses and riders at the Great Turn. The horses screamed in agony, one rider was carried off on a stretcher, and the crowd roared and continued to wager on the outcome.

The next between-race contest was among representatives of the different companies of guards, racing in full armor three times around the track. Several of them collapsed in the heat, clattering as they fell to the scorn of the soldiers watching from the tiers. We played to the Greens, improvising some delayed reactions as the soldiers dashed behind us. The coins flew, and there was actual cheering when we were done. This was the performance that the Emperor's servants watched.

I was touching up my makeup during the next steeplechase when I was tapped on the shoulder. I turned to see a slave beckoning to me.

"You are summoned to perform before the Emperor after the animals are done," he informed me.

I bowed in assent, and he left.

"We did it!" crowed Claudius.

"God, I hate following animals," I said. "I hope they clean up after them."

The last morning race was run. We played to the Great Turn. I noticed Samuel watching from the ramp to the stables. Then the parade of the animals began.

Any ambassador wishing to curry favor with the Byzantine Empire knows enough to bring an animal as a gift, the more exotic, the better. These were kept in the Imperial Menageries, mostly in the Great Palace, but were brought out to amuse and placate the populace during the games.

There were elephants, bears, enormous gray wolves from Russia, and a pair of giant creatures with long, brown-spotted necks that soared high above us. Then came the gazelles, a great, glowering rhinoceros, crocodiles writhing in huge, wheeled tubs. After that, the caged cats—the panthers, the leopards, and the lion we had met earlier—pacing behind wooden slats that looked much too flimsy.

"I suppose if one got out and ate a person, that would be part of the fun," commented Claudius as we began wheeling our cart toward the Kathisma.

"Depending on whom he ate, yes," I said. "Looks like the Eparch would be the people's choice."

There was a sudden rise in the roaring and growling.

"Look," I pointed out. "The bear won."

"Poor little lion," she said.

She set up before the Kathisma, wheeling the cart with its load of bricks, dressed like a laborer. She bowed low, then wiped the sweat off her brow with an exaggerated motion. She pulled a long loaf of bread out and made as if to eat it.

Along comes a Fool, the very picture of avoiding work. But he eyes the bread and rubs his stomach. A quandary: how does he get bread without actually doing anything to earn it? He thinks, pounding on his head. Then—an idea! He sneaks around behind the laborer, taps him on the right shoulder from behind. The laborer looks that way, but the Fool has already danced to the left and broken off the tip of the loaf. By the time the slow-witted worker has turned back to the front, he's short some bread, and the Fool is cramming it into his mouth, hiding behind the cart.

The poor Everyman looks about haplessly, shrugs, and starts

again. The Fool does the same trick in reverse, tapping the left shoulder and going right after purloining another piece. The worker, realizing something is up, does a slow burn. Then he waits, feigning a lack of vigilance.

The Fool, having grown overconfident with his success, barely even attempts to conceal himself on his next try. He taps the right shoulder. The worker fakes right, then whirls to the left and whops the Fool solidly with the loaf.

Which hurt like hell when we rehearsed it at the Rooster. They make good, solid, crusty bread in this city, and Claudius hadn't quite mastered pulling the blow just short of my nose. But this time, she was perfect. I saw a blur of bread, and rocked back into a series of bizarre tumbles, ending in a headstand. The crowd roared.

Oh, the Fool has been caught! He begs, he pleads, he shows his desperation. He indicates that he would do anything to avoid prison, even—gasp!—work. All indicated by dumb show, of course, in the space of a few seconds.

The Everyman relents and dumps the bricks onto the ground. He indicates to the Fool that he should follow his lead. He takes a brick, places it in front of him. The Fool does likewise. The laborer puts a second brick next to the first. The Fool, a little more confident, does the same. Say, this is easy, he thinks. The smugness returns.

Then the laborer, who does this for a living, speeds up, his hands a whirlwind, stacking them quickly. The Fool cannot sustain the pace. He is frantic. His section of the wall becomes a tumbledown affair as every brick he puts on it falls. Soon, he is sneaking glances at the impassive laborer to his left, and stealing bricks from the latter's part of the wall to even the score. Then, he is caught again.

Consternation! There is no more room for redemption. The

laborer, not a patient man, takes a brick and throws it at the Fool.

Who catches it. And then another. And then another.

Brick juggling has its own technique. Oh, you can flip bricks through the air like you would clubs or balls, but that's just basic stuff. The interesting way of doing it is to take three bricks and press the middle one between the two outer ones so that they make a straight line. Then you start switching them in midair while keeping the illusion of the line intact. It's not easy.

Especially when you bring in a fourth brick, and then a fifth. By this time, you don't have to pretend to be in a panic; it comes naturally with what you're attempting to do. And just when I was about to drop them all, in came Claudius to grab one and steady the pattern.

We held for a moment, facing each other in front of the Kathisma. Then she brought a sixth brick into the line, and we had four hands going, our arms shooting in and out of each other's way as if we were a human loom.

We finished by tossing all of the bricks into the air. I caught the first two and held them together, and she quickly grabbed the rest and stacked them neatly on top of my base pair. Then she started stacking more and more, while I looked increasingly exhausted.

The stacking wasn't a random pattern, of course. It allowed me to stagger around while maintaining this crazy tower. Then I tilted the bricks in a peculiar way, and they tumbled into a more stable structure. In fact, it was now a section of wall, identical to the one she had built on the ground. I placed my section next to it, and snatched the last piece of bread from the cart in triumph.

There was thunderous applause from the Kathisma and the

nearby sections. Even the musicians were clapping, which is a rarity.

I glanced over at Claudius and said, "Well done!" Her eyes were shining as she looked up at our audience. We bowed and quickly piled our bricks back onto the cart.

A purse came flying down from the upper level of the Kathisma. I caught it and then fell backward under the impact, provoking more laughter from the crowd. I looked directly at the Emperor, who was guffawing merrily. He waved to me, and I waved back and bowed again.

We rolled our cart back to our pen and relaxed.

"Anything to eat?" asked Claudius mischievously.

I pulled the sections of bread out of my pouch and handed them over. I had eaten only a small portion during the act. With so many repeat performances, if I actually ate the loaf, I would have been too heavy to move by the time we finished.

Claudius added some cheese and nuts from her pouch, and we had ourselves a nice repast there in the middle of the Hippodrome while the chariots careened around us.

The slave who had summoned us before dashed across the course after the first race was over.

"The Emperor wishes you to perform at Blachernae Palace tomorrow afternoon," he said excitedly. Then he bent down and whispered, "You are about to become a wealthy pair of fools. Guard yourselves well."

He dashed back.

"We're in," I said, clapping her on the back. "All right, two more times and we've done the circuit."

"Wait," she said, pointing up. "It's the flying man."

A man walked before the Kathisma wearing the most outlandish costume I had ever seen, and I'm accustomed to motley. His tunic was covered with all manner of feathers, and he was carrying a pair of giant wings, larger even than those of the bronze eagle soaring over us.

"My Lord, Emperor Alexios, long may you thrive," he shouted. "I am here to show you a marvel. I have spent ten years studying the creatures of the air, and have discovered their innermost secrets. Now, I have used this knowledge to devise wings for man. With this, you shall rise above any Emperor who has ever lived. Your armies shall conquer beyond any wall, any moat, any mountain. Nothing shall stand in your way."

Alexios kept a straight face throughout, and motioned to the fellow to proceed. The moment the man turned away from the Kathisma, the entire Imperial retinue began crowding to the front, wagering heavily.

"Are there actually those among them betting he will succeed?" marveled Claudius.

"No," I said. "I think they're only betting on how far he'll land from the column."

The poor, deluded fellow scaled the Column of Constantine Porphyrogenitos, then hauled the wings up after him. He slipped his arms into them, and flapped experimentally a few times. Then he looked around and froze.

I wanted to shout for him to come down, but the crowd was shouting for him to make the attempt. All we could do was watch and see if the fear of shame would conquer the fear of death.

It did. He spread his wings and leapt straight out. For a moment, he sustained the illusion. The crowd held its breath, and the Hippodrome was silent. The silence was broken by a solitary scream, which was in turn broken by a sickening thud.

"Looks like he got about thirty paces," commented a guard standing nearby. "I don't think that breaks the record."

"You owe me dinner," said another.

There was laughter all about, especially from the Kathisma, as the slaves went to remove the poor fellow's corpse from the track. Claudius looked at me.

"They laughed at us, and they laughed at him," she said. "Makes me feel less proud of what we did."

"It could have been worse," I said.

"How?"

"We could have followed him."

The rest of the day was anticlimactic. We did our last two performances and packed up, shaking hands with the gymnasts and acrobats. It was a profitable day all around, and we were in a buoyant mood despite the one fatality. The flier wasn't one of us, so his death did not weigh down our spirits overmuch. All in a day's work at the Hippodrome.

Samuel was waiting to collect his fee, but did not press us for an exact accounting.

"Come back anytime," he said. "We will all profit."

"Thank you," I said.

As we left the stables, we were hailed by a man waiting outside. He was in his forties, I would say, of medium height and build. He still had all of his hair and a humorous cast to his eyes. He was wearing a light blue tunic under dark blue robes marked with an insignia that I didn't know.

"Congratulations on your performance, my good fools," he said. "I would like to buy you a drink if you have the time."

"If it was the end of the world, I would still have time for a drink," I replied. "Lead on, noble sir."

He took us through a maze of side streets to a small tavern near the Venetian quarter. He ordered a pitcher of wine and a bowl heaped with shellfish, and we dug in.

"May we have the honor of knowing who is buying us dinner?" I asked.

"Forgive me," he said, and then he seemed to puff up with self-importance. "I am Niketas Choniates. I am a Senator and the Logothete of the Sekreta."

Claudius looked at me.

"Are we impressed?" she asked.

"I'm not sure," I replied. I turned to our new friend. "You're a senator and the chief of the civil service. Which means you're powerless in two different ways."

He leaned back and laughed until he nearly choked.

"By God, it's true!" he roared. "I am a functionary. No more, no less. The Senate meets every day down in the Great Palace, while the real strings are all being pulled up at Blachernae." He leaned forward, suddenly quiet and serious. "Where the two of you will be entertaining as of tomorrow."

"Ah," I said, unsurprised. "What are you looking for?"

"Fools have a license to mock freely before the Emperor," he said. "Although I did not hear you speak earlier, I assumed that your humor was not merely physical. And in the short space of time we've been talking, you've confirmed to me that your wits are of the highest quality."

"Thank you."

"So, I was wondering what the price of mockery is nowadays."

"It depends on what you want."

"To direct it at an intimate of the Emperor."

"You want to pay me to ridicule someone. Who?"

He shook his head. "First, I must know if you will do it. Otherwise, I might be placing myself in some jeopardy by revealing who my enemy is. Information travels so quickly around here."

"Then I must refuse," I said. "If a person of your stature is afraid of this person, I am certainly not going to take any risks on your behalf. Especially on such short acquaintance. We've only been in the city for a few days. Until we know all of the ins and outs of the palace, who's who and doing what to who else, we cannot afford to play any favorites."

"I understand entirely," he said, smiling. "Well, it was worth the discussion. I truly enjoyed your performance, by the way."

"Thank you."

"Did I detect a satirical tone to your choice of material?"

"Material, meaning subject matter? Or meaning bricks?"

"Both. I thought it might have been intended to be a bit allegorical. We live in a city that depends upon the state of the walls surrounding it. Here were the embodiments of prudent wall-building and prodigal living for the moment, pitched in battle. Believe me, the topic has been of no little concern for those of us who wonder about the future of the Empire."

"Sounds like a worthy topic for debate down in the Senate."

He winced. "That's all we ever do there. We talk. I think that the Senate only exists in case the government is overthrown again. We have no authority until there is no authority. Then we have some—if the army and the people are willing to go along with us. Where were you before you came here?"

"Elsewhere."

"Anywhere near Venice?"

"No."

"Hm. A pity. I'm interested in knowing what they're up to. Crusaders are geniuses at creating difficulty. They always expect you to believe that their cause is so holy that you should just roll over and give them supplies and right of free passage, and before you know it, there's a German army camped in your courtyard. You might want to mention to our Emperor that he should rouse himself from his lethargic revels and think about the walls some more."

"Is this something you want to pay me to do?"

"I thought it was something you would do for free."

"Maybe. I'll think about it." I stood and offered my hand. "Thanks for dinner."

"A pleasure, my friends. Stop by anytime and share some gossip."

We had time to talk during our walk back, each holding one handle of the cart.

"Suddenly, we are a valued commodity," observed Claudius. "Will others be attempting to purchase our services?"

"Possibly. Anyone with access to the Emperor becomes a target. The best course is to refuse all of them and go our own way. I wonder if any of the other fools had been approached like that."

"Would they have accepted such a bribe?"

"I doubt it, but you never know. We're human, and we have our weaknesses. It would be especially tempting if a fool was asked to target someone he was planning to attack anyway. A little easy money on the side."

"I'm so glad that you're incorruptible. By money, anyway."

"Thank you. I wonder who our friend Niketas dislikes so much?"

"Maybe someone will bribe us to make fun of him. Then we'll know."

We pulled up to the Rooster and wheeled our cart in back.

"The next step is to find out the identity of the bald man we smoked out," I said. "It would be nice if we could get him to speak somewhere near Zintziphitzes. If he could identify the voice, then we'd be certain."

"Let's see him tomorrow before we go to Blachernae," she suggested. "Do you want to repeat the brick routine?"

"Not tomorrow," I said. "We'll use the other material."

"Good," she said, stretching. "I am tired of pushing this damn cart. I feel like we've gone over every hill in the city today."

"And how did milady enjoy performing before a hundred thousand people?"

She grinned at me. "I felt like I was ready to fly when we finished before the Emperor, and there was no need for that winged contraption, either. If that logothete fellow hadn't intercepted us, I would have dragged you to the nearest inn and taken a room with a real door in the doorway, thrown you inside, dropped the bar, and had my way with you."

"My dear Claudius," I exclaimed. "For that, I would have turned down the prospect of a free drink. Let me know next time."

We went up the steps, waving to our fellow patrons. I was more alert this time, remembering that Thalia had promised to meet us again. So, it was with little surprise that I entered our room to find the cowled figure standing there.

"Good evening," I said, sensing Claudius tensing behind me. "You've come earlier than expected."

"I was unaware that I was expected," came Father Esaias's voice from under the cowl. "But most would prefer me to be too early than too late."

ELEVEN

That is no country for old men.
WILLIAM BUTLER YEATS, "SAILING TO BYZANTIUM"

I should have spotted it from the hands, once again the only
part of the person I could see. Thalia's were strong, yet still
young and supple. These were old and gnarled, although they
looked powerful enough to break a neck if necessary.

"I figured that sooner or later I would be receiving another
visit from you," I said, switching modes as smoothly as I could.

"Truly, you are a strategist to be reckoned with," commented
Esaias. "Which makes me wonder at the crudeness of your earlier
tactics with my man."

"It seemed like the right approach at the time," I said, stalling
until I found out whom he was talking about.

"He's such a harmless little one," he continued. "At least, he
is now, hawking his useless little talismans to the gullible. He was
quite the pickpocket until the drink and disease destroyed his
abilities. Now, he brings in a small but regular amount, and we
take care of him as we do all of our people."

"It is wonderful what your church does for the needy," I said.

"We look out for them more than the True Church does," he
said. "More than either of the True Churches. Say what you will
about us. We may all burn in Hell, but we will have provided

for each other more than those looking down upon us from Heaven."

He looked out the window, nodded slightly, then turned back to us. Claudius immediately stood with her back to mine and watched the hallway for signs of trouble, her hand on her sword.

"Terrifying the weak is hardly sporting," continued Esaias. "Mind you, it is how I make a substantial part of my living. But all you took was one item, a fact so odd that it aroused my curiosity more than my ire. May I see it?"

I reached into my pouch and removed the ring I had retrieved from the relic seller. I placed it in his hands, and he held it up to the light.

"Demetrios," he pronounced finally. "So it is true that he is dead?"

"According to your man," I said.

"Relic sellers shouldn't be grave robbing," he said sadly. "It only angers the grave robbers, and then I have to smooth things over between them. Without the grave robbers, where would the relic sellers get their relics?"

"It did seem out of his line," I commented.

"One might say that robbery is out of yours," he replied. "Yet the story I've been hearing is that you are seeking out another fool because the two of you collaborated on some theft years ago, and now you're back to claim your share."

I shrugged and said nothing.

"Frankly, I don't believe it," he said. "I am in my own way a fisher of men. I knew both Demetrios and Tiberius. I believe that you are akin to them. You lack that inner stench of true depravity. Oh, do not protest, Fool. I have a nose for that sort of thing. And if you are in fact cut from the same motley as they are, then I suspect that you are a subtle fellow up to some good."

I shook my head admiringly. He was one of those men who

had lived so long in the world that all pretense had been stripped away. Master of the underworld he may have been, but he was the most direct person I had met in this Byzantine city.

"Then, as one subtle fellow to another, where do we stand?" I asked.

"Tiberius and Demetrios both had occasion over the years to seek my help, whether it be information or influence. I had occasion to seek theirs as well. I am proposing, not exactly a friendship, but an alliance. That is, if you are truly their brother and not merely a greedy interloper."

"And how will trust be established? Shall we exchange favors? Must I wear your handkerchief?"

"Good Fool, you will make me blush like a young girl if you continue. No, I propose to exchange something essential to us both. You there, Claudius."

She started, but did not look at him.

"Come now, sirrah," he admonished her. "Do not be overzealous on your master's behalf. I merely ask that you go downstairs and fetch a bucket of water."

"How do I know that you haven't signaled your men to take me the moment I reach the bottom step?" she asked.

"Because if that was my desire, you would have been taken before you even came up here," he replied.

"Feste?" she said, looking at me.

"Go on, Apprentice," I said. "I think I understand what he wants from me."

She drew her sword, and stepped carefully down the hallway, glancing at each doorway before passing it. I watched her descend until her head was completely out of view. An eternity passed. Then I heard her footsteps returning, accompanied by a sloshing sound. I was never so relieved as when I saw her head pop back into view at the top of the stairs.

She placed the bucket between Esaias and myself and assumed her post at the door.

"How many of my people did you spot?" queried Father Esaias.

"Four in the tavern, five more outside," she replied.

"Impressive," he said. "You only missed three."

"You're bluffing," she said. "Four in the tavern, five outside. Not that it matters; they're more than enough."

He stepped forward. "Well, Fool?" he said. "Is it a truce?"

"All right," I said. "You first."

He pulled the cowl back from his head, letting it hang loose down his back. The face was old, the cheeks sunken. An ancient scar ran up his left cheek, crossing where the eye would have been and continuing to the top of his head. The surviving eye was dark brown, a bit rheumy. It was blinking rapidly.

"Look quickly, Fool," he said, showing yellowed teeth. "I do not like the light for long."

"I have you," I said, and he replaced the cowl.

"Now it is your turn," he said.

I knelt before the bucket and washed the makeup off my face, scrubbing every bit of chalk and flour out of the many wrinkles I knew were there. Then I stood.

"You're an older man than I thought," he observed.

"You're about what I expected," I said.

"Few live this long in my profession, and those that do rarely end up comely. This is my true face, and you are now one of the few who may identify me. As I now am for you. Now, you have come to learn what happened to the missing fools."

"Yes. What do you know of them?"

"Nothing. They disappeared. My only concern was with Tiberius, who owed a small amount of money to one of my men, but such disappearances are not infrequent around here. To us, it was a matter of minor curiosity. Should it have meant more?"

"Maybe. How do you feel about the current occupant of the throne?"

That caught him up short. He folded his arms and leaned against the wall.

"Even under the terms of our agreement, that's a dangerous question," he said finally.

"I withdraw it. But apparently, my brethren came across a plot against his life. I think whoever was behind it eliminated them."

"I've heard nothing," he said. "Which means either it doesn't exist, it did exist but was abandoned, or the conspirators are very closemouthed indeed. Yet your brethren disappeared last fall. When is this dethroning supposed to take place?"

"I don't know. That is the extent of my knowledge. But it existed long enough for someone to kill six people to conceal it."

One hand disappeared into the cowl. I tensed slightly, but he was just scratching himself idly.

"This does concern me quite a bit," he said finally. "From my standpoint, I don't want Alexios to be replaced just yet. Thieves depend on the Emperor's walking a fine line between competence and chaos. I go back a long way in this city. I remember when Manuel reigned. The city was well policed back then, and the Vigla were everywhere. It was hard to make a living, and the prisons were a nightmare. But oddly enough, when Manuel died and Andronikos slew his way to the throne, things got even worse. He was so greedy and unpredictable that there were barely enough pickings left on the carcass for the rest of us. So, when the Angeli took over, you could imagine our happiness. Just enough stability to keep the population fat and happy, and just enough incompetence to let us roam relatively unhindered. The ideal balance, a thieves' paradise. And we certainly want to keep it going as long as we can."

"Then I propose this. Claudius and I will be inside Blachernae as of tomorrow. We will share information with you as it comes up. You do the same with us. There may come a time when I may ask more of you. But in exchange, I may find myself in a position to influence things at court."

"A fair bargain, Fool. And, in light of your connection to the late owner of this ring, I will forgo smiting you for your conduct toward my man."

He tossed the ring back to me, and walked toward the door. Then he turned and held up one bony finger in warning.

"This truce will be honored by us unless you violate our trust," he said. "But violations will be taken seriously."

"Understood," I said. "Thank you for your counsel, Father."

He left. We stood at the top of the steps and watched him until he passed through the front door, his bodyguards falling into place behind him.

"Did we just make a pact with the Devil?" asked Claudius.

"Possibly. But he's an intelligent, self-interested Devil. I don't think we lose anything by it."

She looked at me. "I noticed that you didn't mention anything about Thalia or Zintziphitzes. You even implied that Thalia was dead."

"For her protection."

"I thought she was a suspect. Why protect her?"

"Just in case I'm wrong."

We rose early the next morning and searched for the preacher. He was neither in his usual square nor the tavern.

"Still at his place," I guessed. "Shall we descend?"

We ducked into the alleyway where the tunnel began. No one followed us. I lit a candle, handed it to Claudius, and lifted the flagstones. She lowered herself in carefully. I followed and recovered the entrance.

"How do you propose getting that bald man within hearing range?" she asked.

"I'm still working on that," I said. "Maybe Zintziphitzes will have a few ideas."

The rats scampered about freely. They seemed bolder in our presence this morning. Some even came close to challenge us, but a few well-placed kicks sent them squeaking into the gloom.

"We need our escort," I commented as we entered the main drainage tunnel. "The natives are certainly more agitated when he's not with us."

"Feste," she said softly, pointing at the steps to his room.

The rats were swarming up the steps, practically crawling over one another in their haste to get to the top.

"Stay here," I said.

"We have only one candle," she replied. "I'm not waiting in the dark for you to return."

She drew her sword, the sound of the blade rubbing against the scabbard echoing through the tunnels. I pulled my knife from my boot and started kicking my way up the steps.

The rats ran down past us. I climbed to the doorway, knowing what I was going to see, not wanting to see it, but not having any choice in the matter.

They squeak when they are excited or angry. Not a frightening noise by itself, but multiply it by several hundred in a small room under the earth, and it becomes terrifying. They were fighting over him, a small verminous war.

"Old men should be allowed to die of old age," I said, shaking with sorrow and anger. "If you live that long, you should die in your own bed. Not be cut down like this."

"He could have just died," she said, hanging on to me.

I grabbed a torch from the wall and lit it with the candle. The body was prone, one hand stretching toward the shelves. I looked in that direction to see a knife resting on the lowest shelf. There was blood everywhere. His cloak lay in tatters on the floor, his stick broken in two nearby.

"Let's get out of here," I said.

"We can't just leave him," she protested.

"We're outnumbered," I replied, a bit harshly. "This is as good a resting place as any. No point in taking him above ground just to shove him back under. When it's all over with, we'll come back."

"Shouldn't we at least say something?" she asked.

"Go ahead."

She thought, then turned to face the paltry thing on the floor.

" 'Then shall the dust return to the earth as it was: and the spirit shall return unto God who gave it,' " she said softly amidst the squeaking. " 'Vanity of vanities, saith the preacher; all is vanity.' "

"Let's go," I said.

We came out cautiously, seeing assassins in every shadow— and far too many shadows. We each had a torch now, but the light they cast didn't pierce the darkness very far.

"A sword did that," I said. "Maybe more than one."

"Soldiers?"

"You saw the bald man. He had his own guards. He saw the smoke, sent them to check the source. Or maybe someone followed us, despite our precautions, and saw us with Zintziphitzes."

"Maybe," she said dubiously.

"What are your thoughts?"

"Why did he become enough of a threat to be killed like this? Why now?" she asked.

"Because we came on the scene. Our conspirators may be on the march again."

"But why haven't they come after us?"

"Maybe because there are two of us. Or maybe he knew something else that he hadn't told us. Or maybe they plan to kill us later."

We walked on.

"The timing is odd," she said. "There's one other possibility. Did you tell Thalia about him?"

I stopped, cursing for a good twenty seconds.

"I'll take that as a yes," she said. "I propose that the next time she visits, I follow her back."

"No. If she's that dangerous . . ."

"Sooner or later, you have to let me do something on my own," she said. "Besides, it would be easier for me."

"Following a Guild Fool is no simple task. I'm not even sure I could trail her without being noticed."

"I can," she insisted.

"No, and that's final, Apprentice. Let's get through a day at Blachernae; then we'll plan the next step."

She walked on, shaking her head.

I was afraid now. I had been afraid when we entered the city, but the series of successful performances over the past week had dulled the sense of threat. But now I was certain our enemy had shifted his full attention to us.

I felt one more thing. Guild or no Guild, I wanted Zintziphitzes' killer to die, preferably by my hand. What would happen next in Byzantium was of little consequence to me anymore.

We cautiously poked our heads up from the tunnel just in case anyone was waiting there with a mind to take them off. Then we scrambled out, tossing the torches into the hole and covering it up with the flagstones. We walked into the open streets, trying not to look like two fools afraid for their lives.

"By the way, thank you for the words you said over him," I said. "Ecclesiastes is always a good choice for preachers and fools. It ends, 'For God shall bring every work into judgment, with every secret thing, whether it be good, or whether it be evil.' "

North to the horse's ear we went, until the walls that separated Blachernae from the rest of the city loomed before us. The complex was nestled on the Sixth Hill, overlooking both the plains beyond the outer walls and a small beach on the Golden Horn. There were two great palaces beyond the gate, one built by the first Emperor Alexios a century ago, and a newer one built by Manuel, who I suppose found the older palace cramped and dingy. The complex had several churches, a private hippodrome, baths, and the usual guard towers, including the Anemas Tower where our new friend Stanislaus lived. Isaakios had turned his renovating eye on this area as well, to the point of constructing artificial islets in the Golden Horn to accommodate his building frenzies. None of these pleased the eye, although a tower built as a monument to himself was impressive, if only to demonstrate the height of his folly. All were watered by aqueducts from the Hydrales River, one of Andronikos's few positive contributions to the world.

We went around to the servants' entrance. We were expected, fortunately, although we still spent over an hour being conducted from one room to another by a series of slaves and servants, the haughtiness of the manner increasing with the size of the room.

The last servant to face us, a pinched-face fellow named Euthymios, frowned mightily when we entered his chamber.

"You're the ones, are you?" he sniffed. "Certainly a scruffy pair, aren't you?"

"We cannot compare with your magnificence," I said, bowing humbly.

"No, you cannot," he agreed. "I am the chief servant to the Emperor. I have been instructed to allow you to perform, much against my wish, but that is neither here nor there."

"Where is it, exactly?" I asked.

"Before you enter his presence, you must rid yourselves of all weapons," he continued, ignoring me.

"Most esteemed sir," I said. "These are not weapons, they are props. They are the tools of our trade. Juggling without sharp implements is merely passing the time. Juggling with knives and swords is entertainment."

"It's all right, Euthymios," came a voice behind him. The chief servant jumped.

In walked Captain Stanislaus, grinning broadly.

"Well done, my friends," he said. "I saw you at the Hippodrome. Spectacular!"

"Thank you, friend Captain," I said, bowing.

He turned to Euthymios.

"They will be juggling at the far end of the room," he said. "These fellows won't be doing anything dangerous anywhere close. I'll make certain of that. Besides, they don't look suicidal."

"Not in the least," I agreed. "If I get killed during the routine, I don't get paid."

Euthymios put his finger up to the Captain's face, then pulled it back hurriedly.

"This is your responsibility," he said.

The Captain growled slightly, and Euthymios skipped backward and out of the room. The Captain turned and winked.

"Now for some advice," he said. "Stay away from politics.

Laugh when he attempts to tell a joke. Don't insult anyone yet. You'll find out whom you can insult safely soon enough. And if I see any piece of metal come within fifteen paces of the throne, I'll cut you both in half."

He smiled. We smiled back. He led us to a pair of doors and threw them open.

"The jesters are here, Your Greatness," he called, and we walked into the largest room yet and bowed low to an immense throne made of solid gold.

Only it was empty. We looked around uncertainly, and a voice called, "Over here!"

Emperor Alexios Angelos the Third lay upon a couch covered with silken cushions, several of them propping up his legs. The Cleopatra of the flute was present, massaging him gently, no doubt producing some therapeutic effect. The Emperor was wearing a simple white robe. His head was bare, the crown resting on a cushioned stand by the throne. Up close, he looked his sixty-odd years, the powerful physique topped with a somewhat blockish head, his long black hair plaited into a thick braid in back.

He was laughing at our bow to the empty throne, and continued as we bowed again in his direction.

"Oh, dear, I'm starting again," he said, chuckling throughout. "It did me a world of good, you have no idea, my friends. I laughed so hard that I completely forgot the pain in my legs, and that is worth gold to me, do you know? Nothing else has worked so well when they're like this, and the physicians—God, I hate physicians. Monsters of ignorance, all of them, and I've tried all of them. The Jews were the best, although there was this Arab doctor some sultan gave me—some sultan, or son of a sultan, or rival of a sultan currying favor against the sultan, I can't remember—and he was supposed to be quite good, but my advisers wouldn't let me use him, said we couldn't be sure which side he was on, and I'm not always sure which side my advisers are on, but they are advisers, so what is an Emperor to do, hm? I've treated my legs myself, nothing like a good cauterization, but the doctors don't like that; they just keep forcing cathartics or purgatives or who knows what poisons down my gullet, so there you are."

"Here we are," I agreed. "I am thankful if I have been of some comfort to Your Majesty."

"Oh, but you have. You certainly have. I've missed having jesters, used to have a pair of dwarves, quite marvelous little fellows, but they left me; it was so sad. Neither of you are dwarves, are you?"

"No, Your Majesty, but we could perform from a squatting position if that would help."

He roared. "Squatting. Did you hear that, my dear? She's a performer too, plays the flute, Egyptian, don't you know? Plays the Egyptian flute, some reedy little thing, the flute, I mean, not her. Play for them."

She ceased her ministrations and took a piece of bamboo from a table nearby. She brought it to her lips and produced some of the most horrendous sounds I have ever heard passing for music.

Alexios watched her fondly, waving his hand in a vague approximation of the beat. This went on while my mouth slowly began to ache from the rigidity of the smile I wore for her performance. When she was done, we all applauded, the Emperor because he liked it, and we because it was over.

"There, how do you like that? Was it not superb?" he asked, beaming.

"Extraordinary," I said. I made a mental note not to play my flute in his presence. I didn't want to show her up.

"It's the upper lip that's the secret, you know," he continued.

"Both of her lips are gifts from God, but what she can do with that upper one. . . . Well, she's worth whatever concession I gave the Egyptians for her."

He looked at Claudius.

"Does your partner speak?" he asked curiously.

"No," replied Claudius, and he laughed again.

"Well, do something else," he said. "I have nothing but time for entertainment today, although someone's bound to come in and report on some boring thing or another. They always do. It's hard enough being Emperor without having to listen to all that prattling. Isaakios used to actually enjoy that sort of thing, but he thought he was born to this position. Ridiculous fellow, thought he was better than me. I was the older brother, I should have been Emperor first; that's the way things are supposed to be."

"I have an older brother," I said. "Perhaps I should have insisted on his being a fool first. But the honor fell to me."

"Is it an honor being a fool?" he asked.

"It depends on where I am. In this city there are so many that it becomes commonplace."

"A city of fools! Yes, it truly is," he exclaimed.

And you are their king, I thought.

We performed for about an hour. Then the Emperor declared that he needed a nap. He declared this looking straight at the flutist, and she simpered and slunk into his bedchamber.

"I'll have my eunuch see to you," he said. "Captain, take them to Philoxenites and see that they are taken care of. I want the two of you here every day."

"It will be our pleasure, Your Majesty," I said, bowing. "Have an enjoyable nap."

He lurched off, and the doors closed behind him.

Captain Stanislaus came over to us.

"Quite good," he said. "And you kept the cutlery at a safe distance."

"Of course."

"Come with me."

He led us through marble corridors to an office with a view of the Imperial Pier at the Golden Horn. We stepped in to meet our new benefactor.

He looked up from an oaken desk where he had been scribbling something with a quill.

"So these are the fools we saw," he said. "I am Constantine Philoxenites, Imperial Treasurer."

He was the bald man Zintziphitzes had smoked out yesterday.

TWELVE

For where God built a church, there the Devil would also build a chapel....
Thus is the Devil ever God's ape.

MARTIN LUTHER

It is one thing to promise oneself to smite an enemy with one's own hand. But it is something else entirely to do it in a well-guarded palace with a captain of the Imperial Guard standing a foot away. Not every opportunity has to be seized. *Carpe diem*, in my experience, will only get you through a single day. If that.

So, I swallowed everything, hoping it wouldn't come back up immediately, and bowed low. The back of my neck felt uncomfortably exposed, but I came back up unscathed.

"Feste, the Fool, and his assistant, Claudius," announced Captain Stanislaus.

"At your service, my Lord Treasurer," I said.

"I saw you at the Hippodrome," said Philoxenites.

"We marked you as well, sir, for the sun did make of your bald pate an heir. We were forced not to look directly at you for fear of being blinded."

Stanislaus chuckled.

"Amusing, for a lesser sort of mind," said Philoxenites, clearly unamused. "I hope that you can raise the level of your wit when the occasion demands."

"It can soar like a stone from a catapult," I said.

"Then crash back into the earth," he commented.

"Or smash its target to pieces," I retorted. "I have every weapon of wit—the blunt, the sharp, the crude, the subtle, the inflammatory, and the poisonous. All at the disposal of my patron."

"Then you are a mercenary," he said, pleased. "I can work with a man who likes to be paid."

I bowed again. He pulled out a small purse.

"The Emperor likes you," he said, handing it to me. "Otherwise, you would not have been sent to see me. You will be expected at Blachernae in the early afternoon on a daily basis. He's rarely up before then unless there's an occasion that demands it. You may be called upon to entertain before guests, or his children, or to fulfill whatever whim possesses him at the time."

"I understand."

He stood and looked up at me.

"You're a tall fellow for a fool," he observed.

"That's only because you're used to seeing dwarves," I replied. "I am a bigger fool than they, certainly. I had no idea that size mattered so much."

"If you were half your height, you would double your salary," said Philoxenites. "The Emperor likes dwarves. They make him feel superior. Captain, step outside for a moment. I would speak with these fools in private."

Stanislaus looked surprised, but complied with the request.

Philoxenites stepped over to a sideboard with a pitcher of wine and filled three cups, handing us ours himself. He sat on the edge of the desk.

"To the Emperor," he said perfunctorily and drank.

"To the Emperor," we chorused. It was good wine.

"You will be reporting to me before and after you see him," he said. "As long as you are in Alexios's favor, your payments will be guaranteed. Bring me any and all conversation that takes place, and I will sweeten the payment."

"What makes you think I have a taste for sweets?" I asked.

He looked surprised.

"I thought you depended on patrons," he said.

"I have one now," I replied. "The Emperor. Having more than one tends to confuse me. Did the dwarves have to report to you?"

"No," he said. "But they were established long ago. Now they're gone. I am the one who is established here. Don't forget that."

"Then, if I may be so bold, answer me a question."

"What is it?"

"Was that your regular seat at the games?"

He looked puzzled. "Yes, it was. It has been for years. Why do you ask?"

"I only wonder why someone so established would be seated so far from the Emperor."

His face darkened, the color of the choler so deep that I thought for a moment he would strike me. Then he calmed down.

"A fair question, Fool," he said. "I am reassessing my opinion of your wits. The tides that wash against this city come from many directions. They shift and collide so that even the best navigator may occasionally run aground. I am not sure whether the Emperor currently holds me in disfavor. But my seats at the Hippodrome have little to do with that. I frequently carry on the business of the Treasury while there, and it must not be allowed to interfere with the Emperor's enjoyment of the games. I slave to keep him happy, Fool, do you understand?"

I bowed again. "You are a most loyal follower, sir. That makes me curious as to why you wish me to spy on him."

"Not so much for what he says, as for what others say to him. He is receiving bad advice from many. Worse, he is following it.

I care for the Empire as well as the Emperor. Where do you hail from?"

"Most recently from the north. But there are few places I have not been."

"Have you been here before?"

"I passed through many years ago."

"But not under the name of Feste," he said. "I would have remembered that."

"No, milord."

"Hm. Well, you came at a good time. Alexios is in constant need of amusement as he ages, and the vacancy has been too long unfilled. I wish you well."

He opened the door and beckoned to the Captain.

"Show them out," he said. "And provide them with a document for safe passage at night. I expect the entertainment will occasionally last that long."

Claudius and I bowed and followed the Captain.

"What did he have to say?" asked Stanislaus.

"I believe the intention was to exclude you from the conversation," I replied.

"Very good. But tell me anyway."

I stopped.

"Everyone wants to know what everyone else is saying," I complained. "Is there no respect for privacy anymore?"

"Is your loyalty to the Emperor or to the Treasurer?" asked Stanislaus.

"Is there any difference?"

"It depends. What did he say to you?"

"That he wanted me to spy on you, Captain."

He laughed at that. "All right, Fool. Have it your way."

"You don't trust him."

"I don't trust anyone," he said.

"But I thought you said you were loyal to the man who pays you. Isn't that the Treasurer?"

"No," he said, bringing us to the side entrance. "The Hetairia report to the Grand Keeper of the Doors, if you can imagine such a title. He holds the purse strings. Very tightly, in fact, but there you are. But our loyalties are to the Emperor, no matter who actually gives us the gold."

"I'll never understand this bureaucracy," I said. "Will we be seeing you at the Rooster later?"

"Perhaps," he said. He pulled out a document from a desk near the entrance, scribbled a few words, and placed the seal of the Imperial Guard upon it. "Here, this will give you safe passage in case you run into any of the Vigla after sunset."

"Thank you, Captain."

The sun was already setting as we left Blachernae. Fortunately, we had no other errands and were able to take a direct route across the Lycos to the Rooster. All around us, people hastened home, trying to outrun the closing of the gates and the patrols of the Vigla.

"What cowled visitor do you suppose awaits us tonight?" asked Claudius as we walked.

"Thalia said she was going to meet us last night," I replied. "I wonder what kept her."

"I wonder who is keeping her," said Claudius.

"What did you think of Philoxenites?" I asked, changing the subject.

She chewed her lower lip as she considered the question.

"He didn't seem that menacing to me," she said. "He plays his own game, of course, but he seemed more interested in trying to use us than in finding out what we know."

"Yet that could be his way of misdirecting us. We now know that those seats were his at the time Zintziphitzes overheard the

[167]

plot against Alexios. And he certainly has the resources and the soldiers."

"Is he using the Imperial Guard?"

"Probably not, since they don't get paid by him. The Varangians, on the other hand, are paid directly from the Imperial Treasury, so he has a pretty good selection of killers at his beck and call. Given the lack of trust between him and Stanislaus, I'd think the Guards would be a less likely choice."

It was dark when we came to the Rooster. We had to show our pass to one patrol before then, which delayed our return. As it turned out, the sergeant had seen us at the Hippodrome, so we escaped without too much annoyance.

Peter Kamantares, the butcher, was coming from around the back as we arrived, toweling himself off vigorously.

"Hail, fools," he said. "There's still stew, maybe even a few pieces of meat left in it."

"Another souvenir of your trade?" I asked.

"Not today. Michael killed more than he could sell today, so we have a bit of venison to share."

"We are fortunate to live with such bloodthirsty men," said Claudius. "It makes for a rich diet."

"Aye, it does at that," replied Peter. "Although in my case, my clothes are so bespattered that I frighten the ladies away. A considerable drawback, if you ask me."

We entered the Rooster to the usual roar. Except for Asan, the regulars were all there. The Russians were staring disconsolately at the dwindling pile of coins they had left. It turned out that one of them had sought to win their passage back by gambling, but chose one of Father Esaias's establishments. The dice were unfriendly.

Simon brought us wine. The stew was a good one, and we toasted both Michael for the deer and Simon for cooking it.

Despite the presence of the giant Stephanos at the table, there was still ample meat left for Claudius and me. The others were already at the end of their meals and bade us a good evening. Simon began clearing the tables as we each took a second portion.

"It is a hungry business you're in," he observed.

"We were performing before the Emperor," I said proudly. "We entertained him for quite a while, but he neglected to provide a meal for us."

"The Emperor!" he exclaimed. "You have come up in the world. Will you be leaving me then?"

"Not just yet, friend Simon," I said. "There is little permanence in a fool's life, so we will continue here. Especially since we paid you for two weeks in advance. By the way, was there anyone asking for us while we were out?"

"No," he said, thinking back. "Were you expecting someone in particular?"

"No," I replied. "Just hoping some more work would come our way. An excellent meal, my host. Good night."

"No soldiers tonight," remarked Claudius as we went upstairs.

"The Varangians rotated out, remember? And Stanislaus wasn't certain he would be here."

"The place certainly didn't lack for noise," she said. She yawned as we came to the entrance to our room. "I wonder where Asan was tonight. What's wrong?"

I pointed to the floor. "He's here."

He was on his back, eyes still open, a look of surprise on his face. I squatted down by him and rolled him over. There was a single stab wound in the middle of his back. The blood on his cloak was sticky to the touch.

"Someone must have blamed him for trying," said Claudius.

"Did you ever notice that he was of your height?" I said. She looked at me. "Same color hair. Similar cloak, in fact."

She looked down at him. "Someone was waiting in our room to kill us. Asan walked in, deciding to ransack it when we were out."

"And was killed in our place," I concluded, standing up. I looked at the body. "I must say the timing is a bit inconvenient for us."

"More so for him."

"Yes, but here's the thing. Putting aside the attempt on our lives, we now have a murdered man in our room. Not the sort of thing one wants to bring to the authorities around here."

"Don't you think they'll want to help?"

"The Vigla? No, I think they will assume that we killed him; then they will seize us, torture us, and execute us."

She looked at the body. "You're right. Not at all convenient. Very inconsiderate of the murderer, if you ask me." She unshuttered the window and looked out. "We face the rear of the building. It might be easier to lower him out the window than to take him downstairs."

"Sounds good," I said. "Wait. We can keep this simple. We just wait until the others have fallen asleep; then we'll bring him to his own room."

We sat together, keeping vigil over Asan's body, flicking occasionally at the flies that were beginning to gather, until the sounds from the other rooms gradually ceased.

"We must be getting closer," she murmured.

"I suppose so," I said. "Always a good sign when they try to kill you. Makes it easier to find out who it is. The trick is surviving."

"So far, so good," she said.

There was silence at last, broken only by the marching of the Vigla somewhere in the distance. We poked our heads out into the corridors and listened until we heard sufficient snoring from the other rooms. Then we hoisted up our unlucky burglar and brought him to his room. We laid him on his pallet as gently as we could; then I reached down and closed his eyes.

We tiptoed back to our own room without being discovered, then collapsed onto the pallet, holding each other tightly.

"May we sleep now?" she asked. "I don't think our murderer will come back again tonight, and Asan is no longer a problem."

"Something just occurred to me," I said, getting to my feet. "We are going to have to report this to the authorities after all."

"But I thought you didn't want to bring in the Vigla."

"Not the Vigla. The real authority around here. Come on."

We went back out to the street. Despite the freedom of passage conferred upon us by Stanislaus, we kept to the shadows and alleys, making our way toward the Lycos River, looking for a church.

Easy enough to find in this city. Constantinople has over two hundred churches, from the immensity of the Hagia Sophia down to the tiny brick buildings dedicated to saints so obscure that after martyrdom God Himself must have looked at them when they came before His throne and said, "And you are . . . ?"

There was more than one church dedicated to Saint Stephen, of course, but there was only one Saint Stephen's Church on the Lycos. It was a medium-sized brick structure. Despite the lateness of the hour, it seemed to be doing good business. People were coming and going like it was a market day.

We entered through the front doors to find a few dozen men and women crowding the area between the doors and the ikonostasis. Our Lord and His Mother waved merrily from the painted screen, beckoning to the lost souls to walk through the doorways into the sanctuary. The penitents were lined up before a simple wooden chair next to the deacons' entrance that was playing the part of the Bishop's Throne tonight. Father Esaias was seated upon it, a golden alb and stole draped over his customary cassock. A pair of burly priests stood on either side of him, ready to mete out contrition with a pair of stout clubs if need be.

We took our places in line and watched the proceedings. Each person would walk up to the chair, kneel before Esaias, and speak in hushed tones. Frequently, a sack was handed over as a donation to the church. The sacks were of varying size, and many of them jingled. Esaias would extend one bony hand in blessing, usually with some coin in it. On some occasions, the sacks were apparently too small, for the blessing consisted of several blows to the head rather than coin. The recipients of these attacks begged most wholeheartedly for forgiveness, then slunk into the night, no doubt to repent.

"Should we have brought something?" whispered Claudius.

"We are bringing news," I whispered back. "I am not sure that he is going to like it."

Our turn came, and we went up together and knelt before him as the bodyguards looked at us in surprise.

"Forgive us, Father, for we have sinned," I said.

"Wrong church," he replied. "Sin is not necessarily condemned in this sanctuary. Although sinners may be."

"Can we talk privately?"

He looked out at those remaining. "Anything not routine business?" he called. There was none. He turned to one of the other priests. "Father Theodore, take over. Father Melchior, come with me."

Esaias led us down a flight of steps into the crypts below the church. He paused before an altar with a panel depicting Saint Stephen behind it. He crossed himself, then slid the panel aside and led us down another flight of steps into what turned out to be a group of rooms appointed more lavishly than some palaces I have seen.

He reclined upon a red-silked couch and motioned to us to sit on some chairs opposite.

"What is it, my son?" he asked.

"Asan was one of your men?" I asked.

"A lesser thief with aspirations but little talent," he said. "I hear you using the past tense with him."

"He was killed tonight. At the Rooster."

"By you?"

"No, Father. We came to report his death, and to assure you that we had no part in it."

He folded his hands and lay back, the very picture of a dead priest.

"Where was he killed?"

"In our room."

"When?"

"Sometime during the day, I think. He was there when we returned."

"Why was he in your room?"

"We've caught him twice trying to steal from us."

"Then damn him for a fool," pronounced the priest. "No offense."

"None taken."

"Still, there would be no reason to kill him for stealing from you, at least not for anyone else. Do you think that someone killed him thinking he was one of you?"

"That thought did cross our minds."

He stood abruptly and pointed to the floor before him.

"Kneel, sinners," he commanded.

Not knowing what else to do, we knelt. He placed a gnarled hand on each of our heads as if to pronounce a benediction.

"He may have brought his death upon himself," he said. "But it is not true that you had no part in it. Your very presence set in motion the circumstances that led to it. Therefore, under our code, you owe us a life."

"But . . ."

"Or a death. Rise and prepare to accept your penance."

We stood, uncertain as to what he meant.

"The death you owe us will be of the man who killed Asan. I am not interested in any niceties of policy or politics as to this matter. Our society demands retribution. A death for a death. You have become our chosen instrument of revenge."

"But we don't know who killed him."

"Then I expect you to find out. If it is connected with the deaths of your fellow fools, then no doubt you will nose him out, or be killed in the attempt. If that happens, we will continue the quest. On the other hand, the man you seek may be closer to home. Perhaps someone at the Rooster caught him stealing and acted hastily. Have you considered that?"

"No," I admitted.

"You share a house with a hunter, a butcher, a large ruffian who is in fact one of my enforcers, and a band of increasingly impoverished and desperate Russians. It could be any one of them."

"True enough," I said. "What shall we do about Asan's body?"

"Where is it now?"

"We took it to his room."

"A wise course of action. Let events play out as they will. I assure you that Simon will not bring in the guard. He prefers as little notice as possible. Now, go in peace, my children. But return with news of your progress."

Father Melchior escorted us out.

"Make a pact with the Devil, and before you know it you're working for him," commented Claudius.

"I think we all want the same thing, ultimately."

"But what if Asan's death isn't connected to what we're doing?" she asked. "What if it was just something that happened in the Rooster by coincidence? Are we now so beholden to this monster that we have to hunt down the killer and execute him? Asan was a thief. Whoever did this may have been completely justified."

"Then he shouldn't have dumped the body in our room."

"Panic," she argued. "He wasn't thinking. But now it's a death that's wanted, and we have to supply it. That's not justice; that's just another murder."

"We'll think of something. This is all supposition on our part. Look at the bright side. The murderer probably is after us, so we can kill him without agonizing over it."

"Well, that would be a blessing, wouldn't it? God, this foolish life leads to perverse logic. Look, I have a feeling that events are coming to a head, now. I really think you ought to let me find out what game Thalia is playing."

"If you were a full-fledged fool..."

"We don't have time," she interrupted me. "I've juggled for you, played for you, killed for you. Apprentice or not, I can do it."

"No."

"Why are you protecting her?" she shouted. "What does she mean to you after all this time? Somehow, she's part of what is happening here, and you're letting your history blind you to all this. Or maybe it isn't history to you. You've let the past become present again. And how can I possibly compete with her? I'm not even a fool yet. Hell, I'm not even a woman any more."

"Stop it, Viola."

The use of her name caught her up short. She walked ahead

of me, fuming, but by the time we reached the Rooster, she had calmed down. It was around midnight, and no one stirred when we entered.

"I'll take first watch," she said as we entered our room.

I stretched out on the pallet.

"If it is one of our neighbors, who is most likely?" she asked.

"Any one of them is capable of doing it," I said. "What leaps to mind is friend Peter the butcher coming from the back of the building as we came in, having just washed his hands. The man spends his life up to his elbows in blood. What's a little more?"

"He seems like a decent fellow," she said. "But you never know. What about Stephanos? He and Asan both work for Esaias. It could have been a falling-out among thieves."

"Stephanos is more brute than thief," I said. "I doubt that they worked together. If he caught Asan stealing, he'd be more likely to snap his neck and brag about it afterward. I still think Asan was killed because someone thought he was you."

She shivered, sitting in her corner.

"I never knew what it was like being marked for death," she said. "Can't say that I like it much."

"Occupational hazard," I said. "Good night, wife."

She leaned over and kissed me, her beard tickling.

"Good night, my love," she whispered.

I fell asleep.

She didn't wake me for my watch. She didn't wake me at all. What did wake me was a pair of strong hands shaking me roughly.

"Theo!" someone whispered.

I opened my eyes to see Thalia, still in monk's garb, kneeling by me. I sat up.

"What's the hour?" I asked, blinking stupidly in the daylight.

"Midmorning," she said. "And a fine thing for a Guild fool to be caught napping like this."

"But Claudius was on watch," I said. I looked around the room.

Claudius had vanished.

CHIRTEEN

There is in you an impulse to play the clown, which you have held in restraint from a reasonable fear of being set down as a buffoon; but now you have given it rein, and . . . you may be unconsciously carried away into playing the comedian in your private life.

THE REPUBLIC OF PLATO, CH. 37

You'd better get going," Thalia said. "All hell is breaking loose downstairs."

"Where's Claudius?"

"How should I know?" she said, shrugging. "I just got here."

"How did you get in without their seeing you?"

"It's not the first time I've come into a man's bedchamber through the window," she said. "Not the first time I came into yours that way, now that I think of it."

I looked around the room. Viola's jester bag was gone, along with the saddlebags containing the rest of her belongings.

"Looks like he pulled out," she observed.

"She wouldn't do that," I muttered.

"She?"

"He. He wouldn't do that," I said. "I'm not awake yet. What's going on downstairs?"

"One of your neighbors isn't awake yet either. Probably because he's dead. The landlord isn't letting anyone leave until he sorts things out."

"Simon? How is he keeping them in?"

"With a really big sword," she said, grinning her old grin. "I should introduce him to Euphy. She likes men with big swords."

I gave the room a quick once-over. There were no bloodstains where Asan had fallen. His cloak had absorbed everything. Good. Nothing to tie us to him.

"You stay here," I said. "I'm going downstairs."

I staggered down, the very picture of a hangover, and stared sleepily at the assembly.

"Good morning," I said. "Is there some holiday? Why isn't anyone working?"

"Good morning, Fool," said Simon, completely filling the doorway. He held a two-handed longsword in front of him like it was a feather. "Someone's killed Asan."

"Killed?" I gasped. "When? Where?"

"In his room last night," said Simon. "Where's Claudius?"

Damn, I thought. Bad timing all around.

"He rose early," I said. "He's out."

"Out where?"

"I don't know," I admitted. "He didn't say. I overslept. When I awoke, he was gone."

"There's your murderer," said Michael.

"Impossible," I said. "He couldn't have killed Asan."

They turned to look at me.

"Why not?" asked Simon.

"Because he was with me the entire time," I said.

"Until you fell asleep," said Stephanos in an ominous rumble.

"And how do you know when Asan was killed?" demanded Simon.

"I don't," I said.

"Claudius killed him," said Michael.

"He doesn't seem the type," protested Peter. "Why would he kill him?"

[179]

"Does not matter," said one of the Russians. "Was thief. Deserved to die."

Stephanos stood up with a roar, the bench tumbling behind him. He took a step toward the Russians, ready to fight them all at once.

"Stop," said Simon quietly.

Stephanos turned toward him. "Asan was my friend," he bellowed.

"There will be no fighting in here," said Simon. "You sit down, or I'll kill you myself. I swung this blade for Christ. I can swing it against the Devil if I have to."

Stephanos stared at him, then looked down at the blade that was pointed at his chest. He picked up the bench and sat down meekly.

"Now, we don't want the Vigla poking around our lives," said Simon. Everyone in the room nodded in agreement. "Right now, it looks like Claudius may have done it. But he's skipped. As long as he stays skipped, that's fine. If he comes back, I'll deal with him. On the other hand, it may be one of you. Asan may very well have had it coming, but that's not how we do things at the Rooster. You want to kill someone, you take it outside. Otherwise, you will have me to answer to. Am I understood?"

"What about him?" asked Michael, pointing to me. "His companion did this. Are you going to let Feste stay here?"

"He's paid in advance," said Simon. "I have no problem with him. Do you?"

Michael looked at the sword, which was now pointed toward the floor.

"No problem," he said, shaking his head.

Simon stepped away from the doorway.

"Have a productive day, gentlemen," he said pleasantly. "Dinner tonight will be rabbit."

They filed out quickly, leaving me with Simon. He looked at me.

"I don't think Claudius killed him," he said. "You, on the other hand, seem more than capable."

"So is Claudius," I said. "Who do you really think killed him?"

"Most likely someone here," he said. "No one else went upstairs last night, or I would have heard them."

"What are you going to do with the body?"

He went back into his room, then reemerged with a large, burlap sack.

"Do you need any help?" I offered.

"Sure. Get a bucket of water and some rags."

By the time I came back up, the late thief had been unceremoniously bundled into the sack, along with his belongings. In the daylight, I could see that Asan's room was larger than mine. It also featured an actual door in the doorway, with a plank that could be dropped into place behind it. I cleared my throat, and Simon looked at me.

"I was wondering, since this room is now available..." I said hesitantly.

Simon began laughing.

"You're a cold-blooded fellow," he said. "The lad's barely dead, and you want a better room. Maybe that's a reason for killing someone."

"Hardly."

"All right, it's yours as long as you don't fear ghosts. Hard to let out a room where someone's just died. Murdered men tend to prowl around a bit."

"So do murderers," I said. "I like a door I can bar. Especially since I don't have a sword like yours. You were very imposing down there."

He snorted. "Once you've faced a Saracen army, a barroom

seems tame by comparison." He threw me some rags. "Here, you clean up. I'll take care of the body."

I took the rags and began mopping the floor as Simon hauled the sack downstairs. I didn't ask him what he was going to do with it. I preferred not knowing.

I rinsed out the rags in the bucket. There was a small amount of blood on the floor, barely coloring the water. I took the pail out back and emptied it. Then I remembered Thalia and went back to my room.

She was still there, staying out of view from the hallway.

"Where is everyone?" she asked.

"The other inmates have gone to work," I said. "Simon is lugging the body away. I have the feeling he's done this before."

"At the Rooster? Very likely. So, we're alone at last. I'm glad the little fellow's not around."

She had that look going again, a smile dancing in her eyes.

"Give me your knife," I said.

The smile vanished.

"Why?" she asked.

"To satisfy my curiosity."

She reached inside her cowl and pulled it out.

"And the other one, please."

A second slid into her other hand. She gave them both to me. I held them up to the window and inspected them carefully.

"No blood," I said.

"My hands and nails are clean, too," she said, holding them out for me to see. "Of course, if I were a killer, I'd be smart enough to wash up afterward. Curiosity satisfied?"

"Not completely," I said. "You said you would return two nights ago. What happened?"

"I saw Father Esaias come in with a rough-looking bunch. I

thought it would be impolite to join the party, especially since he and I showed up wearing the same outfit."

"And last night?"

She was silent.

"In the last three nights, I have returned to my room to find someone who should have been dead, someone who looked like Death, and someone who actually was dead," I said. "Were you here last night?"

"I thought he was found in his room," she said slowly.

"Claudius and I put him there after we found him here," I said. "But someone killed him here thinking he was Claudius or myself. Were you here last night?"

"No," she said. "I was detained."

"Who detained you?"

"I can't say."

I held up her knives.

"You're unarmed, my dear. And you've been holding out on me. I want to know who you're working for."

Her face turned livid.

"How dare you!" she spat. "After I nearly died for the Guild, you question my loyalty?"

"But you didn't die," I said. "That makes you the only one so far."

"You don't believe I was attacked," she said, shaking her head. "Oh, Theo, I had expected better of you after all this time. You need proof. Very well."

She pulled off the monk's garb. Underneath she was still in man's clothing.

"And I'm not unarmed," she said, dropping two more knives to the ground. "That's the first token of good faith. Here's the second."

She started to pull off her tunic.

"Wait," I protested.

"Come, Theo," she said. "You've seen this body before. Don't play shy with me."

Thalia stood half-naked in front of me, still seeming for all the world the eighteen-year-old fool I once knew.

"Bring back any memories?" she said mockingly.

Before I could say anything, she turned around.

The smoothness of her skin was broken by grotesque scars covering her lower back. I reached forward and touched them lightly. She shuddered violently and clasped her arms tightly across her chest.

"So, Theo, I can come hither and still make myself alluring to a man," she said in a broken voice. "It's the going thither that repels them."

"Get dressed," I said roughly. I handed her back the two knives I held.

She was back to holy anonymity in seconds. Then she turned to face me.

"Do you believe me now?" she asked.

"Believe, somewhat. Trust, no," I said. "Did you know Zintziphitzes was killed?"

Her shock looked genuine.

"When?" she cried.

"Two or three days ago," I said. "We found what was left of him in his room, providing a funeral feast for his four-legged neighbors. Now, someone's coming after me. Any ideas on the subject?"

"No."

"Then get out. Come back when you have something useful to tell me. I have to find Claudius and perform before the Emperor, and I haven't had anything to eat."

"I thought you were going to save me," she whispered.

"That wasn't part of my mission," I said. I started packing my gear.

When I looked up, she was gone.

I tossed my bags into a dead man's room, then went to the stables.

"The short fellow with the beard?" said the stableman. "Came here just after dawn. Collected his horse and left."

"Did he say where he was going?" I asked, my heart sinking.

"No. But he was headed out of town. Rode toward the Rhegium Gate."

"And he left no message?"

"None."

Viola had left me. There was no getting around it. I didn't think it was the attempt on her life that was the last straw. She had more mettle than that. Maybe it was finding herself in league with Esaias that drove her away.

Or maybe it was me, pure and simple. I had been too much the teacher, not enough the husband. Too many restraints placed upon her. She had left Orsino to flee a restrictive role, only to find another one with me.

Live and learn, Theo. Next time you'll get it right. If you ever merit a next time.

I went to visit Zeus. It had been over a week since I had seen him. He had no further information on the subject. I tried to give him a carrot, but he snapped at my fingers so sharply that I had to drop it in self-defense.

Fine, I thought. Yesterday I had three friends in a city of four hundred thousand. Today, it seemed, I had none.

I arrived at Blachernae earlier than expected, but the Emperor was up, lunching and listening to his advisers argue with each other. He saw me and waved a chicken leg.

"Here, boy!" he said, whistling.

Oh, dear, that tiresome routine that emperors do when they think they're being funny. No choice but to turn dog for the moment, scampering about on all fours, sitting up and begging while he held the leg just out of my reach. Finally, he turned to one of his advisers and said, "I'll wager you a bezant he can do a somersault and catch this in the air."

"I accept the wager, Your Majesty," said the man.

Guffawing, Alexios tossed it high, shouting, "Fetch!"

I not only caught it, I caught it with my mouth. Hell, I was hungry, and I was damned if I was going to eat it off the floor.

I sat by the foot of the throne, eating quietly, watching the proceedings. The elder son-in-law, Alexios Palailogos, was there, lounging around in a gold tunic and leggings. Someone who I later learned was Michael Stryphnos, Euphrosyne's brother-in-law and the Grand Duke of what was left of the navy, sat by him, reaching constantly into a bowl of figs between them. George Oinaiotes, the Grand Chamberlain, was standing at a table, pontificating, while Philoxenites watched everything from a seat nearby. Some lesser bureaucrats were scattered about. And, at the rear, stood Captain Stanislaus and two of his men. The captain was watching Philoxenites.

"All I am saying is that the raids on the Black Sea merchants would be much more profitable if we used our own ships," Oinaiotes was saying as I munched away. "Hiring pirates to do the job cuts into our take. They just aren't reliable enough."

"How many ships do we have?" asked the Emperor.

Stryphnos looked a bit blank.

"Can't say, exactly, Your Majesty," he replied vaguely.

"It would help if you would stop selling them," said Palailogos, elbowing him.

"Now, now," said Stryphnos. "I only sold a few. Needed the money. Birthday presents and such. Anyhow, the pirates have been working out just fine. Lovely folk. Give 'em a few titles, a nice sash, and they think they're just like us."

"We have gotten some complaints about these raids," interrupted Philoxenites. "Some of the merchantmen were our own. Imperial piracy is usually directed at other countries' goods."

"Is it?" exclaimed the Emperor, bursting into laughter. "Well, we had better stop doing it then. Robbing Peter to pay Paul, eh, Fool?"

"Aptly put, milord," I said.

"I still say we should restore the navy," resumed Oinaiotes. "It's just more comfortable when they report directly to us."

"Make you earn your keep at last," said Palailogos to Stryphnos.

"But Your Majesty," protested Stryphnos. "Building more ships would necessitate cutting down that lovely forest. Where will you hunt then?"

"He has a point, you know," said the Emperor to the Chamberlain. "It's so convenient when you can go out, kill a few deer, and be back home by sunset. If we chop all that down just to build a few boats, then I'll have to travel an extra day to hunt. And you know how I hate riding that long. Makes my legs hurt even more, eh, Fool?"

"We certainly wish no pain to the royal limbs, Your Majesty," I said. "If the Emperor cannot stand, then the empire must fall."

"Hah! Well spoken, Fool," exclaimed the Emperor. He turned to his flutist, who was standing by the throne. "You see, my dear, it's a play on words, because I am the empire, of course, and..."

She looked at him blankly.

[187]

"Has to work on her Greek," he confided to me. "Knows enough to know what I want, but that's about it."

"Sounds like the ideal woman," I said.

"Watch this," he said, grinning lewdly. He turned to her. "Nap!"

She smiled, picked up her flute, and headed toward the Imperial Bedchamber.

"Is she a treasure or what?" he said, sighing. He made as if to get up.

Philoxenites rose and cleared his throat. The Emperor looked at him irritatedly.

"What is it, Eunuch?" he said.

"Your Majesty, there is the question of your nephew," Philoxenites said quietly.

There was a slight rustle among the rest of the advisers. The Emperor sat back in his throne, his hands resting on the arms in an attempt at a regal pose.

"What of him?" he said.

"We have received word that he has made his way to Hagenau, and is under the protection of his sister and the German court."

"That little whore Irene," said the Emperor. "Quite the operator. Like a cat that keeps landing on its feet."

"Or on its back," I said.

The Emperor gave a quick bark of laughter and patted me on the shoulder.

"He has also made contact with the Crusaders," continued Philoxenites.

"Well, what of it? Let him go on a Crusade. Do the boy some good. Make a man of him at last."

"What if he is seeking an army to turn against Your Majesty?"

"He wouldn't do that!" declared the Emperor. "The boy owes

me his life. I could have had him killed. I could have had his eyes put out. Did I? Did I?"

The advisers shook their heads.

"I was too soft with the boy, I admit it. But I had hopes for him. Thought he might come around, see the light. Didn't think he had any loyalty to my brother after all this time. So, he escaped. Does it matter? Let him hide behind his sister's skirts, or play soldier and get killed by the infidels. Why should he be of any interest to me now?"

"What if he brings the Crusade through here?" persisted Philoxenites.

"Then we'll stop him," said Palailogos confidently.

"Yes! We'll stop him," agreed the Emperor. "The people won't have him here. They don't know him. He's just a runaway boy. What hold does he have over Byzantium? Are there any here who would support his claims? Captain?"

"None, Your Majesty," said Stanislaus.

"Well, then. You are wasting valuable time, eh? Time that I could be spending in my, er, nap."

"Then there is the question of your brother, Isaakios," said Oinaiotes.

The Emperor looked at him through half-closed eyes.

"What of him?" he said, wearily.

"The whole world knows of Your Majesty's mercy and kindness," said the Chamberlain. "Certainly, fraternal obligations have been honored to the hilt in his case. It almost pains me to suggest anything that would be contrary to your natural beneficence."

"Go on," said the Emperor.

"It was Isaakios who arranged for his son's escape. The evidence is irrefutable. Yet you have done nothing to punish him for this transgression."

"I deposed him. I blinded him. Executed several of his supporters. Seems like I've done nothing but punish him. Look, I know where you're going with this, but I'm not going to heap any more misery on his life. I'm Emperor, he's not, and that's all we need to say on the subject. Let him have his petty little plots. It gives him something to do with the day."

"But at least remove him from the Double Column," said Oinaiotes. "Keep him incarcerated somewhere more secure. Restrict his visitors."

"But the Double Column is so comfortable," said the Emperor. "And it has that lovely view."

"Isaakios is blind, Your Majesty," Oinaiotes reminded him. "What use does he have for a view?"

"What think you, Captain?"

"Keep your enemies close, Your Majesty," said Stanislaus. "Always good strategy."

"And you, Fool?" he said, turning to me.

"Your Majesty, I wouldn't dare give advice to divinity."

"Stop the fawning, and answer me. What would you do if he were your brother?"

"If he were my brother, then he would be the brother of a fool and therefore of no concern to Your Majesty."

"Hmph," he said. "Well, I'll think about this. After my nap. For it is that time. Go away, all of you. Eunuch, pay the fool."

He stood, seizing a staff to lean upon. We all bowed, and he left the room.

"Well, Jester, you've certainly wormed your way in quickly," commented Stryphnos. "Now, answer me this. What do you call a man who seeks advice from fools?"

"Emperor," I said, looking directly at him.

Stanislaus hid a smile. I bowed and followed Philoxenites out of the room.

"You didn't have to do much today," he commented.

"Shall I await the end of his nap?" I asked.

"No," he replied. "When he's that insistent upon it, it means he plans to nap for quite some time."

"With a pillow like that, I'm not surprised."

We entered his office.

"Sit down," he said.

I complied, and he paid me. I started to leave, but he waved me back to my chair.

"We need to talk," he said.

"But you were present the entire time I was," I said. "Surely you need no report from me."

"Not about that," he said, scratching his nose.

They came up behind me so silently that the first thing I heard was the slight rush of air as the ropes settled around me. I didn't even have a chance to struggle. I was trussed up in short order, barely able to turn my head to see the two Varangians who did it. I recognized neither of them.

I maintained calm. A facade, of course, but I'm good at those.

"What would you like to talk about?" I said politely.

"You told me that you had come from the north," Philoxenites said. "And indeed you entered the city through the Rhegium Gate, consistent with your tale. But then I receive word from the guardpost at the Anastasian Wall that you passed through along the Via Egnatia. Which means you were coming from the west."

"I'm terrible with directions," I admitted sheepishly. "I must have taken the wrong road at Philippopolis."

"Don't be tiresome," he said, sitting on the edge of the desk. The guards moved my chair up until I was a foot away. Then Philoxenites slapped me once.

"Ugh," he said, wiping the makeup off his hand with a handkerchief. "Very unpleasant. Don't let me do that again. To whom do you owe your fealty? Venice? Hagenau?"

"Neither," I said. "How about you?"

He motioned to one of the guards, who then delivered an expertly placed blow with a club to the side of my head. I saw stars for a moment. The Pleiades, I think.

"Where's your assistant, Claudius?" he asked.

"I don't know," I said. "He disappeared this morning. Ask at the Rooster; they'll confirm it."

"At the Rooster?" he said, laughing. "They'll confirm anything they're paid to confirm. You have to do better with your references, Fool. Who do you work for?"

"The Emperor."

Another blow. I saw Orion this time. It made sense—he was always chasing the Pleiades.

"If you kill me, what will you tell the Emperor?" I said.

He shrugged.

"People come and go around here," he said. "What's another missing fool?"

"So, you did kill the others," I snarled.

He looked at me in surprise.

"What on earth are you talking about?" he asked.

"The murdered fools," I said. "Niko, Piko, Demetrios, Tiberius, Ignatius, Thalia. Even Zintziphitzes."

He looked at me, completely baffled.

"Step outside," he directed the guards.

I heard a door close.

"Now," he said. "What you are about to tell me will determine whether I allow you to live. Are you saying that all of these people are dead?"

"Murdered," I said. "At your behest."

"Why would I want to kill a fool?"

"You were about to kill me."

"But you're a spy," he said. "Or aren't you? When were they killed?"

"Back in November."

He stood and paced the room behind me. I felt something salty run into my mouth, but whether it was blood or tears I could not say.

Philoxenites reappeared, holding a dagger.

"I had no knowledge of this," he said.

"Why should I believe you?"

"What makes you think I was connected to these things?"

"You were overheard at the Hippodrome by one of us, plotting against the Emperor."

He placed the blade against my throat.

"What plot?" he said softly. "When was this?"

"At the games of November first. We know everything now. And if I am killed, it will be brought straight to your rivals here. You won't live to see me buried."

He started to laugh.

"You played this game badly, Fool," he said. "The games of November first? On November first, I was in Adrianople. And I can bring in several hundred witnesses to swear to that before the Emperor."

FOURTEEN

A fool's mouth is his destruction.
PROVERBS 18:7

Now, as much as I enjoy the idle badinage of a fool who is about to meet his maker, there comes a time to speak seriously," said Philoxenites. "If there is a plot against the Emperor, I want to know about it."

"How do I know you're not part of it?" I asked. "How can I be sure you won't just slit my throat afterward?"

"You don't, and you can't," he said affably. "I seldom find it necessary to prove myself to a common ruffian like yourself. So, if you don't talk, I'll just slit your throat now. The way I see it, you have little to lose."

His logic was compelling. Of course, I was the one tied to a chair with a dagger at my throat, so my ability to reason was somewhat hampered.

"Zintziphitzes overheard two men plotting against Alexios," I said. "Back in November. He brought the information to the fools who were working here."

"Why to the fools?" asked Philoxenites.

"Because they had access to the Emperor and Empress, and it was the only way he could reach them," I said. "He thought no one else would take him seriously."

"Then why didn't the fools bring it to the Emperor and Empress?"

"Because they wanted to check this story out first for themselves. And inside of a week, every one of them had disappeared."

"This was in November?"

"Yes."

"But there has been no attempt on the Emperor since then."

"Zintziphitzes believed that the assassins were waiting for a particular event to occur."

"When did you speak with him?"

"A few days ago."

I recounted the full conversation for him. He listened, playing idly with the dagger.

"So, you smoked me out at the games," he said. "I was curious as to what started that little fire, but paid it no further mind. And you decided I was behind this conspiracy."

"You were my chief suspect," I said.

"Your use of the past tense suggests that you have changed your mind," he said, pleased. "Or, that you're being pragmatic."

"I'm still alive," I said. "That counts for something."

"It is too bad that your only witness is dead."

He looked at me for a long time. I couldn't read his expression.

"I saw your friends perform for many years," he said finally. "I couldn't help noticing that concealed amidst the foolery was a great deal of good advice, something that a succession of emperors followed to their benefit. I observed, however, that when presented with the opportunity today, you chose not to give any."

"Any fool can give advice, but the fool who seeks to stay in service should study his situation before doing so."

"A wise policy. Our current lord and master doted on the dwarves. They had been here so long that they understood Constantinople perhaps better than anybody. When they disappeared so abruptly, a few of us suspected that they were persuaded to leave by someone jealous of their influence. But I had no idea that they were murdered."

He stepped behind my chair, out of sight, not out of mind.

"Not that the idea offends me," he continued. I flinched as the dagger touched the nape of my neck. "It's a sound tactic. But, as it didn't come from me, it is one I would like to see fail."

He withdrew the blade and untied the ropes.

"All of these fools you mentioned . . . they worked together?"

"Except for Zintziphitzes," I said, shaking my hands until I could feel them again.

"Which was why he survived for so long," he mused. "And you showed up after hearing about the disappearances. Why you? Who sent you?"

I shook my head. He waved the dagger at me.

"I wish to make two points quite clear," he said. "Firstly, as far as I am concerned, I now own you. You live at my sufferance. Don't be so foolish as to make any attempts on my life. I am certain that you are capable of accomplishing it, but you will not see the sun set again if you do."

"Is that one point or two?" I asked.

"Secondly," he said, ignoring me. "We have not had this conversation. Nor will we be having the several other conversations that we will be having on a daily basis. In the meantime, I will be making some inquiries of my own."

"That's fine," I said. "May I go now, milord?"

He opened the door, and the two Varangians came in.

"Take him away," he ordered them.

I hoped that that meant they weren't going to kill me. Some agreed-upon signal, and off with his head. But I found myself outside the gate to Blachernae in no time at all.

"I saw your act at the Hippodrome," one of them said pleasantly. "I liked it. Me mates said you were good at the baths, too."

"Thank you," I said.

They gave an ironic salute and went back inside. I turned and started gulping air like a man escaped from drowning. Good air in this city, filled with smoke and spices and sweat.

"They say a cat has nine lives," said a voice behind me. "How many does a fool have?"

I turned to see Captain Stanislaus leaning in a doorway.

"And if a coward dies a thousand deaths, but a hero only once, then how many must a cowardly cat die?" I replied.

He nodded in the direction of my Varangian escort.

"Usually when I see those two with someone, the someone is being dumped in the harbor," he said. "What's the secret of your survival?"

"People think I'm more useful alive," I said.

"Are you?"

"Never underestimate the value of entertainment, my good Captain."

I slung my bag over my shoulder. Stanislaus left his post and fell into step beside me.

"I hear you lost a neighbor last night," he said.

"You are exceptionally well informed," I replied.

"And your partner, Claudius, has suddenly left town. Why?"

"I don't know. When you see him, ask him."

"I plan to. It's too bad he broke up the act. You were quite good together."

"It is too bad. But that's life. I've worked solo before."

"Do you think he killed Asan?"

"No. Do you?"

"Possibly."

"Then bring your suspicions to the Vigla. Sounds more like something in their line than yours."

"Listen, Fool," he said, grabbing my shoulder. "You arrive in town, and within a week the Empire takes you to its bosom. Yet in that same time, someone close to you is stabbed to death. You are carrying some evil omen, and this concerns me."

"No need to be concerned on my behalf."

"Why were you so anxious to perform at Blachernae?"

"Because that's where the money is, Captain. Street juggling is fun, but I want to live well."

"Is there a threat to the Emperor?" he demanded.

I looked at him. His normal swagger had been replaced by an air of uncertainty.

"You tell me," I said. "How the hell should I know?"

"Asan was killed in your room," he said. "Perhaps in your place."

"Where did you hear that?"

"A little minx told me. *Stultorum numerus* ..."

"Get stuffed!" I spat, shaking his hand off.

"She said you would know. . . . ," he said falteringly.

"Who said that?"

"Thalia. A fool."

"I heard she was dead."

"But ..."

"Protect your own damn emperor. What does any of this have to do with me?"

"Aren't you a Guild fool?"

"No. They can go to hell. A fool can't even work anymore without the Guild getting in his way."

"I need your help," he said quietly.

I turned in exasperation.

[198]

"Last time I checked, you had the entire Imperial Guard at your disposal," I said.

He looked around to make sure no one was within earshot.

"There's no one I can trust," he said.

"Why trust me?"

"You have no idea what it's like in Blachernae. Everyone is plotting against everyone else. Some for power, some for wealth, some for women, and some just to keep what they already have. It's gotten to the point that even those who want the same thing can't set their rivalries aside long enough to work for it."

"What are you in it for?" I asked.

"I'm a bit old-fashioned. I'm loyal to the Emperor."

I laughed.

"There are so many bizarre things in this city," I said. "A loyal soldier may be at the top of the list. No offense, Captain, but I don't see what good I could possibly do you. I'm just a fool, after all."

"You'll be around Alexios and his retinue. Just keep your eyes and ears open. Jesters may be privy to things that guards are not. And if you learn anything, bring it to me."

"You may have to get in line, Captain. Tell you what... if Thalia's still alive, send her along to the Rooster." I made as if to leave, then turned and leered at him. "We used to have some fine old times, Thalia and me."

Before I could take another step, he was on me, shoving me against a wall.

"If you say one more word about her, I'll kill you myself," he said, choking out the words.

"It's like that with you, is it?" I said. "Be careful, Captain. Cats have claws and teeth for a reason. I'll be at the Rooster."

He released his hold, and I walked away. I glanced behind me once. He was still standing by the wall, arms folded, watching me.

Well, life was getting complicated again. My very presence was stirring things up, which was good as long as I lived to do something about it. I wondered who else would approach me.

The Captain must have had a friend at the Rooster if he knew about Asan's death. Unless Thalia told him. I wanted to talk to her again. Bad enough giving out the Guild's password like that, although we were long overdue for a change. Malvolio had known it, and had used it to gain my confidence back in Orsino, but he had infiltrated the Guild long before I found him out. But I had never discovered whom he was working for, if anyone. It seemed like simple revenge at the time, but now I was beginning to suspect he was part of some larger plan.

That evening, the atmosphere at the Rooster was decidedly subdued at dinner. Not surprising, given the death in the family. The mutual suspicions did not help. Every time someone reached for his knife to slice some bread, hands jumped to waists and sleeves and any other place where a weapon might be at the ready. Many of them looked to me to brighten things up, but I was in a foul mood myself. There had been no word from Claudius, and I was too wrapped up in the Blachernae business to go out searching for her. A good husband would probably have dropped everything to find her, but I guess I had a way to go in that area.

Asan's room—my room—was empty when I retired for the evening. A nice change. I closed the door and dropped the bar, then secured the shutters over the window. I blew out the candle and stretched out in the darkness. Asan's pallet was much more comfortable than mine. Despite the morbid accommodations, the fears for my wife, and the day's intrigues, I fell asleep almost immediately.

I woke in the night as a dark form slipped into bed beside me, holding me tight. It was the wrong dark form.

"How did you get in?" I asked drowsily.

"Window," said Thalia. "It doesn't latch very well. I had forgotten that you had switched rooms. I almost made the Pecheneg trader in your old one a very happy man."

She slid her hand inside the tunic of my motley. I grabbed the hand firmly and removed it. By this point, I was awake enough to realize that she didn't have a stitch on.

"What's the matter?" she said, sitting up.

"I can't do this," I said.

"Why not? Did something happen to you?" she asked. "You said you almost lost a leg. I thought at the time you meant your leg. Did you mean something else?"

"Something happened to me," I said. "I acquired a wife."

"No!" she protested. "Settled down? Not Theo. You're too rootless to be married."

"I'm not rooted," I said. "Just married."

"Where is she now?" she asked.

"Somewhere that way, I think," I said, pointing west.

"All right then," she said, sliding her hand back. I intercepted it again.

"I said I was married."

"I've slept with married men before. It's never been an impediment to either party in my experience. Frequently, it's an enhancement."

"Let me clarify for your edification: Married. And faithful."
She sat up again.

"It's the scarring, isn't it?" she said, resting her hands on her chin. "It's put you off."

"No," I said. "If it weren't for the wife, I'd be happily entwined. We could compare scars in the dark."

"I suppose that sounds like fun. But if she's back west..."

"It's no great feat to be faithful to a wife who's around," I said, cutting her off in midproposition. "The true test is being faithful when you're apart."

"Noble old you," she snorted. "And I suppose you think she's being faithful while you're gone."

"She's a veritable Penelope," I said. "I'll have to kill her fifty suitors when I return."

"Ooh, I know that story! Could I be Circe? Please?"

"It won't work. Most men are swine before they meet you. Your enchantment is of a different sort."

"Flatterer." Thalia stood up, felt around the floor for her garments, and began dressing.

"Why are you so interested in seducing me?" I asked.

She stiffened in the darkness.

"I thought I could weasel my way back into your good graces that way," she said.

"You've gotten it backward," I replied. "Get into my good graces first. Then maybe you'd have a shot at seduction. At least, under unmarried circumstances."

"Fair enough. What task do you have for me?"

"Something I'd rather do myself, but I'm only one fool. Simon thinks someone inside the Rooster killed Asan. I'm laying odds it was friend Peter, the butcher, but that's just a hunch. Do you think you've recovered enough to follow my neighbors around and see if they are who they say they are?"

"Done," she said. "Boring, but done."

She threw on the cowl, then stepped toward the window.

"By the by," I said idly. "How did Captain Stanislaus get hold of the Guild password?"

She froze, then sat down slowly beside me.

"I'm sorry," she said. "It was my fault."

"You had better tell me."

"When I was stabbed and left for dead, I was on my way to meet him. He was one of my lovers at the palace."

"And one of your sources, of course."

"Of course," she said. "When I didn't show up, he became worried. He came looking for me. He's the one who found me nearly dead in an alley. He dressed my wounds, carried me to his rooms, and cared for me in secret."

"By himself?"

"No. He has servants when he's in town. Rank has its privileges. He also had a surgeon come in to patch me up a little better. Not a Guard surgeon, but someone from the Jewish quarter who could keep a secret.

"I babbled a lot when I was there, half in a delirium. When I had recovered somewhat, Stanislaus told me what I had been saying. You have to remember, this was weeks after I had been attacked, and by this time, the other fools were all gone. I was terrified. I had almost been killed, and I didn't even know what I was supposed to know that was so important.

"I had blurted out something about the plot, but he couldn't find out anything when he looked into it. And I was worried that someone from the Guild would show up and not know where to turn for help. I gave him the password, Theo. I probably shouldn't have, but I wasn't thinking clearly at the time."

I patted her on the shoulder.

"It's all right," I said. "I've been thinking we're due for a new one in any case. Did Stanislaus have any suspects?"

"He had so many that he didn't know where to turn first. I think he's hoping that you'll draw them out, and he'll catch them when they kill you."

"I don't like that plan. How about the one where he catches them *before* they kill me?"

"He thinks that killing you makes their intentions a bit clearer."

"Oh. He has a point there."

She leaned over the bed and kissed me gently on the cheek, then climbed through the window.

"Sleep well," she said softly, and then vanished into what was left of the night.

I spent the morning searching for Viola, looking in places we had been before. No luck, and no real way of knowing where to look. I had no time to retrace our route back to Thessaloniki. I supposed if she went that way, I would eventually hear about it from Fat Basil. If I was still alive to receive the message. And if Viola was still alive to send it.

I was unaware of anyone following or watching me, although I was taking the usual precautions. Either I had lost them or they were very good. I assumed the latter for safety's sake, now that I no longer had anyone watching my back.

Knowing about the connection between Stanislaus and Thalia cleared up a minor matter for me. I was wondering how Thalia had learned of our arrival in the city. Obviously, Stanislaus had told her after meeting us at the Rooster, and she started following us soon after.

The sun was soon high enough to tell me to attend to my royal audience. I passed through the gates and doors to Blachernae to find Alexios unattended except for a few guards by the doors. He was slumped on the throne, staring into space, his chin resting on his hand. A pitcher and a full goblet rested on a stand by the throne.

"Ah, Feste," he said. "See? I remembered your name."

"I am flattered, Your Majesty," I replied.

"Sing me something to cheer me up," he said.

"Certainly," I said, picking up my lute.

I sang some comic ditties and some heroic ballads for a while. At one point, he drained his goblet and picked up the pitcher to discover it was empty. He threw it at a door. The thump brought a servant at the gallop, a full pitcher in his hand.

"If I finish this one before the next one comes out," said the Emperor to the man who was quaking visibly, "then I will see how you do against one of my bears at the next games."

The fellow bowed and fled. Alexios turned to me and winked.

"Discipline," he said. "It's how I've come so far."

"Admirable," I replied.

He refilled the goblet, sipped from it, and stood.

"We need a window in here," he grumbled. "I didn't become Emperor so that they could entomb me while I was still living. Where is the sun?"

"When I came in, it was on the throne," I replied.

He made some vague gesture of thanks and started staggering around the room, leaning on a jewel-encrusted cane.

"Ever wanted to be Emperor?" he asked me.

"No, milord."

"You're about the only one who doesn't. I am surrounded by hopeful heirs and ambitious plotters, and those are just the ones I like."

"I hope you find that I am neither, milord."

"You? You are the Emperor's Fool. If an emperor can't trust a fool, who can he trust?"

"Himself, milord."

He considered that.

"I don't know that I can trust myself," he confessed. "I have too many faults. Too many sins. They weigh me down some days. I was as hopeful and as ambitious a man as any I have ever seen, and that's the God's truth."

"If it will comfort Your Majesty, let me say that I have seen worse."

There was a pause as Alexios stared and the guards looked startled; then the Emperor began to laugh.

"Then there's hope for me, eh?" he said. "I must travel more to see these superior sinners. Let me tell you, Feste, sometimes I wonder if it's worth it. I've done all that I have done in order to become Emperor, and now I'm Emperor. What's left? Conquering the world?"

"It's a big place," I said.

"Yes, and it's all we can do to hold on to this little piece of it. I've had my share of those battles, believe me, and that's when I was fighting for my predecessors. Or against them. Been on both sides of a few squabbles. Fought with my father against Andronikos on behalf of the last Alexios to be Emperor; then my father went over to Andronikos, so we all went with him. Tried to come out alive with as many men as I could. That's why they're so loyal to me. When others were all set to fight battles, I arranged some quiet little assassinations. Held the head of the false-Alexios in my hands and averted a war. Caught my brother unaware while he was out hunting. Easiest succession this empire's ever had, hardly had to kill anybody. Didn't even kill my brother!" He paused. "Maybe I should have, you know. It would have been smart. But family is family. I played with him as a child. That's why I only had him blinded."

"Most generous of you."

"And still there are those who don't like me."

"It confounds all sense. Where is your flutist today?"

"Off with the women, having a bath," he said. "Wish I could watch. Maybe I'll have a women's bath built with a hiding place for me. I often wonder what they do when we're not around, don't you?"

"Some things should remain mysteries to men," I said.

"Euphy and I used to bathe together," he confided. "Extraordinary figure of a woman back then. Suppose she still is. Should invite her over to the royal bedchamber one of these days. Just for old times' sake."

"There comes a time when having one's wife becomes the spice that is variety, milord."

"True, true. But in the meantime . . . Ah, there's my treasure!"

The flutist posed decoratively in the doorway, then entered. Small bells decked her fingers and toes, making a pleasant tinkling sound as she walked toward her master. More bells were draped about her body, keeping what little modesty she possessed intact. Apart from the bells, she wore nothing. She had not only bathed, but had had herself oiled afterward. She was downright slippery, in fact, but Alexios seemed willing to make the effort to catch her. She traipsed about just out of his reach as he limped after her, teasing him with sidelong glances and beckoning with her fresh-painted talons. The guards and I watched as she finally let him catch her.

"Well, there's my hunting for the day," he gasped. "Is she not a pretty prize?"

"Indeed. You should have her mounted," I said.

"Oh, I shall, I shall," he said fondly, caressing her hair. "Did you make good report of me to the Empress, my dear? Tell her of how you comforted me with your playing?"

She murmured something in Arabic, and he beamed idiotically.

"I don't understand a word of it," he said. "But it sounds sinful."

I was not about to translate for him. Arabic is a rich language filled with exquisite turns of phrase, especially when it comes to insults, and there's no way I could do it justice in any other language.

"Nap!" the Emperor bellowed, and the flutist danced away into the bedchamber. He would have fallen over had I not leapt forward and steadied him.

"Thanks, good Fool," he said. "You're done for the day."

"It's early, sire," I said. "Shall I await your further pleasure?"

"Not unless you can . . . Oh, I see what you mean. No, go amuse yourself." He leered in the direction of the Belle of the Bells. "I'll ring if I need you," he guffawed.

"Perhaps I could entertain the Empress?" I suggested. I was curious to see how the other half of this domestic bliss operated.

"No need," he said. "She already has a fool."

"I understand that Thalia left her some time ago," I pointed out.

"Thalia?" he said, puzzled. Then he brightened. "Oh, yes. The old one. I liked her. Contortionist. Had dreams about her, I can tell you. Or rather, I can't tell you. Could have had her, but Euphy wouldn't let me. Funny sort of wife, having the say-so over one's mistresses. Glad she let me keep this one. No, she has a new fool."

It is hard to keep a straight face when your heart is leaping in your chest.

"When was this?" I asked casually.

"Yesterday," he said. "Pretty thing. Calls herself Aglaia."

FIFTEEN

The heart of the foolish is like a cartwheel.

SIRACH 33:6

I sat on the parapets of the wall that separated Blachernae from the rest of the city, watching the comings and goings of the world. I could see the Golden Horn over the seawall. Unlike in the Kontoskalion Harbor, the activity here was constant. Ships jockeyed for available berths on both shores, and those that succeeded were relieved of their cargoes before they had even finished tying up. Spices and fish coming in, silks and leather going out.

I heard a commotion from the south, and looked to see the Empress's procession returning from yet another assault on an unsuspecting piece of marble. The pedestrians scattered quickly, accustomed to the comings and goings of this strange and powerful woman, then reformed their patterns after she passed through.

But there was something new today. She was laughing, her deep, throaty bellows rattling nearby shutters and making her hooded falcon shift uneasily on her wrist, wondering at the noise. Her charioteer, whose constant exposure to the sun had so bronzed him that he could have blended in with the statues in the Hippodrome, frequently glanced behind at her, occasionally smiling himself.

The source of this hilarity was a woman in motley, seated next to Euphrosyne, chattering away and making frequent gesticulations. The motley looked as if it had barely been worn, if the brightness of its colors was any indication, and its geometric patterns were so even that it was clear that no patches had been added to it since its creation. The fool was wearing whiteface with rouged cheeks and lips and a pattern of green and blue dots around her eyes, except for a pair of green diamonds under them.

Green diamonds, like the ones I had under my eyes.

The entourage passed through the gate in the wall, and then another one at the end of the palace opposite the one I normally used. I guess the Empress had her own entrance.

I descended the ramp from the wall and waited in an alcove from whence I could see the palace. Toward sunset, the gate opened, and the fool came out, weaving slightly. She didn't notice me until she had nearly passed by.

"Aglaia," I said.

She turned slowly and saw me. She smiled that slightly crooked grin that I knew so well. Not that I needed it to recognize her. I could have done it from the eyes.

"I was racking my brain trying to remember where that name comes from," I continued. "One of the three Graces, was she not?"

"The other two being Euphrosyne and Thalia," she said. "Thalia was Good Cheer, and Euphrosyne Mirth."

"And Aglaia?" I asked.

She came toward me, put her arms around my waist, and held me tight.

"Splendor," Viola whispered in my ear, and then she tilted her head back and let me kiss her for a while.

I took my time doing it. I wanted to get the taste of her back in my memory, strong enough to take with me to the grave. I hadn't known when she left if I would ever get to do this again, and I didn't know even now whether it would be the last time. And there was no rush for me at this moment to go out and do anything else.

"Are you very angry?" she said when we disengaged.

"I was frightened," I said.

"That I would come to harm?"

"No. That I might not ever see you again."

"You didn't think I would walk out on you, did you?" she said, glaring a bit. I took her hand in mine.

"What I thought is that you probably went off on your own damn fool errand," I said. "But if you did decide to walk out on me, it was because I eminently deserved it. I wish you had let me know where you were, though."

"I thought you might try to stop me."

I shook my head.

"In the training of fools, there are many tests," I said. "One is to see if the apprentice will have sufficient wit, initiative, and confidence to get so pissed off at his teacher that he will strike off on his own. Very few take that route. Those who do generally end up being at the very top of the profession."

"You just made that up to make me feel less guilty, didn't you?" she said accusingly.

"No, Duchess. If we ever get back to the Guildhall, ask Father Gerald about when he taught me. Fools resist authority and resent all establishments, which makes training and ordering them about a bit paradoxical. It's even more complicated in our situation because we are married, and I must say, having been through this, that I will never train another wife of mine to be a fool."

She hugged me again.

"There'll be no further opportunity to do so if I have my way," she whispered.

This led to more of that kissing, which was fine by me.

"You're a bit tipsy," I observed.

"I am not," she protested; then she reconsidered as she staggered into the doorway. "All right, a bit," she admitted. "Keeping up with Euphy has its challenging side."

"Tell me how you managed to get in there."

"You forget how good I am at talking my way into places," she said. "It's how I got to be a duchess in the first place. I just walked up to the gate, pounded on it, and said, 'I'm the Empress's new jester.' The guards looked confused and started whispering to each other. I informed them that if the Empress's entertainment was delayed, she would be in a foul mood and inclined to take it out on whoever caused the delay. That got me through the gate. They kept passing the responsibility on up the chain of command, and eventually I was in her throne room."

"Nicely done, but how did you talk your way into Her Grace's graces?"

"That turned out to be the easiest part. She was sitting there, barking at the servants, with that overgrown guard smirking beside her. When I came in, everyone suddenly became quiet. She looked at me, and said, 'What are you?' 'Your new fool, mistress,' I replied. She looked at her chamberlain, who hadn't a clue why I was there, then back at me. 'I gave no orders for a fool,' she says. 'That's why I'm here,' I said. 'If you give an order to a fool, would you expect her to follow it? If you ordered me to appear, I would vanish. But since you ordered no fool, I came as quickly as I could, mistress.'"

"Not bad, Apprentice. Not bad at all. Obviously, she liked it."

"Her chamberlain told me it was the first time she had cracked a smile in a months."

"Good. So, you're in. What have you found out?"

"A few things, but I haven't been there that long. The Emperor's flutist is definitely reporting to Euphy. I think it's the only way she can keep track of him. Euphy has her own baths, and takes all her servants with her. Glorious baths, by the way, best I've had since I left Orsino."

"You haven't had that many."

"Hush, husband. I was a man, and men don't bathe that often, more's the pity. I don't know why you expect us to be..."

"All right, I concede. What did you learn in the baths?"

"Euphy and the flutist chatted in Arabic. I didn't let on that I understood. Mostly about the state of the Emperor's health and reason, both of which seem to be declining. Also, about every single word that was spoken before him. She understands Greek perfectly. That simpering ignorance was just an act."

"It usually is."

"Euphy got quite irate when she heard how often Alexios was bedding this flutist."

"I thought she condoned the activity. Alexios said the Empress had approval of his mistresses."

"She does, but I don't think she expected him to be this enthusiastic. She hauled off and slapped the woman, then apologized and started crying. She said something odd, 'It won't be much longer now.' "

"That's interesting. Do you think she could be behind this?"

Viola chewed on her lip, thinking.

"She's fully capable," she said. "Given how he's treated her over the years, it would be no surprise if she wanted to kill him. And she's been up to her ears in trying to select his successor, especially in choosing husbands for their daughters. But I can't think of any event that the Empress would have to wait for in order to carry it out. It just may have been something she said that I'm taking out of context with my nasty, suspicious mind."

"Stay nasty and suspicious for now, my love. You'll live longer. Anyone looking crooked at you because you're a jester?"

"Not so far. I get paid by her chamberlain, fortunately, so I haven't come face to face with that loathsome treasurer again. I don't think anyone will recognize me as Claudius, but I'll keep my makeup on to be safe."

"Good. Speaking of safety, the password's no good anymore. Don't accept it from anyone. If someone says they're from the Guild, play dumb."

She gave me a hard look.

"Thalia?" she asked.

I nodded. "She says she was in a delirium."

"Well, I have some news about your old lover," she said. "I know where she lives, and I know who her current lover is."

"As to the second, it's Captain Stanislaus," I said, and Viola's face fell. "As to the first, how the hell did you find that out?"

"I followed her," she said simply. "After I so heartlessly abandoned you, I picked up my horse, rode out of town, ducked into the nearest cover, and became Aglaia, Apprentice Fool."

"You've had that motley the whole time?"

"Overconfident, I suppose, but I had it made up in Orsino when I first began training. I have a few other costumes as well, including one of those all-purpose monk's outfits that everyone favors around here.

"So, having transformed myself, I rode back into town through a different gate so nobody would recognize my horse. Then I turned monk and watched your room, waiting for her to show up. Sure enough, she did. She was in there quite a long time, wasn't she?"

"Mostly because I was downstairs defending my errant servant Claudius from the charge of murdering Asan."

Her jaw dropped.

"They think I did it?" she said.

"The timing of your disappearance was a little too close to the event for comfort."

"Oh, dear," she said. "There goes that disguise. At least I'm clear with Father Esaias. I don't think anyone else will care after a while."

"Avoid Stephanos," I advised her. "He seemed very fond of the lad."

"I will. Anyhow, after Thalia came back out the window, I followed her. She went to a building near where the Blachernae Wall meets the seawall. It's by the Cynegion Gate."

"I know the area. Go on."

"Well, lo and behold, who should show up but Captain Stanislaus?" she continued with a wicked smile. "And the greeting she gave him! Mutual enthusiasm, which makes me wonder at the sincerity of both of them."

"Interesting observation," I said, and I briefly filled her in on what I had seen since we parted.

"Stanislaus approached you," she wondered. "This is too confusing. I don't know who is using whom anymore. I couldn't get close enough to them to overhear anything. But she never spotted me, Master. Do I pass that test?"

"You've passed a dozen in the last two days, Apprentice. Now, I'm not sure it's safe for you to return to the Rooster, even with your makeup."

"That's all right. They've set me up in a room in Euphy's side of the palace."

"Can you bar the door?"

"Bar and bolt, both door and shutters. I'm safe enough as far as that goes. How about you?"

"I've moved into Asan's room," I said. "It has a bar for the door, but the shutters need some help." I decided not to tell her how I found that out.

"Asan's room the day after he was killed? That's extremely creepy," she said, shuddering momentarily.

"It's not bad," I said. "I had to mop the blood off the floor, but it's not the first dead man's room I've ever slept in."

She looked at me.

"There was blood on the floor?" she asked.

"Yes. Why?"

"But there wasn't any blood on the floor in our room."

It took great effort not to burst forth in a stream of cursing, but she was a lady again, so I made the effort. And failed.

"Impressive," she said. "You swore in about eight languages in a row."

"Practice, practice, practice," I said. "I'm awfully glad you're with me on this excursion. I completely missed the significance of the missing blood. There was no blood because the bleeding had stopped before he was in there. Asan wasn't killed in our room."

"No," she said. "I have to say that I'm a bit relieved. I've felt a knifepoint at my back for the last two days. Whoever killed him must have killed him in his room and then dragged the body into ours."

"For what reason?"

"To put the blame on us, I suppose. Or to scare us. Or confuse us."

"Well, it worked. We are collectively blamed, scared, and confused. Who do you think did it?"

"Someone sleeping soundly in the Rooster tonight," she said. "Maybe you should knock on each door at midnight and see which one doesn't jump out of his skin."

"Startling this crew under the current circumstances could get a man killed. Believe it or not, I have Thalia checking out the Rooster's denizens."

"You trust her to do that?"

"No, but it keeps her out of the way. And if she's still on our side, maybe something will come of it. It may be that Asan's murder has nothing to do with us."

"You don't believe that."

"No. Look, there's one more thing you haven't considered in this little sortie of yours."

"What's that?"

I hesitated, then went ahead.

"Female jesters have been with the Guild for centuries," I said. "They've been at the Byzantine courts as well. But Byzantine courts being what they are, a lot of the local nobles may not act so nobly when they see you. You'll be considered fair game."

"But I am under the protection of the Empress," she protested.

"And she's both perverse and insane," I said. "She might even find your ravishment amusing if she approves of the conqueror. Or she might order you to go and seduce someone if it will further any plot of hers."

"Oh. I never thought of that. I suppose Thalia had no problem handling that aspect of the job."

"Apparently not," I said, chafing a bit under the constant sniping at my former lover. "But you're going to need more protection than Euphy can provide."

"What do you have in mind?"

I explained my plan to her. We decided to act upon it in the morning.

"I have to go," she said. "She wants me to sing to her at bedtime."

"Would you like to borrow my lute?"

"No, there's a harp there. I'll manage. Kiss me, Fool."

"Very good, milady."

We parted reluctantly.

"Your makeup's smeared," she called over her shoulder as she walked back to the palace.

"So is yours," I called back.

I nearly turned cartwheels all the way back to the Rooster.

Thalia didn't wait for me to return to my room. As I was washing up behind the Rooster, a knife hit the water barrel inches from my face. I looked up to see a cowled figure standing in an alleyway nearby. The hands were hers. I pulled out the knife and joined her.

"Most ladies initiate a flirtation by dropping a handkerchief," I said, handing the knife back to her.

"I've been called a lot of things, but a lady has never been one of them," she said. "Have you heard? There's a new fool in town."

"Yes, I know. Her name's Aglaia. She's with the Empress."

"How long have you known about her?" she asked.

"Just met her today."

"That wasn't my question."

"I've known her for a while," I said. "But I honestly didn't know she was going to show up here."

"So much for getting my position back," she said bitterly.

"You've had plenty of time to get it back," I pointed out. "Maybe she'll give it up. Would you like to try?"

She shook her head.

"Not until the man who stabbed me is six feet under," she said. "I'll settle for three feet."

"Fair enough. What have you learned about my good friends and neighbors?"

"The butcher's a butcher, the huntsman's a huntsman," she

recited. "Stephanos works for Father Esaias, so he is what he says he is, although that means he's on the outside of the law in every possible way. The Russians stick together every minute of the day. They spend their time trying to figure out a quick way of getting their money back. The idea of actually working for it doesn't seem to have crossed their minds."

"Are they all in fact Russians?"

"Yes. I was eavesdropping on their conversations when they were dicing down at the docks."

"I didn't know you spoke Russian."

"Picked it up from a lover who had come here to study for the priesthood."

"I hope you taught him well."

"We taught each other. He'll be a blessing unto his people, Theo. He took back some fond memories, and left me his language and this useful outfit I'm wearing. And that's my report, sir. Not much help, is it?"

"It doesn't eliminate anyone, and it doesn't put anyone ahead of the pack. All right, thanks for doing that."

"What about this Aglaia?"

"She's reporting to me."

"So, you're the chief fool in Constantinople now."

"By default. Remember, at the time the Guild sent me, no one knew you were still alive. Do you want to be the chief fool?"

She shook her head violently.

"I don't even know if I want to be a fool anymore," she said quietly.

"It's been a rough year," I said. "Give it some more time. And don't quit just yet. I still need your help."

"For what?"

"I'll let you know. Keep checking in with me. Good night."

She slipped away.

The Rooster was a little more lively this night. The new resident, the Pecheneg trader who unknowingly almost experienced Thalia's charms, was a good-natured fellow with a taste for gambling. The Russians fell upon him like old friends, plied him with drink, and soon invited him to join them in a friendly game of chance.

Simon caught my eye and nodded. I picked up some empty pitchers and joined him at the bar.

"A message for you from Father Esaias," he said softly.

"What is it?"

"He'd like you to come see him. Nothing urgent, he said, so if you got in late, don't bother tonight. It can wait until after you finish at Blachernae tomorrow."

"All right. If he asks, tell him I'll be there. Any word from my missing partner?"

"I haven't heard anything."

"Any further ideas about who killed Asan?"

He refilled the pitchers with ale and handed them back to me.

"One thing I found rather odd," he said.

"What's that?"

"After I got rid of the body, I went to tell Esaias. I thought that since Asan was one of his men and it happened in my establishment, it would be prudent if he heard about it from me. But when I got to the church, I found out that he already knew about it."

"Really? That is interesting. So, you think someone else from here reported it to him before you did."

"Yes."

"Probably Stephanos. He works for him."

"Stephanos didn't report to Esaias until later. So, he had to have heard about it from somebody else here."

I didn't want to tell him Esaias had heard about it from me. Simon would have decided that I had done it. The last thing I needed now was another person after me.

There was a roar and applause from the Russians as the Pecheneg won the first game. The fellow was excited and fairly drunk, and agreed readily when they proposed a rematch. The trap was set.

"Maybe Father Esaias knew because he gave the order to have Asan killed," I said. "Maybe he found out the lad was running his own games somewhere and not sharing the proceeds."

"Maybe," said Simon doubtfully. "Usually, though, when Esaias makes an example out of people, their bodies are found somewhere open to view so the general public can learn from the errors of others."

"Isn't it wonderful how a priest will take the time to give moral instruction to his flock?" I asked. "Well, good tapster, I am at a loss to explain it. But I will sleep on it, and if anything occurs to me, then I will share it with you in the morning. And so I bid you a good night."

"Good night, Feste."

I went upstairs, barred the door, shuttered the windows more firmly, and had the first uninterrupted sleep I had had in days.

Philoxenites' matched set of Varangians met me at the Blachernae Gate and diverted me to his office before I could see the Emperor. The eunuch looked displeased, but you might, too, if you were a eunuch.

"Why didn't you tell me about this other fool?" he asked.

"I didn't know about her until yesterday," I said. "The Emperor told me, and I went to look her up."

"I want to speak with her."

"Then speak with her," I said. "But remember that she is the Empress's fool, and the Empress may not take kindly to interference with her staff."

"Bring her here later."

"She doesn't work for me, you know."

That brought him up short.

"Isn't she a Guild fool?" he asked.

"No," I said honestly. She was just an apprentice, after all. "But she is an ally. I really cannot tell you more just yet. Shall we attend to His Majesty? I do have work to do today."

He was less than satisfied, but assented.

Alexios was in a good mood. I noticed that the flutist was looking a little worn out, which may have been the reason. A trio of artisans was demonstrating the Emperor's newest toy, a mechanical music maker that played melodies on a variety of golden chimes, silver cymbals, tuned mahogany blocks, and even some plucked strings on a harp-shaped frame. The whole apparatus was played by the turning of a bronze crank at one end, and the effect was both mystical and merry. The Emperor limped around it with a childlike look of amazement, and was so pleased by the effects caused by turning the crank that he did it over and over again, marveling at the combinations of sounds produced. His enthusiasm was such that the inventors became apprehensive that their creation might not withstand his repeated efforts. No doubt the flutist could sympathize.

"Look, Fool," he called. "It does the work of a dozen musicians. Is it not magical?"

"Indeed, milord," I replied. "And I can only thank my foolish stars that it cannot sing and tell stories as well, or I might be out of a job."

"What do you say, my friends?" he asked. "Can you duplicate Feste?"

"That is something that only can be done by the Creator," one of the inventors said humbly. "We may duplicate music because that is something created by Man."

"And yet I am an artificial fool," I said. "For I am a self-made jester. Surely such minds as yours can reproduce the effort."

"It is beyond our capabilities," said the inventor.

"Then, Your Majesty, I submit that these fellows are not so clever after all. For a man as stupid and low as I am can still make himself into a fool, yet these geniuses cannot even do that much."

"There are many things that cannot be duplicated by machines, and I thank God for it," commented the Emperor. He looked fondly at the flutist, who managed a weak smile.

"Now, Feste, I have something to tell you," continued Alexios.

"What is it, milord?"

"Something that will amuse you for a change."

"I am always at the service of entertainment."

He sat back on his throne, grinning broadly.

"You've been challenged to a duel," he said.

Sixteen

That that is is.
TWELFTH NIGHT, ACT 4, SCENE 2

B lachernae Palace had its own hippodrome—smaller than the main one, of course, but covered so that the Emperor could have his entertainment no matter what the weather. It only had space for a thousand of his closest friends, along with their army of servants and an actual army to watch over everyone. Horse racing was an oddity there. The oval was not long enough for horses to build up any speed, but the turns were dangerously sharp. I don't know if horses ever get dizzy, but this would certainly be the place to see it.

The Imperial Box was kept in constant readiness, for Alexios frequently acted upon his whims. On this occasion, he and Euphrosyne actually sat together, talking as if they hadn't seen each other for months.

Word of my trial by ordeal had sped around Blachernae, and all of the immediate family plus assorted cousins piled into the place, along with many of the advisers I had seen before. This was my first glimpse of the three daughters, who sat behind their parents. Anna and Irene chatted happily with their husbands, while Evdokia sat sulkily by and scouted the adjoining seats for marriage prospects.

The Empress was guarded by her charioteer, who smirked at Stanislaus from across the box as only a man with superior muscles may do. The Captain waved at him cheerfully, but kept scanning the spectators, watching for any suspicious behavior.

Then there was a brief fanfare, and I was shoved into the middle of the arena. I stumbled as I came in, which took me through a series of irregular somersaults and handsprings until I crashed into the wall just in front of the Emperor and Empress, which sent me backward through a few more. I then stood up, brushed myself off with as much dignity as I could muster, and then bowed.

Another fanfare, and my challenger zoomed into view, dancing, cartwheeling, flipping, doing all of the tricks I had shown her to perfection, and adding a few of her own invention. Aglaia bowed to the box, and then turned to me and bowed again. I returned the bow as she came up. She saw me bowing, and responded with another, augmented with a series of graceful flourishes of the arms. I saw this, and tried to duplicate it, but my arms got tangled up with each other, and in the process of trying to separate them, my right leg somehow became wrapped up in them until I looked like a human knot.

Aglaia watched me until I succeeded in restoring my limbs to their proper positions. Where Thalia had been feline in her performances, Aglaia used her shorter height to be more mouselike. Her expressions shifted rapidly and constantly, and where Thalia undulated, Aglaia scampered. She suddenly dashed by me and gave me a good, solid kick in the rear; she was standing safely out of reach before I could even blink.

I growled at her, becoming the bear to her mouse, and started lumbering after her, grabbing at her clumsily. But she ducked under my arms and darted around me, giving me another swift kick for my reward. We continued in this fashion for a short time; then I stopped, breathing heavily, wiping the sweat from my brow. She stood apart from me and laughed.

I walked over to my bag and pulled out a club. She stopped laughing and eyed me warily. I pulled my arm back to throw it at her. She motioned for me to stop, then reached into her bag and pulled out two clubs, waving them menacingly at me. I countered by producing two more. She matched with her third, and we each started juggling.

"How stands the duel so far, milord?" I called to the Emperor.

"It's a close match," he pronounced. "She's very good."

"How say you, milady?" asked Aglaia.

"I stand by my champion," declared Euphrosyne. "But this fellow is a talented fool. You work very well together."

"There's a reason for that," said Aglaia. "Empress, may I present my husband, Feste?"

"My Lord Emperor, may I present my wife, Aglaia?" I added.

Alexios looked at Euphrosyne, and they burst into laughter.

"Did you know about this, my dear?" he roared.

"Not an inkling," she said, gasping. "How marvelous!"

"Now, there are a number of advantages to having a jester for a wife," I said.

"And for a husband," said Aglaia.

"For one thing, many marriages are undermined because one spouse suspects the other of being a fool," I said.

"But in ours, we know it for certain," said Aglaia. "So, there's nothing to worry about. And, whenever we have a disagreement..."

"Which we never do," I interrupted.

"Yes, we do."

"Do not!" I shouted.

"Whenever we have a disagreement," she repeated, glaring at me.

"We never..."

"Or an interruption," she shouted angrily, "then as fools we may freely do things that are forbidden to normal people."

"Like what?" asked the Empress.

"Like throwing clubs at each other," she said, and the duet began.

"And knives," I added, bringing them into the routine.

"And swords!"

"And axes!"

And the arena was filled with sharp objects flying through the air, and we beamed at each other through it all, husband and wife at last.

We performed acrobatics, improvised couplets, played our instruments, and entertained for well over two hours. Aglaia was Viola Unbound, the intangible restraints of society along with the very real restraints of Claudius's costume left behind in the transformation. We filled the space with laughter, and there was no saying where Feste's contributions left off and Aglaia's began.

The principal couple enjoyed themselves royally. We even noticed them holding hands, much to the astonishment, even the consternation, of their family. And I think I even saw Philoxenites chuckle once, which was a triumph as far as I was concerned.

We finished to great applause, and Alexios was feeling so good that he actually invited Euphrosyne to lunch with him. She accepted happily, and all rose as they left the box.

"That was quite possibly the most fun I have ever had," said Aglaia as we packed up.

"I was thinking as we performed that this is the fourth guise I have seen you use since I've known you," I commented.

"And?"

"And I was thinking how lucky I am to have such an ever-changing woman. Most husbands need mistresses for variety."

"Mm. Well, I think the plan worked. Everyone knows we're married and under the joint protection of Euphy and her husband. My virtue should be unassailable, now."

"Damn."

"Why?"

"I was hoping to assail it later."

She grinned.

"I have the afternoon off," she said. "Would you like to see my room?"

We took a walk afterward. Away from Blachernae, away from intrigue, away from an Emperor we were trying to protect, away from the desperate scheming around him. We crossed the Lycos, and soon the city noises faded behind us and the lowing of cattle reached us from a nearby farm.

"This is such a bucolic setting," commented Aglaia. "Too bad there's that enormous wall blocking the horizon."

There was a low, grassy foothill before us. Beyond it, the meadow gave way to the rise of the Xerolophon and the Pillar of Arkadios surmounting it. I spread my cloak on the grass and stretched out on it, watching the cattle wander about. Aglaia sat next to me.

"You seem preoccupied," she observed. "Strange mood for a man after lovemaking."

"Preoccupied? How can you tell?"

"You weren't checking to see if anyone was following us."

I looked back toward the north.

"Was anyone following us?" I asked.

"No," she replied. "I'm sure of it."

"Good. Thank you. I've been thinking about our situation, but I haven't come up with anything new. How about you?"

"Well, there's one thing," she said hesitantly. "I don't think it's worth much, but Euphy's been shopping her unmarried daughter around pretty aggressively."

"Evdokia wants a husband. It's nice of her mother to take an active interest."

"I was wondering if it could be more than that," she said. "She wants a qualified male heir for the empire. Maybe if she finds the right man for Evdokia, she will have no further use for Alexios. Maybe that's the event everyone is waiting for."

"Maybe," I said.

She lay back and sighed.

"I don't think much of the idea, either," she said. "I also found out that Captain Stanislaus used to be her bodyguard and official statue-whacker."

"And occasional bedmate, I suppose."

"Definitely."

"I wonder if he was Thalia's lover at the same time, or if that came later."

"At the same time, I heard. That's why Euphy persuaded her husband to take him on. She was angry at Stanislaus. But she threw the Egyptian lass into the deal."

"Interesting. It also gave her another set of eyes and ears on her husband, if Stanislaus was reporting back to her. But I'm still not sure what it all means."

We lay there quietly for a while, watching clouds.

Accomplishing nothing.

"Do you know why we're not being followed?" I asked irritatedly, sitting up and looking back at Blachernae.

"Why?"

"Because whoever is plotting this knows we're not even close," I said. "Zintziphitzes was killed because he was a threat. Asan was killed, and I don't know why. But we've been so misdirected that it's not even worth keeping an eye on us, much less killing us."

"I guess from that perspective not being killed is kind of insulting," she replied.

"We have somehow been led down the garden path to a wrong tree, which we are now barking up. And I have this feeling that we're going to be too late."

"Don't say that," she said, sitting up and putting her arms around me.

"And it's more than just this," I said. "I get the sense that this may be part of some greater plot. Somewhere at the bottom of all this is a threat to the Fools' Guild. We've been operating behind the scenes for centuries without anyone being much the wiser, but our little secret band of manipulators is no longer a secret. First Malvolio infiltrated us; now we're being cut down one by one here."

"Except for Thalia," she reminded me.

"Those scars were real, and they weren't self-inflicted," I said. "Say what you will about the rest of her story, there's no question someone stabbed her in the back."

"Probably a jealous woman," muttered Aglaia.

"Peace, good wife," I said. "You have nothing to fear on that score. You are far superior to her in every respect."

"Including foolery?" she asked.

I kissed her. "Yes, including that. She can outdo you in tumbling, but that's about it."

We stood up and looked around. Still nobody watching us. All we could see were some cattle herders who had been there before we came, and a group of soldiers guarding some kind of construction activity.

"Varangians," I said, catching sight of their colors.

"Isn't that Henry?" she said as we walked in that direction.

"So it is," I said. "I wonder when he got back."

The Englishman hailed us from the top of another hill. The soldiers who we had most recently seen bathing were standing around, watching teams of prisoners linked by chains at their necks. The prisoners were attacking the hill with shovels, heaving the dirt into wagons. When a wagon became full, it was hauled over to a nearby ravine and emptied of its cargo.

"Hello, Feste," said Henry, coming over to join us. "What have you there? Looks like a woman under all of that whiteface."

"It is indeed, good Henry," I replied. "Meet Aglaia, my wife and colleague."

"Wife!" he exclaimed. "I had no idea you were married." He doffed his helmet and bowed. She returned the salute. He looked at her closely.

"I would almost swear that we've met before," he said. "Aglaia's your name?"

"It is," she replied. "But Aglaia has never met Henry, and Henry has never met Aglaia. You must be confusing me with another fool."

"That must be it," I agreed. "So, what brings you back into town so soon? It was just a few days ago that you were rotating out to the Double Column to guard Isaakios."

"Ah, they finally decided to stop coddling the old fellow," he said ruefully. "They're moving him to the prison at the Anemas Garrison tomorrow so they can keep a closer eye on a blind man. Since it's in Blachernae, it falls under the jurisdiction of the Imperial Guard. I tell you, it's no way to treat an emperor, deposed or not."

"It certainly isn't," I agreed.

"So, instead of cushy, meaningless guard duty at the Double Column, we get to stand around in the heat and watch these prisoners work."

"And what exactly is it that they are doing?" asked Aglaia.

"Well, milady," he said, scratching his head. "What they are doing is digging up this hill, the one we are standing upon, and taking the dirt, and dumping it into that ravine."

"I see," she said. "Thank you for that explanation."

"Oh, that's not an explanation," he said. "That's just what they're doing. What you wish to know is why they are doing it."

"Not every fool is in whiteface, I see," she said, smiling.

"What comes of hanging around you lot," he said, smiling back. "Well, one fine day, as it was told to me, the Emperor was riding back from a hunt, and passed by this very spot."

"Oh, happy spot, to be passed by such an Emperor," I said.

"It was not a happy day for the spot, as it turned out," continued Henry. "He had had a bad hunt, and was in a foul mood. His eye fell upon that ravine over there. He said, 'I do not like that ravine.' He then saw this hill."

"The one we are standing upon," said Aglaia.

"Indeed, milady. And he said, 'I do not like that hill much, either.' And then, being the all-powerful monarch that he is, he gives an order to have the hill leveled, and the dirt used to fill in that ravine, thus killing two birds with one stone."

"Thus does tyranny make the world flat," I said. "And you get to stand around and watch it happen. Fortunate old you."

He spat.

"It's ridiculous," he said softly. "There are walls to rebuild, ships to construct, troops to train. The empire is falling apart, and he has us doing this. Do you know why? Because when it's done, he's going to have more vineyards put in, because the imperial imbibing requires more wine than there is in all of Byzantium. I tell you, the old Emperor wouldn't have treated us like this. But that's why Alexios does, because the Varangians were Isaakios's favorites."

"That's too bad," I said.

"So, how is it with you? Last I saw, you were getting ready to play the Hippodrome."

"I did well. The Emperor liked me so much that I am now a regular visitor at Blachernae."

"What happened to Claudius?"

"Vanished. I suppose he got tired of being treated like a servant."

"Hm," he said. He glanced at Aglaia for a moment, then shook his head. "Say, did you happen to see who won the guards' footrace?"

"As a matter of fact, I did. Sorry, it wasn't a Varangian. An Imperial Guard named Lasparas."

"I knew it!" he crowed. He turned and shouted up the hill. "Hey, Cnut! Come down here. You owe me money, boy!"

Cnut came strolling down the hill.

"What for?" he said.

"Lasparas won the footrace at the Hippodrome."

Cnut's face fell, and he dug into his pouch and threw a coin to Henry.

"I can't believe I keep losing like this," he said. "I'm going to have to give up betting at this rate."

"It might be a sound policy," I agreed. "How long has it been since you've won one?"

"Must have been nearly a year ago," he said.

"Right," agreed Henry. "When Simon won that footrace on the Mese."

"Simon used to race?" I said. "I never would have guessed."

"Like the wind," said Henry. "We used to bet on him regularly.

Well, a pleasure to see you both. I'd invite you to perform at the baths again, but seeing as you have a lady partner now . . . unless she could do the act blindfolded."

"I'll have to practice that for a while," said Aglaia. "Well met, good Henry."

We walked off.

"Good thing I'm wearing whiteface," she commented. "I swear I was blushing underneath." She stopped and looked at me. "What is it?"

I grabbed her by the shoulders.

"When I told you Simon was a Templar, you said something was odd about that. What was it?"

She thought back.

"I was almost asleep," she remembered. "But I remember you saying that, and I said you wouldn't expect to see a Templar here."

"Why not?"

"The Templars are set up along pilgrim routes to the Holy Land. We have a couple in Orsino. Constantinople was never one of their stops, because pilgrims usually go by sea once they reach Italy or Dalmatia. The Byzantines prey upon pilgrims, so they avoid Byzantium like the plague. I suppose he could have just retired here, but I thought it was an odd choice. The ones I've met generally retire near active Templar sites."

"You're right, you're right," I said excitedly.

"Why is this important?" she asked.

"A year ago, Simon was running races," I said. "Now, he walks with a limp."

"So, he hurt his leg," she said.

"Yes, but when? When I was bathing, after you had gone to see about the horses, he joined me. We compared notes about our scars."

"Men," she shuddered.

"He told me that his limp was the result of a spear thrust during the Crusades. But he couldn't have been winning footraces a year ago if that was the case. So, he's lying about how he got it."

"Why?"

"Did you hear the one about the man who challenged a dwarf to a duel?"

She looked at me, realization dawning.

"How does it go?" she asked softly.

"He was in over his head. The little bastard stabbed him in the leg."

"Niko," she breathed. "It must have been. But we have no way of proving this. And how does it tie in to the plot to kill Alexios?"

"It doesn't," I said triumphantly.

"Now, you've really lost me. Why not?"

"Because there never was a plot to kill Alexios. We've been chasing around after something that doesn't exist and never has. That's why we haven't been followed."

"Wait a minute. If there's no plot, why were all the fools killed?"

"I didn't say there wasn't a plot. I said, there was never a plot to kill Alexios."

"But there is a plot?"

"Yes."

"A plot worth killing that many people?"

"Yes."

"And who is this plot against?"

"The Emperor."

She stood there, fuming.

"As someone once said, 'That, that is, is,' " she said. "There is not a plot against Alexios, but there is a plot against the Emperor."

"Correct."

"I am thinking about plotting against you right now," she said. "Alexios is the Emperor, is he not?"

"Last time I checked."

"I give up. Exactly what are you talking about?"

"What were Zintziphitzes' words when he repeated the conversation he overheard?"

She closed her eyes and summoned up the conversation. " 'This will be interesting. I've never killed an emperor before.' "

"Very good. Think about that for a moment. Not *the* Emperor, *an* emperor."

"But that's silly," she protested. "How many emperors..." Then she stopped.

I smiled at her, and she smiled back.

"There are two emperors," she said. "That that is, and that that was. The man who kills Isaakios will be killing an emperor. That's what you're talking about."

"Correct, my love. And I think that man is Simon. I don't know if he's acting for the Knights of the Temple, or if he's working for someone else, but he's in place, waiting."

"Waiting for what?"

"Waiting for Isaakios to be moved to a place where Simon has access. The Varangians are still protective toward Isaakios despite their avowed loyalty to the current Emperor. There's no way they would plot against him. So, arrangements had to be made to remove Isaakios from their hands. Only Alexios has been dragging his feet on that. He only made up his mind to do it today."

"But Isaakios is being moved into another prison. How does that make it any easier to get at him?"

"Because the prison at the Anemas Garrison is controlled by the Imperial Guard. They owe Isaakios no loyalty."

Aglaia thought for a moment.

"Zintziphitzes said the conversation came from Philoxenites' box at the Hippodrome," she said. "Philoxenites wasn't there on the day it happened. Simon delivered wineskins to the games, so he could have met someone there easily. And if he was meeting an Imperial Guardsman in an empty box, nobody would suspect anything because the guards are supposed to be patrolling there." She snapped her fingers. "When we first met Stanislaus, it was at the Rooster. Kind of a long way to go for a drink. We thought he was checking us out for Thalia."

"But first someone had to tell him we were there. And he knew about Asan's death. I thought he had heard about it from Thalia, but maybe his source is Simon. Considering that he told her he was having me watched to see who was trying to kill me, and not only is there no one trying to kill me but no one else watching for anyone trying to kill me, then that was a lie. And since he's been one of the people urging Alexios to transfer Isaakios to Anemas, that makes him a prime candidate for this conspiracy."

"Captain Stanislaus, the loyal soldier."

"He's loyal, all right. But not to Constantinople."

"To whom, then?"

"He came through with Frederick on the last Crusade. He came back here rather than go all the way home. I'm guessing he's still working for the Swabians."

"Still, we have no proof. We have evidence of some lies, but nothing we can use to convince anyone."

"The only proof we can get is to catch them in the act and stop them."

She looked at me.

"In order to catch them in the act, you are going to have to be with Isaakios," she said.

"Yes. I have some ideas on how to do that."

"I have a feeling I'm not going to be happy about any of them."

"Probably not, but if I'm right, we don't have much time. Isaakios arrives at the garrison tomorrow."

"What do you want me to do?"

"Go get Thalia."

"Why?" she asked indignantly. "What can she do that I cannot? And how can you trust her to do anything?"

"I want to find out if I can trust her. If I can, then I can use her. Bring her to Father Esaias's church. Use the password—don't let her know you're just an apprentice. Tell her it's urgent, and make sure she doesn't leave any word for Stanislaus."

"All right," she said.

"Viola?"

"Yes, Feste?"

"She carries four knives. Keep her hands in sight."

"All right."

I hurried down the river to Saint Stephen's. It was late afternoon, and the penitents had yet to gather. Father Melchior was standing inside the entrance. He nodded when he saw me and motioned me toward the steps to the crypts.

"I am expecting two of my colleagues to join us," I informed him. "Two women."

"Very good, my son. I shall escort them down when they arrive. You are expected. Go right on in."

I went downstairs to the altar, knocked on the secret panel, and entered when it slid open. Father Theodore was standing just inside, sword in hand. He brought me to Father Esaias, who was sitting on a chair, sipping from a jeweled goblet. He beckoned me forward, and I knelt in front of him.

"Greetings, my son," he said. "How may I help you in your hour of need?"

"O Ghostly Father," I said. "Teach me that I may go to prison."

SEVENTEEN

The voice I hear this passing night was heard
In ancient days by emperor and clown.
KEATS, *ODE TO A NIGHTINGALE*

I must confess that I have never received such a request," Father Easias said. "Most of my flock consult me on how to escape from prisons."

"I have my reasons."

"A fool with reasons," he said thoughtfully. "Well, basically there are two ways to go to prison. You could say something nasty about someone important, but since you are now the Emperor's Fool, you have license to ridicule both high and low. Or, more certainly, you could commit a crime and get caught."

"Let me clarify," I said. "I need to get into a specific prison, perform a certain task, and then get out again."

"Which prison?"

"The Tower of Anemas."

He sat back and folded his hands.

"I may not be of much help to you here," he said. "We stay out of Blachernae. We don't want to rouse the sleeping giant. As long as they can wander their walled-off portion safely, they assume the rest of Constantinople is similarly crime-free."

"I see."

"It's too bad you don't want to go into the Praetorian prison.

We have a lovely set-up there. The warden pens them in by day, then releases them to loot at night. We all split the take, and the Vigla roam the streets looking for felons who are already locked up. We have the same deal at the Chalke prison. But we can't get at Anemas. Am I to understand that you have found the man you are looking for?"

"I believe so."

"And he is currently in the Tower of Anemas?"

"No. But if I am correct, he will be soon."

"I think that you had better tell me everything."

To think, of all the people in this city, our greatest ally might be this master of corruption. Yet I needed his help. So, I told him my suspicions. To my relief, they made sense to him.

"There is a simple solution," he said. "I send my men to kill Simon now."

"Simple, but not the best solution," I said. "First, he's not that easy to kill. Second, if you just kill him at the Rooster, the conspiracy remains intact. He's just the arrow. We need the men holding the bow. If, on the other hand, we catch him in the attempt, then we have something to take to the authorities."

"What authorities? Will you make a case to the Emperor?"

"No. He may not care that much. I have an idea on that subject, but I need to live through this first part."

"Very well. While we're waiting, I'll send one of my men to keep an eye on our erring tapster."

Father Theodore slipped out of the room.

"I am expecting two of my colleagues to join us," I said.

"Your wife being one, I expect. I heard about her arrival and rapid ascent in the Empress's retinue. Quite a talented woman."

"She is."

"And the other?"

"Thalia, former fool to the Empress."

"I thought you said she was dead," he said sharply.

"I did. My apologies."

"It's sad when there cannot be complete trust between people," he said. "However, under the circumstances, you are forgiven. Why do you think Asan was killed?"

"He had an unfortunate habit of poking his nose where it didn't belong. My guess is that he discovered something about Simon, and tried to use the information to pry some money out of him."

"And Simon did what anyone would do in response. He killed the lad, and then threw him into your room to divert suspicion from himself."

"And to throw me off the scent for a while. I thought the killing was meant to be an attempt on one of us."

Father Theodore returned, escorting two cowled figures.

"The ladies have arrived," he announced.

The cowls came off to reveal a pair of fools: one, an old lover; the other, my wife.

"My dears," said Father Esaias, rising and approaching them. "These bare quarters are graced by such loveliness. Mistress Thalia, I am delighted to see you alive."

"Thank you, Father."

"And, my lady Aglaia, I have heard so much about you in such a short time that I must kiss your hand in greeting."

She rolled her eyes at me as he did.

"Actually, we've already met," she said.

"Have we? Surely not. I would have remembered such a charming encounter."

"What she is saying is that Aglaia was Claudius," I explained.

Thalia turned to look at her in shock.

"You're Claudius!" she exclaimed.

"The same, mistress," said Aglaia in Claudius's voice. "I suppose that means you won't want to flirt with me now."

"And you're Theo's wife."

"It's Feste, now," I said. "Please remember that."

"Nicely done, Apprentice," said Thalia, looking her over critically. "I couldn't have managed that disguise. But then, no one could possibly mistake me for a man."

"What a coincidence," returned Aglaia sweetly. "I couldn't manage your disguise. But then, no one could possibly mistake me for a slut."

I held my breath as the two of them glowered at each other, waiting to see if either would go for a weapon.

Thalia grinned suddenly. "Insult given, insult received," she said. "You pass, Apprentice. All right, Feste. What's this all about?"

"I think we had all better sit down," I said, and we took our places around the table.

"Some wine?" offered Father Esaias.

"I wouldn't say no," said Thalia, and he poured for everyone. "But I thought this was a meeting of some urgency."

"So it is," I said. "First, we have to discuss your future."

"Meaning?" asked Thalia.

"Whether or not you are going to have one," I said.

She started, spilling her wine. Father Theodore was standing behind her, sword at the ready.

"What is this about, Theo?" she asked.

"The time has come for you to make a choice," I said. "The Guild or your lover."

"Stan? What does he have to do with any of this?"

"He is part of the group that killed our colleagues."

"No," she said, shaking her head furiously. "He couldn't have done that. He loves me. He saved my life."

"He may very well love you. He may have saved your life despite having first arranged for your death. Or maybe once you survived the attack, he decided it might be useful to keep you alive in case the Guild sent someone else. You gave him the password. Who knows what else he learned? Did you tell him that Zintziphitzes had overheard the conversation between the conspirators, and could possibly identify their voices?"

She was silent for a long moment, then nodded.

"I'm sorry," she said. "I thought he was helping me."

An enormous wave of relief passed over me. I had thought that we would end up killing her.

"Zintziphitzes lived on while the other fools were killed," I said. "But then I made the mistake of sharing what I knew about him with you. And within two days, he was murdered. Which meant that either you killed him, or you told someone who did."

"The dangers of trusting a lover," she said. "I guess we both made that mistake, eh, Theo?"

Aglaia stiffened for a moment. I patted her hand, and she relaxed.

"Will you help us now?" I asked her.

"Yes. Name the oath you want me to take, and I will swear it."

"Swear by Zintziphitzes' tomb," I said.

"Then by Zintziphitzes' tomb, I will do whatever the Guild requires of me."

"Are we satisfied?" I asked the others. They nodded, Aglaia reluctantly. "Let me tell you what I think is happening. Last year, Isaakios and his daughter, Irene, managed to arrange for the escape of his son, Alexios. Irene no doubt drew upon the resources of her husband, Philip of Swabia. The escape was in early autumn, but the planning must have been going on for some time.

"However, Philip had more than just an interest in reuniting his wife's family. He's one of the powers behind the Crusade that's gathering in Venice."

"But what does a Crusade have to do with all of this?" asked Thalia. "They want to liberate the Holy Land."

"Most of them do. But others see the Crusaders as an available army. The Swabians have had their eyes on this city ever since the last Crusade came through here. The Byzantines treated the Swabians and their allies badly. Philip lost his father, Frederick, and a brother on that journey. He hasn't forgotten. Once Alexios was in his hands, he had a ready-made cause to rally the troops around: to restore the boy to his rightful position as Emperor."

"And puppet, of course," added Father Esaias.

"Of course. But there was one stumbling block. The boy Alexios's path to the throne was as the heir to Isaakios. But you cannot inherit something until the prior claimant dies. So, Isaakios's life became forfeit. And if he died in an Imperial prison, then they could add revenge to the boy's claim of right.

"So, even as the escape was being arranged by Irene, her husband Philip set into motion this conspiracy, using Swabian agents who have been in place since the end of the last Crusade, still loyal to the memory of Frederick Barbarossa. It was necessary for them to have Isaakios transferred to Anemas to rid him of his Varangian protectors, so Stanislaus maneuvered his way from the Empress's court to the Emperor's. And it took him this long to convince the Emperor to move his brother. He probably has been suggesting the idea privately to other Imperial advisers, any number of whom might want to rid the world of Isaakios for their own reasons.

"Then Zintziphitzes overheard that fateful conversation. He brought it to the fools, and somehow during their investigation, they made the conspirators aware of them. One of the fools must have been taken first and tortured to give up the rest. Or maybe the conspirators decided to eliminate all of the fools just to be safe. But they never knew about Zintziphitzes, for he was not part of the Guild."

"And your proof will be if Simon shows up in Anemas to assassinate Isaakios," said Aglaia.

"Yes. I mean to be in there to stop him. Which brings us back to how I can manage that."

Thalia laughed suddenly.

"It's simple," she said. "You're the Emperor's fool. Have him send you in to entertain the prisoners. It will be an act of charity that will assuage his guilty soul."

We looked around at each other.

"That will work," agreed Father Esaias. "But you will have only the one opportunity. If you have the wrong day, then it will be hard for you to get back in on short notice."

"Which is where you come in," I said to Thalia.

"How?" she asked.

"Find out from Stanislaus when the deed is to be done," I said.

She gave me a hard stare.

"You mean, sleep with him and get it out of him that way," she said bitterly.

"You've been sleeping with him," I pointed out impatiently, "for a few years, now."

"But this is different, and you know it," she snapped. "This isn't pleasure anymore. But that's all right with you, isn't it? That's what I've become—Thalia, the Guild Whore."

"Don't you understand?" I shouted. "This isn't about you. There is an invasion coming! A bloody war that could kill thousands and lay the empire to waste!"

She sat in silence, stunned. I took a deep breath and continued.

"But if we keep Isaakios alive and take away the boy's claim to the throne, then that may be the one thing that can stop the war. Everyone in the Guild has done horrible things for the sake of peace. Why should this be any different?"

"You don't have to sleep with him," Aglaia said softly to Thalia. I turned to look at her. "You can get the information another way. Given what he's done to you, and to your friends, I wouldn't waste any more time on him. Get him alone, get him undressed, then hit him with something hard and tie him up."

"And then?"

"I've been told you carry four knives," said Aglaia. "Use all of them."

Thalia looked at her, and smiled slowly. It was the coldest smile I have ever seen in my life.

Father Melchior came in and whispered something to Father Esaias.

"Simon's not at the Rooster," Esaias informed us. "His belongings have been cleared out. Someone else is tending bar and cooking for him, but he doesn't know where Simon went."

"Gone to ground," I said. "Probably already in Blachernae somewhere."

"I'll be back in the morning," said Thalia. "I'll have the information."

She left.

"I have to go, too," said Aglaia.

"One of my men will escort you to Blachernae," said Father Esaias. "And I'm having another follow Thalia, just to be safe. I am now going to turn my back for a moment so that the two of you may embrace."

He stood and contemplated a bust of Homer by the fireplace.

"Good night, Apprentice," I said, and I kissed her.

"What terrible things will I be doing for the Guild, I wonder?" she asked.

"None tonight," I said.

She left.

"Would you rather stay here tonight?" offered Esaias. "It's the safest place in the city for you."

"No, I'll go back to the Rooster," I said. "I want to keep up appearances in case anyone wants to check up on me."

"Very well," he said. "But Stephanos will be watching your door, and more of my men will be guarding the Rooster."

"Thank you. I'm putting you to a lot of bother."

"It's no bother," he said, and I could see him smiling under the cowl. "We're up at night, anyway."

I woke before dawn. When I opened my door, Stephanos was standing in the hallway, watching the stairs. He nodded to me politely as I passed him, then went into his room to sleep. I walked outside to see the sun rise, but clouds blocked it from view. I did my stretching and tumbling exercises, the same routine that they taught me at the Guildhall so many years ago. The left leg was limber, but warned me of an oncoming storm. As if I needed to be told.

Father Esaias was up and about when I arrived at Saint Stephen's. A tray of bread, still warm from the oven, was on the table, and he motioned me to help myself. A good fool makes sure that he eats, no matter what, so I forced myself to swallow some.

There was a rap on the panel, and Father Melchior brought in Thalia. She sat down wordlessly and helped herself to a goblet of wine, which she gulped in a second. She refilled it, then held it in salute to me.

"To the Guild," she said, and finished it off.

I waited.

"It's tonight," she said. "Simon's somewhere in Blachernae. The Imperial Guard changes shifts at sundown. The two men guarding the entrance at night are in on it. Simon will be carrying a wine-skin for delivery to the prison garrison. Then he will continue on to the lowest level, where Isaakios is being held."

"And Stanislaus?"

She held my gaze steady.

"He won't be reporting for duty today," she said. "And that's it for me."

"Thank you, Thalia. That was good work. If I survive the night, I'll try and get you restored to the Empress's court."

"You don't understand, Theo," she said. "I meant, that's it for me and the Guild. I'm not doing it anymore. I let all of you down."

"No, you didn't. You were nearly killed. You can't blame your-self for that."

"Yes, I can. I was careless, and then I let myself be used. And Zintziphitzes died because of that."

She started crying.

"And eight years ago, you abandoned me without so much as saying good-bye," she continued. "That hurt so much."

"I left you a note," I protested.

"A note. After all we had been for each other, you couldn't find me. Then you show up years later married to another fool, and treat me like a common drab."

"I'm sorry," I said. "For everything."

"I'm not in a particularly forgiving mood right now. I've just spent the night torturing a man to death, Theo. For the Guild. For another one of our useless battles. We can't change anything, Theo. Can't you see that? The forces against us are too powerful."

"I don't accept that," I said softly. "But if you want to quit, go ahead. What do you want me to tell the Guild?"

"Tell them I'm dead," she said. "I might as well be. Tell them that I died with the others. Thalia is no more. I have to flee Constantinople, anyway. I've murdered an Imperial captain."

"Here," I said, handing her my purse.

She opened it, and stared at the money.

"This is too much," she said. "I can't take this."

"I don't need it," I said. "We're set. Here, take it. It will help you find a new life somewhere. Buy yourself a small farm; find yourself someone who will be around all the time. Have a family."

She tucked it into her waistband and stood.

"I ran away from a farm when I was nine," she said. "From a father who beat me when I wouldn't submit to him. I was on the streets for two years until the Guild found me and made me a jester. I may not be a jester anymore, but I will never go back to a farm."

"You could work for me," offered Esaias. "I could find a great deal of use for a woman with talents like yours. And I don't mean prostitution. I mean thievery, the most honored of crafts."

"Thank you, I suppose," she said. "But I must turn you down, Father. No offense, but I haven't sunk that low yet."

And she walked out.

"Oh, but you will, my child," murmured Esaias. "Of that much I am certain."

I picked up my bag and lute and slung them over my shoulders.

"You could go to the authorities with what you know now," commented Esaias.

"With the words of a dead man, as related by the woman who has killed him and fled?" I said.

"Perhaps not," he said. "Good luck, then. Our desires converge on this venture, albeit for different reasons."

"Thank you, Father," I said.

He made the sign of the Cross over me, and I left for Blachernae.

The Emperor was in a black mood when I arrived.

"It's wrong, Fool. All wrong," he muttered. "I shouldn't have listened to them. So what if he's blind? Anemas is still a hellhole. It's where we put people to suffer. It was a weak moment when I gave in, and I can't go back on it now because I'll look indecisive, and I can't have that."

"I understand, milord," I said. "Still, it is a shame to think of him so immured, lacking even the simple entertainment that he had before. The confinement of the body is not nearly as grievous as the confinement of the mind."

"I am trying to see how that is supposed to cheer me up," he said. "That's what I pay you to do."

"Merely a preamble to what I was about to suggest, milord."

"What's that?"

"That you would do me great honor if you would permit me to go into this underworld and entertain your brother, if only for the one night. It might ease the transition for him."

He looked at me, his eyes watering.

"Good Fool, you put me to shame," he said. "Your generosity of heart and spirit rival any that I have seen in the Church."

"Your Majesty flatters me," I said, bowing. Actually, I considered that faint praise, but it was not the moment to debate the point.

The Emperor turned to his guards, then stopped.

"Where is Captain Stanislaus?" he complained.

One of the guards stepped forward.

"A maidservant left word with us this morning," he said. "The

Captain is ill, and did not wish to expose Your Majesty to any contagion."

Nice touch, Thalia, I thought.

"How very considerate," said Alexios. "Well, fetch the Keeper of the Imperial Inkstand, would you?"

The guard vanished, and soon returned with the official, a grandiose fellow in maroon robes. He did not actually carry the inkstand and pen himself, but with two snaps of his fingers directed a pair of servants to kneel before the throne and proffer the sacred items on silver salvers to the Emperor.

"How long do you plan to be at it?" he asked.

"Sire, I will go upon completion of my duties to Your Majesty, and will stay there all night if need be."

He took a piece of paper, scribbled on it, and then sealed it.

"There," he said, handing it to me. "You will be rewarded for this, I promise you."

I bowed and tucked the document into my doublet.

There still was the day's entertainment to get through, but fortunately I was dismissed shortly after his luncheon. I needed to get inside before the evening shift came on. I couldn't risk being stopped by Stanislaus's compatriots.

Aglaia intercepted me before I left the palace. I transferred my juggling cutlery to her so that I could pass inspection at the prison. We discussed our plan of action.

"There is one basic flaw in your idea," she said as she walked me to the Empress's entrance.

"What is that?"

"Simon will probably be armed. You won't be. He's bigger than you, he's faster than you, and he has already killed several of our colleagues, all of whom had Guild training. What makes you think you can beat him?"

"Because I know he's coming. And because, at the bottom of it all, I am the master of survival."

She placed her hand on my cheek.

"You had better be right," she said.

"I will see you in the morning, Duchess," I said, and kissed her lightly on the forehead.

"Not nearly good enough," she said, and pulled my head down to hers.

The Tower of Anemas was set against the wall that protected Blachernae from without. It was named for some long-forgotten prisoner. There were various legends as to who he was, my favorite being that he was the architect who designed the tower, only to find himself its first resident upon its completion.

The garrison was next to the tower, providing quarters for several squadrons of the Imperial Guard. No bathhouses here, but a nearby gate led to a small beach by the Golden Horn given to their exclusive use.

The entrance to the prison was at the base of the tower. Some noblewomen, either wives of prisoners or just good people on missions of mercy, were leaving as I came up, some weeping, some carrying empty baskets, all clutching handkerchiefs to their faces. The entryway exuded a pestilential odor, although the guards seemed oblivious to it. The storm predicted by my leg hit just as I walked through the door, sheets of water cutting us off from the rest of the world.

I showed my order from the Emperor to the guards outside. They motioned me into a small office where the commander of the day watch read it over carefully.

"Well, nice of His Majesty to care," he said. "Hands against the wall, spread your legs."

I complied while he patted me down for weapons.

"You're a thorough man," I observed. "Keep it up, I might begin to enjoy it."

"I already am," he said. "What's in the bag?"

"My props for entertaining," I said, holding it open.

He inspected it, emptying its contents out onto the table. Although I had left my knives and swords behind, the clubs gave him pause.

"You could kill a man with these," he said, hefting one and rapping it on the wall.

"That wasn't my intention," I said.

"Nevertheless, I'm keeping them here," he said. "You can take the rest. I'll have one of my men take you down."

"Down?" I asked, gathering my lute and remaining gear. "I thought the prison was in the tower."

"The tower guards the wall," he said. "The prison is beneath it."

He gave an order, and one of his men took a lit torch from a sconce in the wall.

"This way, Fool," he said.

I followed him through another door that led to a flight of steps leading down. When we reached the bottom, he seized an iron ring at our feet and pulled open a heavy wooden trapdoor over another stairway that vanished into the darkness six feet beneath us.

"He's down there," he said.

"Thank you."

He watched as I started cautiously down the steps.

"What about the torch?" I asked, turning to look back up at him.

"It stays with me," he said.

"But there's no light down there. How am I supposed to perform?"

"Not my problem," he said. "Have a good time."

My head had barely cleared the entrance when the door crashed over me, eliminating whatever view I still had of the world. I heard bars set into place over it, and for a brief, panicky moment wondered if I had been betrayed, tricked into some oubliette and abandoned. There was a rough, wooden rail on my right, fortunately, and I gripped it tightly as I felt for each step with my foot. I do not know how many steps I descended. I was beginning to think that the stairway might go straight to Hades, and that I might meet Orpheus himself coming back up, when I suddenly hit floor and the railing ended.

I ventured forward slowly, reaching out with both arms. Before I had gone five steps, a voice cried out, "Halt!"

"Hello?" I said.

"Please move two steps to your right," it continued. "You were about to kick over the slops bucket."

"That would have been messy," said another voice to my right. "Tell you what; stay where you are, and I'll move it out of your way."

"Thank you," I said.

I heard a chain rattle, and sensed a body shuffling quickly in my direction.

"Got it," said the second man. "I'm putting it over by me in case anyone needs it."

"I'm sorry," I said. "But I can't see anything."

There was a low chuckle coming from all directions.

"Join the club," said another. "The Fraternity of the Gouged. Don't worry, you'll get used to it."

"Poor fellow," said a deep voice. "Are you in much pain?"

"Thank you for your concern, but I am not blind," I said.

"Really? Then you're in the wrong dungeon. You really should complain," he said, and the room echoed with the raucous laughter of the others.

"I am in the right room," I said. "That is, if this is where the Emperor is."

There was silence.

"Who are you?" came the deep voice.

"I am Feste, the Fool," I said. "I have been sent to entertain the Emperor Isaakios."

"Over here," said the deep voice.

"Are you the Emperor?"

"I speak for him," he said.

"Then how am I to know if he is here?" I asked. "For I am to entertain him, or my mission will fail."

"You're no fool," said an older, querulous voice. "You're an assassin."

"Excuse me?"

"You heard me," it continued. "You think I don't know why they brought me here? My brother is going to have me killed."

"Hush, my sovereign," said the deep voice. "Don't give away your location."

"My Lord Isaakios," I said. "I am here at the Emperor Alexios's behest. . . ."

"I am the Emperor," he shouted. "He is a usurper!"

"Forgive me, my Lord Emperor," I said. "I am just a jester. I have been sent to entertain you. If it will ease your mind, I will remain where I am, safely out of reach."

There was a pause.

"Are you truly a jester?" asked Isaakios.

"By King David, I swear it," I said. "By the First Fool, Our Savior, I swear it. By a pig's bladder, by a rotten vegetable hurled from a balcony, by a maltuned lute and the bottom of a cask, I swear it."

"He speaks as a fool," said one of the others.

"Well, if you are a fool, juggle for us," said Isaakios.

"Excuse me, milord?"

"Prove your foolish mettle. Juggle."

"Juggle in the dark for an audience who cannot see? Milords, this is more of a metaphor than a performance."

This provoked a few chuckles.

"The fools at my court could juggle blindfolded," said Isaakios.

"As can I," I replied. "But if you blindfold the audience, you don't have to juggle that well."

"But we can hear," he said. "Please."

I felt in my bag for three apples and sent them into the air. I felt the men stirring about me, leaning forward. The strangest performance I have ever given. In a sense, it was pure faith all around. I threw apples into the air, trusting my ability to do it accurately, knowing I had succeeded when they landed precisely in the opposite hand.

"What is it that you are juggling?" asked the deep voice.

"Apples, I think," I said. I passed one in front of my mouth and took a noisy bite out of it without breaking the flow. "Yes, apples," I said, crunching loudly. "Want one?"

"I have not had an apple in ages," he said. "Toss one over here."

I threw one in the direction of the voice. A second later, I heard him pluck it out of the air. "And one for the Emperor?" he requested. I threw him another, and heard this one caught as well.

"You're very deft, my friend," I said.

"He's become my bodyguard," said Isaakios. "Thank you for the apple."

"You may want to have him taste it to make sure it's not poisoned," I said.

"I already did," said the deep voice.

[257]

"What about the rest of us?" cried another.

"Dear me, I hope I brought enough," I said, and started tossing apples around the room to where voices called for them. It took a dozen apples to feed my audience, and all I had left to sustain me through the night was the one I had taken a bite from at the commencement of the routine.

We sat around, munching in the darkness.

"What time of day was it when you entered, Fool?" asked Isaakios.

"Late afternoon, milord. I understand that you arrived this morning."

"Yes, along with my friend with the sepulchral voice," he said. "Interesting place, this tower. I remember touring it once when I first came to Blachernae. Never wanted to go back, although I put my share of prisoners here. None of them in this room, fortunately."

"No, sir," called another. "You are among friends, here."

"Perhaps, Fool, you might have some insight into a philosophical debate we were having before your arrival," said Isaakios. "We were discussing Plato's allegory of the cave. Are you familiar with it?"

"I read it a long time ago, milord. Could you refresh my memory?"

"In it, Socrates posited a cave with prisoners chained so that they could only look straight ahead at a wall. They had no experience of the world outside the cave. All they knew of it was from a parade of shadows cast upon the wall in front of them, made by men behind them carrying objects before a fire. To these prisoners, the shadows were reality."

"I remember it now, milord," I said. "And what was your debate about?"

"Whether we, as blind men in a dungeon without light, but with knowledge and memories of the world, are better off than Socrates' unenlightened prisoners. What say you, Fool?"

"It seems to me, milord, that knowledge is better than ignorance."

"Yet, those prisoners did not know that the world could be any better than what they already knew. We do. With this knowledge comes despair. With ignorance comes bliss. I would conclude that we are the worse for our situation."

"Then you are the fool, milord, not I."

"Your argument being what?"

"From good old Ecclesiastes, milord. 'I the Preacher was king over Israel in Jerusalem.' Just as you were king, milord. And he does say, 'For in much wisdom is much grief: and he that increaseth knowledge increaseth sorrow.'"

"So, he agrees with me."

"No, milord, for he still concludes that 'Wisdom excelleth folly, as far as light excelleth darkness.' So you see, milords, you cannot even begin to compare yourselves to Socrates' cave dwellers, for you are wise, and your wisdom lights up this wretched space so that no shadows may deceive you. This preacher, they say, was the wisest man who ever lived, and how may a fool such as I even begin to gainsay him?"

"You're a bit of a preacher yourself, aren't you, Fool?" observed Isaakios.

"Just a seeker of knowledge, like all true fools."

"Then I hope that you may find it in your travels."

"Thank you, milord."

"Did they let you bring any music with you?"

"I have a lute, milord. Shall I play?"

"That would please all of us."

I needed no eyes for this, of course. I began a soft melody, thinking to sing through the night. But the tune prompted Isaakios to speak again.

"I owe my life to a fool," he said.

"Really, milord? How could one as lowly as me preserve such an exalted person as yourself?"

"It was during Andronikos's reign. Were you in Constantinople then?"

"No, milord, but I have heard tales told."

"The worst ones are all true, yet they do not begin to encompass the depravity of that monster. He relied upon auguries of all kinds to guess who would be the man to depose him. One day, the suspicion fell upon me, and he sent his favorite executioner, a fellow with the inappropriate surname of Hagiochristophorites, to arrest me. I was living in the southwest part of the city, then, as far from Blachernae as I could get. I was lying in my bed, oblivious to all danger, when a voice roused me, crying, 'Awake, Angelos, for the hour of your doom is at hand! Take your sword in hand and strike a blow for your city. Your city will follow you if you do.' "

"Remarkable," I said.

"No sooner had I sword in hand than this executioner burst into my courtyard with his attendants. I had no time for armor. I leapt upon my horse and rode at him, shrieking at the top of my lungs. I took him by surprise and cut him in two.

"And then I galloped all the way down the Mese to the Hagia Sophia, calling to all along the way to join me, telling them what I had done. I stood on the pulpit and confessed my crime, and before I knew it, I was leading a revolution."

He sighed.

"I had thought that the voice came from Heaven," he said.

"That I was chosen to become Emperor through Divine inspiration. And when I became Emperor, I thought that I myself was divinity.

"But then, one day some years later, one of my fools was entertaining. A fellow named Chalivoures. Did you know him?"

"I did, milord. A most witty fool."

"He was, he was. With a most distinctive voice. I suddenly recognized it as the one alerting me to my oncoming assailant. I tried to thank him, but he denied any knowledge of what I was talking about. I could tell that he was lying. Finally, he allowed me to reward him. I gave him free rein in the Imperial Wine Cellar."

"A most generous reward," I commented.

"In retrospect, not so generous," said Isaakios. "He drank himself to death within the year."

"A happy death for a fool," I said. "One I myself might have chosen."

"Still, it was quite a comedown to learn that one's divine inspiration was out of the mouth of a common jester. And a few years later, I was deposed by my loving brother. So much for divinity."

"He treated you most cruelly," said one of the other prisoners.

"No, he did what I would have done in his place," said Isaakios. "Indeed, he had my blinding performed by the best of surgeons to ensure my survival. Andronikos would have just done it himself and butchered the job in the process."

He stopped, contemplating his fate. I strummed quietly on, and could soon hear snoring from a few of my companions.

Then I heard a chain rustle as one of them sat up.

"Someone's coming," he said quietly.

I stopped playing and stood up. I couldn't hear anything, but I trusted the powers of the blind in this instance. Sure enough, a slow, heavy tread approached the dungeon. Then the bars were removed, the trapdoor lifted, and light from a single torch filled the area.

I held my hand over my eyes until they adjusted to the sudden return of sight. Around me, the prisoners were rising to their feet. I could see them for the first time. Some were chained, others loose. In the corner farthest from the steps was a robust, red-headed man who could have been anywhere from forty to ninety, accompanied by a larger man with a matted, black beard.

A pair of massive boots. That was the first glimpse I saw of Simon as he came into the room. Massive legs, body, head. A torch in his left hand, and in his right was the same giant sword with which he had faced down Stephanos in the Rooster. A lifetime ago, it seemed. A lifetime lasts only as long as a person lives. Mine suddenly seemed too short.

"I was wondering when you would show up," I said.

He looked at me in surprise.

"Well, fancy meeting you here," he said. "Good. Saves me a trip."

"Who is he?" said a man to my left.

"One who wishes to kill Isaakios," I said. "And myself. Answer me a question, good tapster?"

"Why not?" he said, placing the torch in a crude sconce in the wall. "You're not going anywhere."

"Are you in fact one of the Knights Templar?"

"No, no. Merely a uniform I acquired from someone who wasn't using it anymore. I kept it in my room figuring you'd be sticking your head in sometime. Thought it might give you something else to think about."

"It did. You and Stanislaus must have had quite a few laughs on my account."

"We've laughed about many fools," he said. "And we'll have one more to laugh about later."

"I'm afraid you'll be laughing alone," I said.

He hesitated slightly, then held the sword in front of him.

"Is he dead then?"

"I'm afraid so," I said. "I hope you were paid in advance. But answer me this: if you're not a Templar, what are you? Where did you train?"

"I trained with an old man," he said. "On a mountain."

"The Cult of the Assassins," I said, nodding. "But now you're for hire."

"Yes," he said.

"Who hired you?"

"Part of the payment was for my discretion."

"Interesting. Oddly enough, I trained with an old man as well."

He gripped his sword with both hands, looking calm and relaxed.

"I've met several fools who trained with that old man," he said. "All of them dead, now. I put little stock in his training."

"Point taken," I said. "But I was his best pupil."

"As I was for my teacher."

"Excellent. Then we will see whose education is most fit for this match. And remember, my friend, that I will be having the assistance of these fine gentlemen."

He laughed as he surveyed the room.

"And remember, Fool, that in the country of the blind, the one-eyed man is king," he said, baring his teeth. "I have a sword, Fool. All you have for a weapon is that lute, and a sword beats a lute in my book."

"True enough," I said. "But I also have a bucket of slops."

I picked it up and heaved its contents at his head. He ducked, as I had planned, and the stream of human waste splatted against the torch set in the wall. The flames sputtered and went out.

"In the country of the blind, the advantage belongs to those who have lived there the longest," I said. "Gentlemen, the assassin's torch is out. You will know him by his smell."

Bodies rushed silently by me. I heard heavy chains swung through the air, a sword whistling through the darkness. Something metal hit something metal, and I heard a man cry out in pain.

"Fool," whispered the deep-voiced man at my ear. "If you have any weapon at all, give it to me. I will take care of him."

I snapped the strings on my lute and slid my hand inside its hollowed body. There was a dagger secured inside, hidden from the probing hands of the Imperial Guards. I handed it to my new ally, and waited.

There was a thud, a gasp, and a series of gurgling noises that quickly subsided. Then there was silence.

"He's dead, milord," said the deep-voiced man.

"Well done," said Isaakios. "My companions, my brethren. I am indebted to all of you. But is this not merely a temporary victory?"

"I think not, milord," I said. "They wanted an outside assassin so that no one could say the Imperial Guard killed you. At least, that's my guess. We'll try to convince your brother to transfer you back to the Double Column. The attempt on your life should persuade him."

"Who are you, Fool?" he asked. "Who do you work for?"

"I was a friend of Chalivoures," I said. "Hate to see his efforts go to waste."

I don't know how long we remained there. I could hear the rats as they discovered Simon's body. I fantasized that they were the

same ones who Zintziphitzes once befriended, but that was unlikely.

We slept in shifts. Blind men keeping watch, imagine that. But
they had accomplished what several Guild fools had not, so in
this particular place, there was no one I would rather have had
as my fellow soldiers.

I woke as one of them shook me.

"Someone else is coming," he whispered.

We all stood. Footsteps, bars moving, the trapdoor creaking
open. Then several Imperial Guards came down with torches and
drawn swords. They stood around and looked at Simon's body.
The haft of my dagger was sticking out of the front of his throat.
His sword lay beside him.

"What happened here?" asked an officer.

Isaakios stood before us, erect and in command.

"This man was allowed into our cell with weapons," he said
severely. "He has made an attempt upon our very life. We demand
to know who is responsible for this outrage."

The officer glanced around at his men.

"Where are the night watch?" he asked.

Uncertainty, shrugs from the others.

He looked at the rest of us, settling finally upon me.

"What are you doing here?" he asked.

Quaking, I held my Imperial Order in front of me.

"Begging your pardon, General," I squeaked. "I don't know
exactly what happened, it was so dark, but this man, the dead
one, he came in shouting for the head of the Emperor, and there
was fighting, and I couldn't tell who did what, I just want to get
out of this horrid place, I'm the Emperor's Fool, he sent me here,
he's expecting me back, he'll be livid if I'm not there."

"Get him out of here," ordered the officer. "Then we'll try
and sort this mess out."

I bowed quickly to the prisoners and was hustled up and out of the Tower of Anemas.

It was dawn. The storm had passed. The sun was rising across the Bosporos, and Aglaia was standing outside the prison door, waiting.

"Good morning, Fool," she said.

"Good morning, milady," I replied. "I trust you slept well."

"Not a wink," she said. "I saw Simon go in around midnight. I never saw him come out."

"If you want to see him come out, we can wait for a bit," I said. "It may take a while. He's rather heavy."

She wrapped her arms around me.

"I guess the Rooster will be needing a new tapster," she said.

"I suppose so," I said. "I was thinking of moving out of there, anyway. I'm tired of the place."

She led me back into the palace, where I slept for a whole hour before I had to work again.

EPILOGUE

Herein thou hast done foolishly: therefore from henceforth thou shalt have wars.

II CHRONICLES 16:9

Despite Tantalo's efforts, the city of Zara could not reach a peaceful accommodation with the Venetians. When the siege commenced, the Christian citizens hung crucifixes over the walls to rebuke their Christian attackers. Nevertheless, the city was taken in November and many put to the sword.

Aglaia had brought our information about the conspiracy to Philoxenites while I was spending the night in the Tower of Anemas. We believed that he would appreciate the usefulness of keeping Isaakios alive in case the Crusaders followed his son to Constantinople. Always good to have options. The two Imperial Guards who allowed Simon entry to the prison disappeared that same night. A few more residents of Swabian origin quietly vanished over the next few months. When I mentioned this to the Imperial Treasurer, he shrugged, and the two Varangians in his office looked studiously out the window.

My wife and I decided to take a set of rooms south of the Blachernae wall, the better to give us the run of the entire city. Palaces are so confining. We continued to entertain our royal clients on a daily basis, but also performed in the various markets, just to keep in touch.

A letter by way of a sympathetic merchant reached Fat Basil in Thessaloniki. A month later, I saw a stripling youth in muddied motley juggling six rings while balanced on one foot. What made the trick even more remarkable was that the foot was on top of a six-foot pole. His name was Plossus. He was a new graduate of the Guild, and quickly learned the ins and outs of this vast city. He settled near the Hippodrome, and became a great favorite of the factions there.

A few weeks after that, I heard a commotion as I sat on a low wall, eating some figs. A crowd of children appeared, skipping and dancing alongside a small cart pulled by a pair of brown donkeys. The driver was a dwarf who shouted foul and abusive taunts at the children while hurling handfuls of sweets to them. He noticed me as he passed and nodded slightly.

He called himself Rico, and his surly exterior was matched by a facility for invective unrivaled in my experience. I liked him immediately. When I introduced him at court, the Emperor took one look at him and virtually bleated with delight, a noise Rico would take and imitate hilariously on many an occasion.

Rico became the Emperor's favorite, a position I gave up gratefully. I preferred roaming the squares and taverns, poking around the dark alleyways, making friends in the unlikeliest of places, cultivating my sources of information. One day would find me gossiping with Niketas Choniates on the goings-on in the Senate, another dining at midnight with Father Esaias, trading useful rumors and speculations.

The Emperor set the dwarf up in Niko and Piko's miniature palace. We pitched in to clean it up. Aglaia took a deep breath, and vanished with Rico into the escape tunnel with some blankets. They collected the remains of our little colleagues, and we buried them secretly that night. A few days later, we did the same for Zintziphitzes.

A new troubadour, a Bolognan who called himself Alfonso, began riding the circuit from Thessaloniki to Constantinople. Thanks to him, Viola finally managed to send a letter to her children, assuring them that she was alive and well.

"But not safe," she told me.

"I never promised you safety," I said.

"No, you didn't," she agreed.

A few months later, Alfonso returned with letters from both Mark and Celia, and Viola read them to herself at every spare moment.

Not that we had many. It was a constant whirl of performing and spying, maneuvering and occasionally ducking. On the occasion of the New Year's games, we devised a special group performance, finishing with the five of us—Rico, Plossus, Alfonso, Aglaia, and myself—standing at the five points of a giant silver pentangle in front of the Kathisma, with all of the nobility of Constantinople, the Senate, the various armies, the factions, and the people watching.

What they could see was five fools juggling clubs. What no one in the entire Hippodrome but us could hear was how we began.

"For Ignatius," said Alfonso as he started.

"For Demetrios and Tiberius," said Plossus as he joined him.

"For Niko and Piko," said Rico, tossing his clubs high over his head.

"For Thalia," said Aglaia, for the two of us had agreed that the Guild need not know that she had survived.

"For Zintziphitzes," I said, bringing the old fellow back into the fold at last.

"For the Guild!" we cried as one, and the clubs leapt across the center in a star pattern, so that each club eventually was touched by all of us. So we remembered those who were gone.

And I often wondered where she went, and how she managed, but Thalia was never seen in Constantinople again.

The seasons passed as we continued on. One day, just past the summer solstice, Alfonso showed up and with a bland expression handed me a small scroll. I read it with delight, and looked up to see him grinning broadly.

"Tell the others," I said. "We'll celebrate at our place tonight."

I had an appointment to meet my wife that afternoon. We had taken, on those rare occasions when we had free time together, to wandering around the city like tourists, seeing the sights. We had arranged to meet at the top of the Pillar of Arkadios, fulfilling a wish she had expressed our second day here. I made a few purchases, then shouldered my bag and hurried along the Mese up the Xerolophon. The pillar stood on an immense base, and was constructed of giant, hollowed-out blocks placed one upon another, with windows carved out of the sides providing a variety of views as you climbed the spiral steps to the top.

It was at the summit of this great tower that I found my beloved, gazing out to sea, as the sun ambled down the Via Egnatia toward Greece, Rome, and beyond.

"A beautiful sight, isn't it?" she said.

"Yes, it is," I agreed, and she smiled when she saw I was looking at her, not the sunset.

"There are a lot of fishing boats out there," she observed. "We shall eat well tomorrow."

"We shall eat well later," I said. "I have some good news."

"Oh?"

I pulled out the scroll and read from it.

"From Father Gerald: 'In light of your apprentice's successful completion of a variety of tests under your tutelage, and in view of her prior noteworthy accomplishments and sheer worth, it has been decided to accept her as a member-in-full of the Fools' Guild. She will henceforth be given the rank of Jester, and shall be known within the Guild as . . . ' "

"Let me guess," she said. "Claudius."

"No," I said. "Claudia. They've decided to let you continue being a woman. Congratulations, my love."

"Thank you, Master. Must I still call you Master?"

"Never again. I've brought you something."

I handed her a bulky item in a soft, cloth sack. She reached inside and pulled out a lute.

"It's lovely," she exclaimed, and kissed me. She immediately tuned it and began playing.

I dug into my bag and produced another instrument, a large, triangular wooden frame with strings of varying lengths. I took a pair of soft mallets and started tapping them on it, producing a pleasing sound.

"What's that?" she asked.

"A local instrument," I said. "They call it a cembalum. I've been meaning to learn how to play it. After all, when in Rome . . ."

We started improvising a duet.

"Oh, did I mention that I am with child?" she asked me in the middle of it.

"No, you didn't mention that," I said, and we played on for a bit. Then I put down my mallets and held her close.

"Is it all right?" she asked.

"It's wonderful," I said.

"I do like this city," she said. "Do you think we can stay here?"

"I suppose that's up to the Guild," I said. "But we'll be together, wherever we are. I promise you that."

"That's fine," she sighed.

I held her, watching the sun set, seeing so many miles out the fishing boats returning. So many.

Too many.

"What's wrong?" she asked, as I stood to get a better look.

"Those aren't fishing boats," I said. "That, my dear, is the Venetian fleet."

AUTHOR'S NOTE

But the disadvantage with sources, however truthful they try to be, is their lack of precision in matters of detail and their impassioned account of events, we refer to a certain internal faculty of contradictory germination which operates within facts or the version of those facts as provided, sold, or proposed, and stemming like spores from the latter, the proliferation of secondary and tertiary sources, some copied, others carelessly transmitted, some repeated from hearsay, others who changed details in good or bad faith, some freely interpreted, others rectified, some propagated with total indifference, others proclaimed as the one, eternal and irreplaceable truth, the last of these the most suspect of all.

THE HISTORY OF THE SIEGE OF LISBON, JOSE SARAMAGO

In my continuing efforts to verify the chronicles of Theophilos the Fool, I have searched every contemporaneous historical source I could find. Alas, the Fools' Guild succeeded in suppressing almost every reference to its existence. What little I could find consists mostly of passing references to individual fools.

However, there certainly were fools in Constantinople, and I can think of no better start for the aspiring Byzantine or foolish scholar than to turn to the works of Niketas Choniates, a contemporary of Theophilos. And I can think of no better introduction to this remarkable historian than *O City of Byzantium, Annals of Niketas Choniates*, as superbly translated and annotated by Harry J. Magoulias. It was published by Wayne State University Press, and I add my voice to those who would see it reprinted, at least in paperback form.

Choniates, unusual for historians of his era (and ours), reported what he knew objectively. He had no particular axe to grind, although he had a healthy mistrust of superstition, gleefully recording every instance in which someone relied upon omens to his or her detriment. He had a sly wit and was deft with an insult, usually well deserved. It is not surprising to find that he and Theophilos were acquainted, although Theophilos rates no mention in the *Annals*. At least, not under that name.

It is from Choniates that we hear of Chalivoures and Zintziphitzes, and that the Emperor Isaakios "delighted in ribaldries and lewd songs and consorted with laughter-stirring dwarfs . . . he did not close the palace to knaves, mimes, and minstrels." He even reports an actual jest made by Chalivoures, one of the few surviving examples from any jester:

> Once at dinner Isaakios said, "Bring me *salt*." Standing nearby admiring the dance of the women made up of the emperor's concubines and kinswomen was Chalivoures, the wittiest of the mimes, who retorted, "Let us first come to know these, O Emperor, and then command *others* to be brought in." At this, everyone, both men and women, burst into loud laughter; the emperor's face darkened and only when he had chastened the jester's freedom of speech was his anger curbed.

Now, to get the joke, you have to recognize, as Professor Magoulias does in a helpful footnote, that the Greek words for *salt* and *others*, *halas* and *allas*, are homonyms. You see, it's a pun. Okay, so it doesn't really work in English, but if you were a twelfth-century Greek, you would be on the floor right now. I mean, it just killed back then.

You now see why translation is such a difficult art.

I am still working my way slowly through the manuscripts preserved at the Irish abbey I mentioned in my note on the translation to *Thirteenth Night*, the first of these accounts. In that note, I speculated that some of Theophilos's manuscripts made their way from the abbey to Shakespeare by way of Will Kempe, an actor in Shakespeare's troupe. However, an alternative route has been proposed by Peter Tremayne, author of the entertaining and meticulously researched Sister Fidelma mystery series. Tremayne, who is a much better historian than I am, has kindly consented to my quoting from his letter:

[Shakespeare] could have made the connection through Edmund Spenser (1552–1599), the English poet (*The Faerie Queen*), who went to Ireland as part of the Elizabethan conquest. Spenser was rewarded with 3,000 acres of land confiscated from the Irish, some of which was confiscated from my direct ancestor. Spenser was given Kilcolman Castle in north County Cork, near Doneraile. Kilcolman Castle stands a few miles north from the townlands of Ballyellis. My ancestor . . . was hiding out at the time in the guerrilla band led by Donal, the illegitimate son of Donal IX. . . .

If I recall, *Twelfth Night* was written by Bill Shakespeare around 1600. In 1598 my redoubtable ancestor took part in the attack on Kilcolman Castle. It was burnt down . . . [as] part of a concerted plan to drive the English back out of Cork. Spenser had to flee for his life with his family and followers. . . . He arrived back in London where he died shortly thereafter "for lack of bread" as Ben Jonson reported.

I could envisage the ailing Mr. Spenser, having fled from

Ireland, selling the manuscripts, which he had plundered from the Irish abbey during the conquest, to Shakespeare in 1598 to raise money to buy some food!

Very possible, Mr. Tremayne, very possible. And as the Bard himself said, "And thereby hangs a tale."

Of course, Shakespeare stole that line from Theophilos.